Suddenly SPYING

Gin Mackey

PGP

Pink
Granite
Press

For Dick

Your belief in me breathed life into my writing

I love you so much!

Have You Already Read This Book?

If you wish to keep a record that you have read this book, you may use the space below for your initials.

Chapter One

Water coming out of the stern? I sprinted down the dock toward my sailboat. Why was the bilge pump on? Scrambling below deck to the living quarters, I waded through the flood, heaved aside a cushion and stuck my finger into a lift hole in the bench seat, revealing the engine. Water spurted from a disconnected hose. I grabbed what was closest—since the boat was also my home, it was a fistful of underwear—and crammed it in to staunch the flow. The metal clamp holding the hose in place had broken. I hustled to my parts drawer, grabbed a spare. After positioning the new clamp, I yanked out the underwear, muscled the hose into place, and tightened the clamp. Whew. And yuck. I was covered in grime and soaking wet.

And now I was late, too. After quickly changing, I hurried above deck. Pulling my hair into a ponytail as I went, I hopped onto the dock. The name on the hull had originally been *DREAM BOAT.* Only the faint outline of the "R" and "E" remained. It read *D AM BOAT* now.

***

Platters clattered to our dining room table and silence descended as the family dug into Thanksgiving dinner.

When the phone in the kitchen rang, Uncle Ned waved to my mother he'd get it. A moment later, he returned and sat down, a conspiratorial smile on his face. "Guess who's coming for Thanksgiving?"

"Give us a hint," I said.

He made an upward swooping motion with a massive drumstick. "Able to leap tall locomotives at a single bound."

I said, "Isn't it tall *buildings—*"

"Faster than a peeing bird." Aunt Deirdre made a sideways swooping motion.

"Faster than a *speeding bullet*, Aunt Deirdre, not a—"

"Look," Uncle Ned said, jumping to a stand, pointing toward the ceiling with the drumstick. Everyone looked. "Up in the air," he shouted. "It's a bird! It's a plane! It's—"

"It's Giselle." But I said it like it was the coming of the plague. I stared at the gargantuan turkey carcass. "This *is* Thanksgiving. Isn't it rude to come at the last minute?"

"She probably just stopped a bunch of people trafficking in nuclear warheads or something and got freed up," Uncle Ned said. He shrugged. "She's a spy. It happens."

"We're just happy our little star is coming," Aunt Deirdre said, clapping her hands.

"She called from her car. She's bringing a friend. They'll be here any minute."

My mother turned to me, lips pursed. "Nora, dear, you don't mind moving, do you?"

"What? Not the—" My mother nodded. It was too late to put the leaf in the table. Stomping to the closet, I pulled out the junior-sized card table Giselle and I used when we were kids. I moved my dishes and crammed my rear into a tiny chair as mom and Aunt Deirdre scrambled to set two more places at the big table. "Hey! It's not like she's royalty."

The front door opened. A hush descended as Giselle swept into the room, arms open wide to her audience. She posed briefly, the better for us to gaze upon her chin-length, Marilyn-blonde, perfection of a coiffure and to note her diamond earrings with matching necklace.

With her was a tall man with green eyes and curly hair she introduced as Jesse. Sitting like an oversized five-year-old at my table-for-one, I craned my neck for a better view.

"That must be her boyfriend," Aunt Deirdre whispered down to me.

Giselle's life was perfect in every way. Why wouldn't she have the perfect boyfriend? I felt a flash of guilt as I thought of Kenny. Hey, I was just *looking*. I was too far away to touch.

Jesse sat beside her, and everyone passed them platters of food. Giselle pushed away her wine glass, emptied a large tumbler of water back into the pitcher, and refilled it with Pinot Noir.

A short time later, Giselle started down the hall to the bathroom. Before each doorway, she stopped, looked in the room, and darted past. On her way back, she made a sudden turn into the dining room and scanned the perimeter. She sat down and resumed eating.

In her absence, Uncle Ned had stepped into the kitchen. Giselle didn't notice him come back. Passing behind her, he put his hands affectionately on her shoulders. Giselle twisted around suddenly, grabbed him, and was just about to pin him to the turkey carcass. Everyone froze. I could see the flash of realization hit her eyes; she grinned and did a quick playful one-two double jab boxing move. "Just kidding with you, Uncle Ned."

"Ha! You got me good!" he yelled in delight, giving her a

good-natured one-two back.

Everyone laughed. But Giselle's rapid-fire breaths didn't seem to match her smile. Had she been kidding? Why had my sister picked now to drop by so unexpectedly? And why the hell was Giselle so jumpy?

***

The entourage formerly known as the family followed Giselle to the living room. I stayed behind, stacked dishes, and headed to the kitchen. From the other room I heard a group, "Ooooh," Giselle's voice and laughter. I moved quietly. I didn't want to have to go in there.

Jesse came in. "Can you tell me where the wine is, Nora? Giselle wants another glass."

"Sure." As I got out a bottle and the corkscrew, he noticed an oversized bulletin board on the kitchen wall. Postcards with exotic postmarks had been attached to every available inch surrounding a central portrait. A row of three small, lit candles sat below.

"Giselle?" he asked, pointing to the picture. I nodded. He walked over, took it in for a moment. "This almost looks like a... like a..."

"Shrine?" I said for him.

"Kinda."

"Uh huh." I handed him the bottle. As he disappeared, I glanced again at the picture of Giselle. She was the oldest. She'd always been the favorite. But it still hurt.

I tiptoed upstairs to my old room. I'd been out of the house for years, but my mother hadn't changed a thing. Museum of Nora.

I heard stomping on the stairs, and Giselle blasted in. Her

cell phone rang. When she saw the number, she stiffened. "My boss. Can you give me a minute?"

In the hall, something made me stop, my eye to the crack between the door and the jamb. Her hands shook so badly, Giselle put the phone on speaker and set it down. I strained to hear.

"You can have all the time off you want," the boss said, "if you can find someone to do the job for you. Far as I know, everyone's pretty busy."

A voice on the phone interrupted. "International terrorist for you on line one, boss."

"What? Don't they know it's Thanksgiving? All right, hold on." Then he was back to Giselle. "I gotta go, Giselle, unless you being a little overworked is more important."

Giselle squeezed her eyes shut and bit her lip, close to losing her fight with tears. Was this connected to how jumpy she was? Her voice thick and weary, she said, "Okay."

"Remember," he said, "it's your assignment unless you find somebody else to take it on."

As I walked in, Giselle picked up a small wooden boat on my desk and blew dust off it. The boat held tiny figures I'd glued in it, including myself at the wheel. "Nora, remember that school-on-a-schooner thing you used to talk about? Taking kids to exotic places for adventure learning? All that wind-in-your-hair, learning-by-doing crap?" Giselle bounced the boat along as if it was bounding on waves, pulled her hair back as if it was blowing in the wind, did a little hula dance.

"So?"

"You're still at Bob's Bikes and Boats. You'll be a hundred before you have money for a schooner. Besides, you would've done it by now if you were going to. It's been nine years."

"It has not." But I did the math. She was right. How could so many years slip by?

One of the tiny figures fell to the floor. I picked up the bed with one hand and retrieved it.

Giselle tried to lift the bed. She couldn't budge it. "You're strong. You go to a club?"

"Working on my boat's all the workout I need."

She assessed me like a piece of possible produce. "Hey, let's do something tomorrow."

"I have to work a half day." And why the sudden interest in hanging out with me?

"After work. I'll meet you there." Not waiting for an answer, she ran back downstairs.

I put the tiny figure back in the boat. "School on a schooner." A wave of sadness rocked me. Back in high school, I already loved sailing. I'd planned to have a seagoing school for girls. My eyes filled with lost-hopes tears as the dream emerged full force—a sixty-foot schooner, all shiny wood and gleaming decks, dancing across the water with sparkling white sails, filled with girls excited to be traveling to the Caribbean, New Zealand, Thailand.

I had a boat, sure. But it was a thirty-footer with a beat-up body, patched sails, engine trouble, and leaks so bad I was afraid to take it out of sight of Portsmouth Harbor.

I looked at the little figures on the boat. The one next to me, I'd labeled "Dreamboat!!" I remembered back to the man I'd dreamed of since I was a teenager. He was tall, sandy-haired, a look of intelligence, kindness and humor in his eyes. Gentle but strong. He loved the outdoors and the sea and sailing. In short, he was wonderfully perfect. My tears rained on the little boat.

Footsteps on the stairs again. Swiping tears away, I

rushed to the door, the boat behind my back, and smacked right into Jesse. He saw my tear-smeared face. "Hey, are you all right?"

I backed to the bed and sat, fighting tears. But I hadn't expected the look of caring in his eyes. Taking the boat from behind my back, I handed it to him. "A dream I used to have. A school on a schooner."

"Cool." He sat beside me, taking in the tiny figures and all the other details. Turning toward me, he put his hand on my shoulder. "Dreams die, Nora. But only if you let them."

***

A voice intruded from downstairs. "Nora!" My mother.

"Oh, that's what I came up to tell you," Jesse said. "Your mom's looking for you."

I went out to the top of the stairs. Below, my mother held up two bags of trash. "I'll take those, Ma," I said, hurrying down the stairs. Jesse followed. He grabbed one of the bags and we walked out the front door toward the street. A car stopped and the window slid down.

"Isn't it nice your sister the spy made it home for the holiday, Nora?" the woman said.

"Yeah. Just great." The car drove off. "Friend of my mother's from bingo," I said.

He stopped. "You know that's supposed to be a secret, right?"

"Of course it's a secret. A secret only the family knows."

"But that lady knew."

"Okay, the family and selected trusted friends the family decides to tell."

A kid from next door wandered into the yard, autograph

book and pen in hand. "Hey, Nora," Larry said, "can I see your sister the spy?" I waved him in the direction of the house.

Jesse looked at me. "Okay," I said, "the family and selected trusted friends and neighbors the family decides to tell."

Two little old ladies walked by. "The neighborhood spy lives there," one of them stage-whispered to the other.

"Tell me something I don't already know," the other one said.

Jesse looked at me again. "Okay," I said, "the family and selected trusted friends and neighbors the family decides to tell, and—"

"And everyone else," Jesse said.

I shrugged. "We're Irish. We're not that good at keeping secrets."

We plopped the bags at the curb and turned back toward the house. Giselle appeared at the front door and trotted out. Jesse continued toward the house while I waited for Giselle.

"Gotta get something in my car." She walked into the street, toward the driver's door. Her phone rang. As she grabbed it from her pocket, a noise from up the street made me spin.

A shiny black sedan. But instead of slowing, it sped up. Giselle had turned away from the noise, the phone to one ear, her finger in the other. The driver was veering *towards* her. Adrenaline electrifying me before conscious thought had a chance, I yanked Giselle back toward the sidewalk. At the last second he straightened and shot past us. Geez, that had been close. I glimpsed a dark-haired man in a lime green shirt. "Get off your cell phone," I yelled at the car.

"I was only on for a minute," Giselle said, jamming her

phone in her pocket.

"Not you, the— Never mind." Giselle grabbed her bags as I gestured at the retreating car. Cripes, he could have killed us if we hadn't gotten out of the way. Some days, doesn't it just seem like everyone is out to get you?

Chapter Two

Giselle and I had just stepped inside the house when I heard footsteps coming up the walk. Giselle continued into the living room as I turned and saw my boyfriend, Kenny, dressed in his auxiliary police uniform. I held the door open for him.

"Hiya," he said.

Giselle's voice sounded from the living room. "Hey, where is everybody?"

"Is that Giselle?" Kenny said, brushing by me. "I should say hi." I followed him inside.

"Hey, Handsome," Giselle said to Kenny. I thought she was kidding and almost started to laugh. Then I looked at him. He was handsome—tall, dark haired and blue eyed—I'd just stopped thinking of him that way. Jesse came in and handed Giselle another drink as she started telling her spy stories to Kenny. She swooped her hand though the air as she described chasing bad guys through Romania. Booze slopped out. She listed so far to the left it wasn't only the booze that was going to end up on the floor.

Jesse quickly moved behind her, one arm encircling her middle and the other grabbing for the drink. "I'll get that for you, Giselle," he said. In a fluid motion, he took the glass, steadied it and her. He'd either done that before or he had excellent reflexes.

I took the glass from him. Giselle kept right on talking to Kenny.

When the story ended, Kenny turned his attention to Jesse. Puffing up his chest, he said, "I was a wrestler in school. State champ."

"Wow," Jesse said, smiling. "Me too, in Kansas."

"New Hampshire's bigger," Kenny said, crossing his arms.

"Kenny," I said, "size doesn't mat—"

"Kansas is twice as big in size. Nine times bigger in population," Jesse said. There wasn't anything contentious in the way Jesse said it. Simply stating the facts.

"Oh." Outranked on the state issue, Kenny still didn't look like he was done talking.

"Uh-oh," I whispered to Giselle. "Why do I feel a testosterone test brewing?"

"Kenny's jealous," Giselle whispered back.

"Why would he be jealous of Jesse?" Odd. He usually wasn't a green-eyed kind of guy.

Kenny slipped off his coat and flipped it toward a chair. I snagged it mid-flight. "Kenny, put your coat on." I got behind him, trying to grab his arms and stuff them back in the jacket.

He ignored me, intent on Jesse. "How about a friendly match?" He rolled his sleeves.

Jesse shook his head and put his open hands up, signaling no. "Nah, that's okay."

"You want a sandwich, Kenny?" I asked. "I can make you a nice turkey—"

"They raise chickens out there in Kansas, Jesse? That's what I heard. They raise chickens." After flapping his elbows like chicken wings and clucking, Kenny scrunched into a wrestling-ready stance.

Jesse slipped off his coat. "Really," he said, removing his tie. "You know what I heard? I heard the New Hampshire state animal is the bull. More bull here than just about anywhere." He started to get into the proper stance. Just before Jesse was set, Kenny grabbed Jesse's wrist with one hand, his opposite hip with the other, swung him to the floor and jumped on him.

They remained stationary for a moment, then Jesse scrambled from under Kenny. Jesse wouldn't be caught by surprise again. The hard set of his jaw and laser eyes said so.

Giselle and I glanced at each other and hurried to either end of the couch to move it back against the wall. She had another glass of something she didn't want to put down, so instead of lifting her end of the couch, she raised her foot and gave the couch a shove toward the wall. I heard the crunch of plaster and went over to see. A chunk of former wall sat on the floor.

I moved the coffee table myself. But I wondered if we'd already woken mom and dad from their nap. Hopefully they were in a tryptophan stupor from all that turkey.

Kenny and Jesse circled each other, looking for an opening. Then Jesse sprang. He dropped to his knees and pulled Kenny into a fireman's carry on his shoulders. Before Kenny could react, Jesse continued the move, dumping Kenny head over heels onto his back. He hit the floor hard, with a "whoof" of expelled air, inches from the now teetering grandfather clock.

Jesse waited for Kenny to catch his breath. You'd have thought Kenny would have given up, but no. They went at it some more. They kept at it so long Giselle and I ended up flipping through magazines on the couch. But when I glanced up, I noticed something. All Jesse's moves now were defensive moves, none aggressive. I went back to my mother's *Better Homes and Gardens*. Giselle went to find more booze.

"He's bleeding!" Kenny yelled in a happy victory voice a few minutes later.

I looked up. "Oh, for heaven's sake." Giselle came back into the living room and Kenny began giving her the play-by-play. I helped Jesse into the kitchen. "Sit here." I pulled out a chair at the table, then got a cloth and dabbed at the cut under his eye. "He just couldn't quit until he drew blood." I shook my head. "What you did out there, Jesse..."

Jesse peered at me through one good eye and one half-closed one. "Yeah?"

"That was nice." Jesse had let him win.

He gave me a smile so easy and open, I... I hoped Giselle realized what she had in him.

His cut stopped bleeding. I got out ice and brought him back to the living room. When he was comfy on the couch, holding the ice to his face, I went back into the kitchen to clean up.

I returned a few minutes later to find Kenny and Jesse in conversation at the front door. "Bye, Nora," Kenny yelled. "Gotta get to work." The door slammed and he was gone.

I hung out with Giselle and Jesse for an hour. When Giselle headed upstairs to unpack, I said, "I better get going. I'm taking the boat out first thing tomorrow."

"You have a boat?" Jesse asked.

"I live on it."

"You live on a boat?"

"A thirty-foot sailboat. But the engine's been sounding

funny."

"Can I come? Maybe I can help."

"I'm going out before work. Eight o'clock. It'll be chilly."

"That's okay."

"What about Giselle?"

"I think it's safe to assume she'll be—"

"Hungover—"

"Asleep."

"That's what I meant," I said quickly, "asleep." As I opened the door to leave, the phone rang. Kenny. I talked to him, then headed to my truck. As I got in, I wondered what clothes Jesse had packed. Early morning on Portsmouth Harbor in November could be wicked wintry.

***

"Hi," I said a few minutes later, slipping into the passenger seat of a beat-up Chevy.

Kenny turned away from the apartment building he'd been watching. His short hair bristled from under a ratty Red Sox cap. As soon as I closed the door, he reached across the old Chevy and pushed the button down, locking the door. His arm grazed my breasts. We'd been going out so long, it barely registered.

Kenny'd been called in on a stakeout. Operating in my capacity as lunch lady, I passed him a fast-food bag, its bottom soggy with grease. "Someone dangerous in there?" I asked.

He opened the bag, grabbed a limp French fry, and shrugged. "Triple murderer." After popping the fry into his mouth, he pulled out a double burger, tore off a two-inch square of the wrapping, set it on the dashboard, and created a mound of ketchup for fry-dunking purposes.

I glanced toward the building. "A triple murderer? That definitely sounds dangerous."

"Not really. All the people he killed were members of his family."

"Well... It was dangerous to them, wasn't it?"

"Yeah, but it's not like a serial murderer who goes out looking for victims. This guy's more a crime of passion kind of guy. His family pissed him off so he killed them."

"What'd they do? Hide the remote?"

He turned to me, a fry hanging from the side of his mouth. "Oh, you read about it?"

"Maybe I shouldn't be here if I might get killed."

"I'm here," he said.

"You're a cop and you're armed! I think maybe I'll head on—"

"Wait. I want to talk to you." He bit into a little apple pie thingie. "Mmmm. It's still warm. They congeal if they're not hot. Thanks, Nora. Thanks a lot."

I laughed. This was my life. Another stakeout, another meal on wheels.

"Why didn't you tell me your sister was coming for Thanksgiving?" he asked.

"Didn't know she was."

"Giselle hardly comes home at all now. And she has that wimpy boyfriend. He's a crummy wrestler," Kenny said. "Another ten seconds and I would've—"

"He *let* you w—"

"Oh, almost forgot. Something for you in my shirt pocket."

I waited.

"Nora?" he said, eyebrows arched, waving his sticky

apple-pie filled hands in the air.

"Oh." I reached over and pulled out a small velvet box. "What is this?" I asked as if it might contain an itty-bitty bomb. I opened it. Sitting in the satin lay an engagement ring.

"It was my grandmother's," Kenny said. "Let's get married, okay?"

"Married?" I felt fuzzy dizzy, like I'd really need to sit down if I wasn't already. "Why?"

"Why not? Seems like about time."

Was there a four-year dating maximum I didn't know about? We had been going together for a long time, but marriage? I dunno, it wasn't something I'd really thought about.

"We could get married in the spring, before softball starts. For the honeymoon—"

I smiled at the thought of a honeymoon. I'd always wanted to travel, see exotic places. Scout them out so when I had my school-on-a-schooner I could take the kids incredible places. Maybe this could be a start. We could go to Polynesia or someplace like that for a—

"—one of my buddies said we could use his cabin in the White Mountains for a couple of days. It'd only take us an hour to get there."

Poof! My vision of cruising the warm waters of the Polynesian Islands in my bikini shriveled and died.

"That way, I won't miss any of the bowling league finals either," he said, finishing the last of the apple pie. A gunshot sounded from the building. "Think about it, okay? And let me know." He leaned over and gave me a sticky kiss. "I gotta go." He wiped his hands on his pants, opened the car door, trotted across the street, and disappeared into the apartment building.

I drove home. Turning at the driveway beside Bob's Bikes and Boats, I headed to the parking lot behind it, right by the dock. Back on the boat, I cuddled up in my sleeping bag. I thought about my life, the dreams I used to have. There was a whole big world out there. But I wasn't part of it. Kenny and I might be the only two left here from our high school graduating classes. Everyone else had gone on to other things. For him, life here was right. But did I want to live the rest of my life in Portsmouth?

I thought I'd end up with a man like the dreamboat in my tiny schooner. What I had was Kenny. Did I want to marry him? What if I turned him down? Would I ever be asked again?

Was there any such thing as happily ever after? Or did people just settle? Was that what I was going to do? Settle for my decrepit boat? Settle for Bob's Bikes and Boats? Settle for Kenny?

Let my dreams die?

I sobbed into my pillow. Maybe I was.

Chapter Three

The next morning, I felt the boat rock. Kenny got seasick as soon as he set foot on the dock, so it wasn't him. I went above deck. "You made it, huh?" I asked Jesse.

"Yeah." Arms crossed over his chest, he bounced from foot to foot. "Nippy, isn't it?"

"Let's find you some warmer clothes." He followed me below. When he'd zipped on a sweatshirt and a fleece jacket, I stood on my tippy toes and pulled a hat onto his head. My hand touched his cheek. "You're freezing."

"Not too bad."

"Liar," I said, laughing. "This is what my dad would always do when we were kids." I took his hand between mine, rubbing back and forth quickly to generate some warmth. Then I did the same to his other hand. He had nice hands. They felt strong and—

"That feels good," he said.

I looked up, smiling. "Told ya." He had kind eyes. I liked looking at his face. As that realization hit, I dropped his hands like I'd been burned. What was I thinking? The man was Giselle's boyfriend. And I was practically engaged to Kenny. "I... Coffee will help, too," I stammered. He turned to the side to try to give me room to pass, but my front slid against his back. He wouldn't think I was coming on to him, would he? I poured him a cup of coffee.

"Thanks." He glanced around, curious about the boat. I understood suddenly that the awkwardness was all on my side. "I've never been on a sailboat," Jesse said.

I shook my head. "I can't even imagine that. Learned to swim when I was four, could sail by the time I was eight. First job I had when I was sixteen was as a lifeguard."

"Not much waterfront in Kansas." His eyes crinkled as he smiled.

I told Jesse about the engine trouble. "She's been starting harder for a while now. This morning I checked out the battery cables, belts and hoses, antifreeze and oil levels. Everything looks okay." He asked me a few questions as I put the engine cover back on. "How do you know about diesel engines?" I asked.

"I grew up on a farm. The tractor had a diesel. Lots of similarities. In fact, Kubota makes engines for sailboats and tractors."

"Didn't know that," I said, wiping my hands. "I'll start her up." He followed me to the cockpit. When I turned the key, the starter motor cranked, but the engine didn't turn over. On the fourth try, she sputtered and coughed to life. We motored out into open water, listening to the engine run for a while. I shut it off and we talked more about the problems I'd been having.

"How old's your boat?" Jesse asked quietly.

"About fifteen."

"She's an old girl. Motor's tougher to start, losing power, running harder. Nora..."

"What?"

"I think you already know."

I sighed, throwing the rag down. "Yeah." The problems

I'd wanted to ignore were not going to go away. "The engine's cooked."

"She's all worn out. I know what that means for a car. Is it as bad for a boat?"

"Ten thousand dollars," my voice caught, "to fix her." Ten thousand I didn't have.

"I'm sorry, Nora."

"No biggie." But I fought back tears as I turned away to start the engine. This time, it wouldn't catch at all. "What is a biggie is that we use the motor to get to the dock."

"That is a problem. You don't have the control without it."

"Exactly," I said. "We can sail in, but it's a lot more difficult."

"We could call a tow."

A brisk wind blew at maybe fifteen, twenty knots, unusual for this time of day. "The weather's kicking up. A tow can take time." I grinned at him. "And it wouldn't be as exciting."

He shrugged and grinned back. "I'm game."

"We'll use the main sail to get near the dock." I glanced at the telltales on the mast. "When we're very close, we'll head directly into the wind. We'll lose power, but the momentum will keep us going. We'll move slowly toward the dock without crashing into it." *If everything goes exactly according to plan.*

He nodded he understood.

"At the dock, your part is critical, Jesse. See that?" I pointed to a T-shaped piece of metal attached to the cabin top. "That's a cleat. The dock line loops around a cleat on the boat. Right before we hit the dock, you jump on and wrap the line around a dock cleat."

"That's what stops the forward motion."

"And what keeps us from crashing into the other boats."

"Got it."

"I'll be right behind you to help get the other dock lines on."

"Let's do it," he said.

"Coming about," I hollered. The boom whipped across the boat as we changed direction and the wind took the sail. We hauled toward the dock.

As we neared, I pulled in the sail slightly to slow us. We attached lines, one to a cleat near the front of the boat and the other near the rear, so they'd be ready once we docked. We then attached the third line to a cleat midship. This was the line Jesse would use when he jumped onto the dock, the crucial first connection between the boat and the dock that would make us stop. We carefully coiled the lines. They had to be free of snags.

If we were off by more than a few seconds, I'd hit the next boat, the *Santa Maria*. She was a spanking new forty-foot Hinckley, by far the most expensive boat on the dock.

"How much does this thing weigh, Nora?"

"About five tons." We were twenty feet away from the dock. "Get ready, Jesse."

He moved to the side of the boat, a little forward, and grabbed the end of the dock line. He crouched, waiting to spring. The gap continued to close. Ten feet, six, four, two—

"Now, Jesse!"

He leaped toward the dock, hitting with a thud, but the dock bounced under his weight. He lost his footing, went backward.

"Jesse!" I screamed.

We kept moving toward the *Santa Maria*. Jesse

scrambled to his knees, then half-crawled, half-ran dog-like to the cleat, whipping the line around and pulling.

He didn't expect the line to be slippery. But it was nylon, and I could see it sliding through his hands. For agonizing seconds the boat continued moving. I leaped to the dock and grabbed the rope, and together we pulled, groaning as we strained. I could feel the boat slow, slow... and finally stop.

I ran to the bow of my boat. She was an inch away from the *Santa Maria*. Jesse and I looked at each other. He started to laugh. I started to shake.

"Thanks, Nora. That was fun."

Okay, so he had an odd idea of what a good time was. Otherwise, I thought my sister Giselle had found herself a pretty nice guy.

***

Just before ten that morning, I stepped off my boat, glancing at the harbor. Got quiet this late in the season. Working boats stayed in all year, but lots of the pleasure boats had already been hauled out. Their owners were long gone, leaving town as soon as the warm weather did.

I hightailed it across the parking lot and up to the shop, buttoning my white work shirt over my striped pullover and jeans as I finished my sixty-second commute. The shop sat on a slope. The top half, at street level, provided motorcycle repairs and supplies. The bottom half, devoted to selling boat supplies and doing repairs, opened at sea level. One of the benefits of working here was that Bob, the owner, gave me a deal on my docking fee. Another was he let me use tools to make repairs on my boat, tools too expensive to buy.

Usually the day after Thanksgiving was a holiday. But the

Ironman Biker Rally that weekend had all the diehards rushing to get their bikes ready. We were open until two.

The hours flew by, and then Giselle, in spike heels and a trench coat cinched at her waist, strolled into the waiting room. She sat down amidst a group of bikers clad mostly in blue denim and multi-colored tattoos. I gave her a wave. "We can leave as soon as my boss gets here."

A loud bang sounded. Giselle rose to a crouch, gun drawn, wild eyed. Every guy in the room pulled his weapon out, too. No one seemed sure of the source of the threat, so guns, knives and chains now pointed in a variety of directions. For a few seconds, there was tense silence.

"Ah," I said, "I think a bike backfired out there." I pointed my thumb toward the garage.

"Oh," Giselle said. She smiled sheepishly and pocketed her weapon. The others did, too.

Everyone resumed chatting, reading, or sitting sullenly with arms crossed, looking mean.

The door to the waiting room flew open and smacked against the wall. Hulk Hallowell stood in the doorway, glaring in my direction. "Where's my bike?"

I stood up slowly. "It's not ready yet, Hulk."

"Whaddya mean it's not ready?" he yelled.

"One guy called in sick and another had to go get a couple of stitches. So it's not ready."

"Whaddya mean it's not ready?"

"What part of 'not ready' don't you understand, Hulk? I'll say it more slowly for you. Nooot reeaaady. Not *gonna* be ready until tomorrow."

He glanced through the glass door into the garage. "There's guys working in there. They better fix my bike. And they better do it now." He looked again at the door.

"Now, Hulk," I said, "let's be reasonable here."

Three of the other guys stood. They wanted in on the fun.

"Come on, guys," I said. "Not today." But they didn't sit down. I sighed, then did a forward flip, landing in the middle of them. I had no idea what I was going to do next, but two of the guys threw punches at me, so I did a cha cha move out of the way and let them clobber each other. When the third guy grabbed my wrist, I twirled toward him, used a tango step to hook his leg with mine and he slammed into his seat.

That's when I saw Hulk make his move. He strode to the door, opened it, and looked back. I pirouetted, did a couple of quickstep moves before taking a flying leap onto my desk, shoving it so he ended up pinned in the door. I scrambled up on the desk and got him in a headlock. "As I was saying, Hulk, let's be reasonable. We had a bad day at the shop. You understand?"

I'm guessing he would have squeaked out a yes if I hadn't been cutting off most of his air. "And there are a bunch of guys ahead of you who also want their bikes." Loosening the headlock a fraction, I turned his head toward the others. "See?"

"Yeah, but... I'm riding a Moped until my bike is fixed. It's embarrassin'."

"That's the standard loaner. They are, too." I gestured with my head toward the others.

"They are?" The guys in the waiting room nodded. I turned Hulk's face so he could see outside to the Mopeds hidden behind the building. "Ohhh. I didn't realize."

All the guys started talking at once about how mortified they were riding Mopeds. I let Hulk go and he was soon deep in conversation, commiserating with the others.

Giselle walked up to me. "How'd you do that?"

"What?"

She swept her hand across the shop.

"Oh. I kind of make it up as I go along. Took a daylong self-defense class once. Rest of it's from dance classes we had as kids, I guess."

"Miss Deana's Dance Expressions?"

"You could tell, huh?"

"Oh sure. Ever use any square dancing moves?"

"I throw in an occasional do-si-do," I said, "but a lot of these guys are into line dancing, so you lose the surprise factor."

"I see." The shop phone rang. "When's your boss coming?" Giselle asked quickly.

"Shouldn't be long." While I answered calls, Giselle pulled a laptop from her pocketbook, started typing as quickly as I'd ever seen anyone type, and making calls on her cell. When the shop phone stopped ringing, I walked over. "Whatcha doing?"

"A little project planning. Just finished." She snapped her laptop shut.

We walked toward the exit as Bob entered. "Hey, you can't go anywhere," he said to me.

"It's two o'clock."

"You're gonna have to help out in the garage for a couple of hours so we can get some of these bikes out of here. Get the guys the parts and stuff."

"She will not!" Giselle said.

"She will, too," Bob said.

"Screw you," Giselle said. "She can do better than this."

"Yeah? You're fired!"

"You can't fire me. I don't work here," Giselle said.

He turned on me. "Then *you're* fired."

"*I'm* fired? But I didn't even—"

"No, but you *should* have," Giselle said, ushering me out. "They can't treat you like—"

"That was my job!"

"Believe me, Nora, it's no big loss." She flounced ahead of me.

Was she right? Just last night, hadn't I been wondering about the same thing? "Maybe I do need a change."

"If you're going to find a new job, you need a new look. Come on. I'll drive." As we walked beside the building toward the lot, I trailed behind, thinking about my life. Giselle dug for her keys. "I just had them." Still focused on the contents of her bag, she crossed to her car.

A guy in a black jacket over a lime green shirt, with dark glasses and a baseball cap, came around the corner of the building. He didn't appear that different from the other bikers, except he had his gun out. "Oh, for the love of Mike," I said. "Another tough guy who has to have his bike right now? This is *not* a good time to mess with me." I thought about just letting him go shoot up the place, but instead gave his gun hand a swift kick. The gun catapulted skyward. As he raised his hands to grab it, I kneed him in the groin. I snagged the gun on its return trip and sent it sailing into the ocean. I really felt like beating the crap out of the guy, but I'd have to wait for him to uncurl from a fetal position, and Giselle was already in the car. Luckily she hadn't noticed what had happened. She was a bundle of nerves as it was.

I got into her metallic silver Corvette and she accelerated toward the center of town.

We'd driven half a mile when I said, "I get my hair cut up here on the right." But she didn't slow. I pointed as she sped by. "Wait, I go to the one there, next to the butcher shop."

Giselle glanced over at my hair. "Honey, you go *in* the butcher shop." She skidded to the curb a block further down. "You need help. I'm taking you to mine."

***

We approached a shop with a sign in French so frilly I couldn't read it. As we entered its swank interior, I realized it probably said Salon Expensív. Why did Giselle even have a place here at home? Maybe because she spent more on grooming than most people spend on housing.

I looked up at the list of services and prices. Manicure, pedicure, facial, seaweed wrap. "I could give someone a seaweed wrap for a quarter of that price and still make a profit."

"Shh," Giselle said.

"Hello. Seaweed is free. You can go to the beach and roll around in it all you want, no charge. And aren't there laws against price-gouging in this state, because—"

"Welcome, Giselle and her leetle seester," the receptionist said. "Eve is ready for you."

"Ready?" I said. "How could she—"

"This way," Giselle said, pushing me toward a chair where a petite woman waited. She'd livened up her pixie cut with a spiky orange ponytail sprouting from the top of her head.

I sat down, and Eve snapped a smock open and whipped it around my neck.

My hairdresser always asked me what I wanted, but Eve turned me toward her so Giselle could see what she was doing. Eve began to cut. "More off the sides," Giselle said, "and layer it so it poufs." Eve cut and pouffed and pouffed

27

and cut until Giselle said, "Good."

"Gee," I said, "if it's not inconvenient, could I take a peek?" Eve gave the chair a spin.

Giselle scootched down so her head was next to mine. "Like it?" she said into the mirror.

"I'm an auburn version of you."

"Great, huh?" She pulled out her makeup case and eyed me. I thought about stopping her, then thought about finding a job, and kept still as she applied eyeshade, mascara, and lipstick.

There had always been a family resemblance, but now I looked remarkably like Giselle.

Giselle paid. She'd gotten me fired so I let her. "What a terrific change," she said.

"You were always prettier," I blurted as we walked to the car.

"No, I try harder," Giselle said. "I slather makeup on every day. I flip through magazines for the latest fashions. I teeter around on these stupid spikes. You think it's easy?"

"Maybe not."

"I've always tried to look hip. While you go for—I don't know—what is that?"

I gave myself the once-over. "Frumpy?"

She threw her hands up. "You can do something about that, Nora."

"Yeah, but you're skinny."

"*You* wear horizontal stripes. You don't have to wait for a Get Out of Jail Free card to stop doing that." She pulled me into an alley. "Take off those clothes."

"Here?" I asked.

Giselle unbuttoned her flowing trench coat. "Yes, here. You wouldn't believe some of the places I've had to change clothes. Hurry up. We're swapping."

Glancing around to see if anyone was watching, I heard a zipper. I looked down. *My* zipper. "Hey!" Giselle pushed my jeans down around my feet. "What the—" As I bent to pull them up, Giselle grabbed my tee shirt and yanked it over my head.

She stared at my big-girl white cotton undies and sports bra. "That is so pathetic," she said, shaking her head.

"Gimme back my—" Instead of my shirt, she threw me her trench coat so I could hold it for her. She didn't seem to care that I was already down to my skivvies. I held it in front of as much of us as I could while she removed her short, black silk wrap-around dress. This left her standing in a sexy black bra and a tiny lacy thong, also black, which she immediately covered by pulling on my tee shirt. She handed me her dress.

"Is this what it feels like to get mugged?" I hurried into the dress. Giselle adjusted the neckline so my bra didn't stick out. Since I'm two inches taller than Giselle, the dress was even shorter on my five foot ten frame. But it covered me up, and it actually fit.

In the bike shop, I'd gotten used to wearing clothes that tended toward the sexless. If I wore anything that even suggested curves, the guys thought I was a sex kitten.

A wolf whistle sounded from above. Men who worked in the second-floor offices lined wide-open windows. "How long have you been there?" I asked.

"Long enough," one said, and he whistled again. I looked over at Giselle.

"They're whistling at you, Nora." She backed away.

At me? I smiled up at them and twirled. Was what they were doing sexist? Maybe, but right now, that was all right with me.

I slipped into the heels Giselle had taken off. After staggering like I'd spent the day at Fat Belly's Bar and Grill, I got the hang of it and headed toward Giselle.

"Wait, wait, wait." She put up her hand to stop me.

"What?" I asked.

"You're dressed sexy but you're still walking frumpy."

"Walking is about getting there."

"It's a lot more than that." She walked, bouncing her hips back and forth in an exaggerated fashion. "It's about your attitude. It's gotta say, 'Wouldn't you love to see this in a bustier and boots?' You *own* them."

I tried it again.

Giselle groaned. "This is gonna be a lot of work," she muttered.

"Hey, I heard that."

I walked, Giselle corrected, I walked some more. Soon I was strutting up and down that alley in Giselle's sexy clothes and Giselle's expensive haircut, feeling pretty darn good.

Giselle trotted up to the main street and beckoned me. When I got there, she pointed at a man with a gorgeous, willowy redhead on his arm, strolling along the sidewalk. "Go!" she whispered.

I sashayed in his direction, eyeballed him, giving it all the attitude I had. When the redhead stopped to look in a window, he slipped his arm from hers and kept coming, eyes riveted on me. As I blew by him, I felt him turn and follow.

The redhead hurried to him. Giselle hurried to me. "You nailed it! You could *be* me."

"I could?"

"Sure. A little work. A little change in attitude."

We stared at each other.

"Would you like to be?" Giselle asked.

"Be you?" I asked, confused.

"I could use a vacation. But I got an assignment. My boss said I just need to find someone who has time to take it on for me. You could come with me, all expenses paid. I'd be helping you, of course. We'd be in it together."

Slowly I said, "I don't have a job."

"That's what I'm saying."

"But doesn't it take a lot of training to become an agent?"

"I don't know if I'd say a *lot.* Some. Definitely some. But I could teach you."

"Isn't it dangerous?"

"Some assignments. But not all of them."

I nodded, nibbling on my lower lip. "I'll think about it."

We got in the car and Giselle drove back toward the dock. I could feel her glance at me a few times, but I didn't say anything. There was so much to think about.

She pulled behind the shop and stopped. "You're coming, right?" she asked.

"It's been five minutes!"

"I'm just asking."

"I'll let you know tomorrow." I got out of the car.

"Hey, I forgot to tell you," Giselle hollered, driving off. "It pays fifty thousand dollars."

Chapter Four

"Fifty *thousand* dollars?" I clapped my hands together. "Hoo! Hoo!"

I had to figure out what I was going to do. I ran to the boat, ditched the black dress for comfy pants and my favorite ratty sweater, and kicked off the stilts. I could only take this dressing up crap in small doses. As I scrubbed makeup off my face, I decided to talk to dad.

***

He sat in the kitchen eating pumpkin pie from the pan. "You do something to your hair?"

"Got it cut," I said, grabbing a fork from the drawer and digging into the pie.

"You look like—"

"I know. Hey, I'm thinking about going with Giselle. Help her with an assignment."

"*You?*"

"I feel like I need a change." I ignored the voice in my head that said most people start by taking a night class or changing their shade of lipstick or something.

"Oh." A thoughtful expression crossed his face. "I don't know what's wrong with Giselle, but something's not right.

If you go, try to help her, Nora. It's not just for her. It's for everyone. She's a family legend. If anything happened to that, it would be like finding out Babe Ruth never hit all those home runs. Or like finding out the U S of A isn't the greatest country in the world. Know what I mean?"

"Sure," I said softly.

Giselle had taken Jesse to the airport. He was on his way back to Washington. She appeared in the kitchen as I pulled on my jacket. "Where you going?" she asked.

"The boat's coming out of the water until the spring. I signed a contract for a winter rental a couple of weeks ago. I have to meet Mrs. Shatkin, the landlady, to pick up the key."

"Can I come?" she asked quickly. "You know. Just to see it."

I shrugged. "Let's go."

Giselle offered to let me drive her car. I took the coast road south. I loved this stretch of shoreline, but it was especially beautiful now, so close to dusk. We meandered by a mix of beaches, clam shacks, motels, and mansions. Tourists flocked here in the summer. But now was my favorite time of year, the quiet off-season. At Hampton Beach, I pulled into a small lot.

Giselle assessed the modest apartment building. "The Farnsworth Estates?"

"She thought that sounded better than Shatkin Apartments." This wasn't Giselle's idea of fine living, but it was clean, cheap, and sliding glass doors led on to a tiny deck overlooking the Atlantic. As we got out of the car, I saw Mrs. Shatkin going into the building on its far end.

At the front door, Giselle read a list of rules written in large letters. "Rule 1 No spitting off the decks. Rule 2 No smoking. Rule 3 No swearing. Rule 4 No drugs. Rule 5 No guns."

We trotted upstairs to my apartment. The door was ajar. Before I could show Giselle around, she made a sweep of the rooms. The fact that the unit was an efficiency made it easier. We went out on the deck to see the view. As we returned to the living room, the front door suddenly swung open.

In an instant, Giselle drew her gun. "Freeze!" she yelled.

Eighty-seven-year-old Mrs. Shatkin stood statuelike, bug-eyed in fear, only her eyeballs moving in her skinny frame. "Giselle," I said softly, "say hello to Mrs. Shatkin." I whispered to Giselle, "She has a heart condition!" I said to Mrs. Shatkin, "It's okay. This is my sister."

Mrs. Shatkin remained stationary. But as soon as Giselle put away her gun, Mrs. Shatkin slammed the door shut and pointed to it. The list of rules prominently displayed outside the front door was also, for my convenience, prominently displayed on the back of this one.

"You broke rule five," she said, glaring at me. She read from the door. "Rule 5 No guns." Mrs. Shatkin crossed her arms. Not exactly radiating a let's-chat-about-this vibe.

I dove in anyway, rapid-fire fashion. "There are five rules, but only one got broken. I don't spit off the deck. I don't spit at all, except when I'm brushing my teeth. And I don't smoke. Some people say they don't smoke when what they really mean is they don't smoke anything but marijuana. I don't even do that. That brings us to the next rule. Drugs, which I don't do, except as prescribed by my physician. Even then, lots of times I don't finish them. And swearing? I only swear when it's definitely warranted, like if I hit my thumb with a hammer. For example, 'That hurts like a son of a bitch.' That time doesn't count though, because I was imagining really hitting my thumb. Or I might swear if—"

"You're outta here." Mrs. Shatkin jerked her thumb skyward like a big league umpire.

But I was on a roll. I turned toward Giselle. "Or I might swear if my sister did something so stupid I lost my winter rental. Shit!"

"Tough toodles," Mrs. Shatkin said.

"I pretty much follow eighty percent of the rules eighty percent of the time. That's not so bad, is it? You don't really expect perfection, do you?"

"Yes."

"What about second chances? Don't I get a second chance?"

"No."

Glancing outside, I spied a "Winter Rentals Available" sign in front of another building. "Fine. I'll take my business elsewhere." I pointed to the sign.

"I own those, too."

I threw up my hands. "Give me back my security deposit and I'll figure something out."

"If you break a rule, you don't get your security deposit back. Read it and weep." With a couple of folds, she made a paper airplane of the rental agreement and sailed it in my direction.

Giselle ran ahead of me. I was so mad, she might have been running *from* me. As I stormed out the front door, I was surprised by a man in my way. I barely saw his face; mostly I focused on the gun he held. "Gimme that." I banged the gun on the list of rules next to the door. "Can't you read?" I looked up toward my former apartment. "Hey, Mrs. Shatkin," I hollered. She appeared on the deck. "Another scofflaw." As the man grabbed for the gun, I jerked it away, and he pitched forward toward a dumpster. I lifted the lid, and between his momentum and sticking my foot in front of him, he propelled himself right in. I closed the lid and locked it.

The dumpster stank of garbage. His lime green shirt would be slime green in a minute.

Mrs. Shatkin looked down. "He doesn't live here," she said.

"Now you won't have to bother processing his application." Placing the weapon by the door, I yelled to Mrs. Shatkin, "But you might want this for when he gets out." I glanced toward Giselle's car. She'd been digging for something and missed the latest gun fun.

As I trudged past the man's black sedan toward the Corvette, Giselle turned toward me, waving a newspaper. "I have the ads," she said. "Want me to help you find another place?"

"Why? So you can take *another* shot at ruining my life?" I yelled.

Chapter Five

The next morning, I drove to my parents' house to meet Giselle. My hair felt more like it used to. No hair spray, no product, not blow-dried to a perfect bob, just pulled back and clipped at the back of my head. Giselle and I no longer looked like twins.

In the kitchen, I poured myself coffee.

"You've seen a little of what my life is like," Giselle said, glancing at her clothes, her jewelry, and out the window at her Corvette. "Might be an interesting change for you, Nora. And you'd make a bundle. How can you lose?"

"I haven't decided yet."

"I'll go with you to the assignment," Giselle said, as if she hadn't heard the "haven't decided" part. "We got lucky. It's a great vacation spot. The guy you're after is wealthy."

I'd kind of forgotten there'd be a "guy" and I'd be "after him." My mouth felt dry.

"I'll show you the ropes," she continued, "and when you're ready—I'll be on vacation and you'll be making tons of money."

"Where would we be going?"

"Someplace sunny by the sea. Come on. We need clothes for the trip."

Giselle drove us to the fashion outlet stores in Kittery,

just north of Portsmouth. I traipsed after her into Jones New York, Dana Buchman, Nine West, and an assortment of other designer stores, ending with Anne Klein. By then, we could hardly carry all the bags.

We headed back to Portsmouth. "I don't know what I'd tell Kenny."

"Why do you have to tell him anything?"

"He asked me to marry him."

"What? When did this happen?"

"Thanksgiving night."

"Why didn't anybody tell me?"

"Nobody knows yet. I haven't had a chance to—"

"Are you nuts? He was cheating on his girlfriends in high school. Me, for example, the little bastard. I thought we were in love. Until he took up with Amy. Then he came groveling back, saying it was all a mistake. I wouldn't marry him if he was the last man on earth. Face it, Nora. Chances are he's still a cheating prick."

"That was a long time ago. He's changed."

"Where is he?"

"On a detail down by the pier, I think. Why?"

In Portsmouth, Giselle took a side road toward the pier. Once we had a clear view of the main street, Giselle parked. Next to a construction site, Kenny leaned against a cruiser. Not a lot to do. Only one lane of traffic could get by. When cars approached from both directions, Kenny played traffic cop, stopping one and waving the other one on.

As we got out of the car, Giselle's phone rang. She was going through her pockets trying to find it when the rev of an engine coming from up the street made me turn. It almost looked like the same black sedan that had just missed us in front of the house on Thanksgiving. He sped towards us.

This guy was a menace. Probably sexting with his girlfriend or something. I yanked Giselle out of the way as he whizzed by, a hairsbreadth away.

"Hey, cut it out." Giselle was still trying to find her phone.

"That guy almost—"

"Found it," she said, pulling her phone out.

I should report that guy before he killed someone. But I was too late to get the license number.

Giselle had missed the call. She tucked her phone away. "I just have to get something from the trunk. Get back in the car. I'll be there in a sec."

From the front passenger seat, I watched the black sedan that had almost hit us. Ha! He was stuck in the construction traffic. He was going nowhere. Served him right.

Getting in the car, Giselle handed me a small piece of plastic. "Here."

"What is this?" I asked, examining it.

"A listening device. It amplifies sound, in case you're not close enough to hear."

"Spy gear," I said. "How exciting." I positioned the device in my ear.

Giselle grabbed a bag from the back seat. Out came a clingy hot pink sheath. She ripped off the tags with her teeth, then slipped her shirt over her head and shimmied out of her pants.

I saw a blur of pink, and a second later Giselle's head popped out of the top of the dress. She poked her arms in the sleeves and pulled the dress down around her rear. Without another word, she opened the door and walked in Kenny's direction. But she didn't just walk, she *walked*. I could feel the heat coming off her. Kenny faced the other direction, but his babe radar picked up her movements. He stopped.

"Don't do it, Kenny. Don't turn around," I said softly.

He turned around and saw her. By then she was crossing the street. She glanced at him.

"Don't do it, Kenny. Don't head in her direction," I said.

He stopped traffic in both lanes and headed in her direction. He was about three feet from her when suddenly Giselle's right leg buckled. She was pretending she'd twisted her ankle.

I sat up in my seat. "Don't do it, Kenny. Please don't do it."

Giselle reached out her hand. Instead of grabbing it, Kenny put his hands around her waist to steady her. She latched on to his forearms.

"Kenny! I could have broken my ankle if you hadn't caught me." I saw her give his arms a squeeze. "My," she said, gazing into his eyes and smiling, "I love a man who works out." A shit-eating grin lit Kenny's face. "Thanks so much for helping me. I wish I knew a way to express my appreciation." They moved closer. "Can you think of anything I could, you know, do?" Her voice dripped with possibility. Their faces were two inches apart.

"Don't, Kenny. Just don't do it, okay?" I said aloud.

Giselle gave Kenny a whopper of a kiss. She didn't even look like she was acting.

"How about a late dinner tonight—at my place?" he asked.

She let out a sexy growl. "See you then."

His hands dropped to her ass and he pressed himself against her. "Oh yeah, baby. See you then." He whimpered as she walked away. In a soft voice, he talked to himself. "You know what I'm going to do to you when I get you alone, baby? I'm going to—"

I yanked the device out of my ear. "Ewww."

Kenny hadn't done the deed, but I had no doubt he would have. That was betrayal in my mind, so of course I thought he was scum. But instead of feeling heartbroken, I felt oddly relieved, almost giddy—as if I'd just had a narrow escape. It had taken Giselle seconds to seduce him. Had other women done the same thing? All the fears about my relationship with Kenny burst to the surface. I broke into a sweat.

I had almost married the wrong man.

The people in the stopped cars had watched the Kenny and Giselle show. With no one directing traffic, two drivers decided to go at the same time and crashed into each other. One of them was the black sedan. The drivers got out to yell at Kenny and each other. Giselle plopped back in the car.

There was nothing left to stop me. "What time should I be at the airport tomorrow?"

"Five o'clock," she said.

"I thought we were going in the morning."

"We are."

Chapter Six

The alarm dragged me out of a deep sleep. Three in the morning. Not that it mattered much. I'd tossed and turned for most of the night anyway. I'd stayed at my parents' house. Trudging to the kitchen, I downed a cup of instant coffee. My cheerfulness index inched up. I hoped the same could be said for my mental abilities.

Giselle had said if she wasn't home, she'd meet me at the airport. I hadn't asked any questions about whatever spy business she was up to. I peeked out the window. No Giselle-mobile. I got ready and made the short drive to the airport.

As I walked toward the outdoor luggage check-in, I thought I saw Giselle in the distance. The woman wore the kind of huge sunglasses that make you look like an insect. A floral scarf covered her hair. I kept watching, and yes, from the walk I could tell it was Giselle. I waved.

"How did you know it was me?" she asked as she approached.

"You're dressed the way Hollywood stars dress when they don't want anyone to recognize them, but it's so obvious, you can't keep from staring to try to figure out who it is."

"Are people looking?" She clutched my forearm, her fingernails digging into my skin.

"No," I lied. "Nobody's even awake yet."

"Oh good." She let out a sigh, and I pried her fingers off my arm.

We checked our bags. "I'm glad you're paying," I said. "Must be expensive."

"Not as expensive as you'd think," she said. "Hurricane season hasn't ended yet."

Part of my brain screamed, "Flee now." The part hollering, "Show me the money" wrestled it to the ground. Giselle handed me my ticket, slipping hers into a dark blue rectangle.

"That almost looks like a passport," I said.

"It is a passport." She snapped her head up. "You have yours, right?"

"Not exactly, no. Why would I need a passport?"

"To get out of the country."

"You said a place sunny by the sea. I thought we were going to—"

"Where? Disney World?"

"Around here when people say that, they usually *are* going to Disney World."

"There are lots of other sunny places to go in the world besides Disney World."

I glanced at my ticket. "Barlanadana. Barlanadana? I've never even heard of it."

"Barlanadana Island. It's so small, most people don't know about it. It's past Bermuda. But not as far as the Caribbean. I think. I've only been there once. But you're not going if you don't have your passport. I could have given you one of mine," she said, fanning out an array of fake passports, "but the ticket's already in your real name."

"I'm sorry. I know you've had assignments outside of the country, but I thought one time you mentioned working for the FBI. And the FBI works inside the US."

"Do I look like FBI? They're all dark and drab, not stunning and alluring. These shoes alone—"

"I admit that part didn't make sense, but I was sure one time you said you did. You work for the CIA? See, that's the source of my confusion. It's the CIA that works outside the US."

Giselle rolled her eyes.

I jammed my hands on my hips. "Oh, so you thought I would just suddenly know everything by some kind of special spy osmosis or something? So I was a little confused," I said, my voice getting louder by the word, "never having been a spy and all."

Giselle clapped her hand over my mouth. "Shhh."

"Mmmf, mmmmf."

"I can't understand a word you're saying."

I removed the hand still clamped over my mouth. "Shouldn't we go get my passport?"

"Right. We have to hurry." She scanned the slowing cars. A midnight-blue Mercedes roadster stopped. Leaving the car running, a man got out of the driver's side and opened the trunk. The passenger met him at the back of the car. "Get in the car, Nora," Giselle said to me. As she moved to the driver's door, she said to the man, "We're with the government."

"Hey, that's my car!"

"We need to commandeer your car for an important mission. Wait here."

"I can't go anywhere," he yelled. "You're taking my damn car."

Giselle burned rubber getting us out of there. "Wow," I said, "you can do that?"

"Not really," Giselle said.

"You mean we just broke the law?"

"Technically, yes. But I prefer to think of it as exercising my judgment in the service of my country." She sped down the road.

"My passport's at the house." When we arrived, I ran in, got it, and ran back to the car.

Giselle stared into the rear view at a truck coming down the street. "Hang on, I'm gonna lose this guy." She careened around the corner and took off for the airport. But in a busy area, a light turned red. Giselle slid so far down in her seat, she couldn't see out the windshield. "You'll have to direct me."

"What? Sit up!"

"I'm not going to sit up and risk getting—"

"*I'm* not going to get killed because you can't see where you're going." I tried pulling her up but she scrunched further down. The light would change any second. "Swap seats." She scootched over to the passenger side as I scrambled across her. The light turned green.

"Lose him," she said.

"That's the newspaper delivery guy. I don't think he's actually after you."

"Lose him. Lose him. *Lose him.*"

"Okay. Okay. *Okay.*" We approached a rotary. I'd never outrun him here. Instead, I slowed so he could catch up with me. I sped up and he did too. When we were almost past an exit road, I shouted, "Hold on." I veered toward the exit, skidded off the pavement, and fishtailed across grass before bumping back onto the exit road. Messy. But it had forced the truck to continue around the rotary.

"Thanks," Giselle said, exhaling a big breath of air.

In the rear view mirror, I saw the truck swerve onto the grassy center of the rotary. He slowed for a split second, but then instead of moving with the flow of traffic *around* the rotary, he headed directly *across* it, in our direction. A tractor-trailer entered the rotary going fast; he'd never stop in time. Brakes squealing, he barreled into the smaller truck, knocking it on its side, pushing it in its path until, amidst the screech of metal, the trucks came to a stop past the edge of the rotary.

Maybe that wasn't our newspaper delivery guy.

My heart pounded. Getting on the plane seemed like a good idea right about now. I glanced at my watch. "We're too late. The plane takes off in five minutes. By the time we—"

Giselle got on her phone. "Carl, I'm late for the Barlanadana flight."

"You have someone who can rebook us?" I asked as she disconnected.

"Rebook us? No," Giselle said, giving me a "duh" look, "I had them hold the plane."

"Okay, let me get this straight. You had someone hold an international plane full of hundreds of passengers because I forgot my passport."

"Sure," she said. "But only for an extra fifteen minutes."

I shot her a look as I jammed my foot on the accelerator. I took the turn into the airport on two wheels, skidded to a stop in a swirl of burning-rubber smoke at the terminal. Flipping the keys to the pissed-off Mercedes owner, I sprinted for the plane alongside Giselle.

Chapter Seven

The other passengers glared at us as we made our way down the aisle to our seats. Maybe they'd think it was Giselle's fault.

"She forgot her passport," Giselle announced loudly, nodding in my direction.

Maybe not.

As soon as we took our seats and buckled up, the plane started backing. I leaned toward Giselle. "I have a few questions," I whispered.

"Shh," she said.

I lowered my voice even more. "Can you tell me—"

"Shhhh!" she said, spewing spit, eyes spinning in their sockets. Either that was her little signal too many people sat nearby to be able to talk or she was about to have a seizure.

I kept my questions to myself. But as the stewardess went over safety instructions, I wondered if a water landing would be an improvement over actually making it to Barlanadana.

Jumbo jets didn't fly directly to the small island. By the time we landed at our stopover, waited for the propeller plane to arrive, and made the white-knuckle trip to the tiny airport on Barlanadana Island, it was midafternoon.

I stumbled off the plane behind Giselle into brilliant sunshine. We retrieved our bags and zigzagged through a chaos of locals in tropical colors and farm animals to the outside car park.

"That's ours." Giselle pointed to a sleek yellow number.

A chicken stood atop the car. I shooed it, but the chicken squawked and stayed put. All of the locals in the vicinity stopped suddenly and stared at me, menace in their eyes. "Giselle, what's going on?"

"You know how cows are sacred in India? Here it's chickens."

"Now you tell me."

"Kiss the chicken," she said.

"I'm not going to—"

"There are strict chicken protection laws. Chicken-shooing gets you six months hard labor." The rumbling of the crowd increased. "And this group's not looking too friendly."

"Do I have to kiss it on the lips?"

"Technically, chickens don't have lips. I think on the head's okay."

I kissed the chicken, gave it a pat. I threw in a curtsy for good measure. The chicken hopped off the car. The crowd smiled and nodded and continued on their way. I sagged against the car with relief, then started to get in. "Guess we won't be stopping at KFC, huh?"

Giselle hit the gas as the crowd spun and pounded after us. When we were safely out of range, I looked at her. "How come I'm in the driver's seat and the steering wheel is over there?"

"They drive on the left down here." She squealed out of the airport onto the main road. A car hurtled towards us. We were going to have a head-on collision.

"Look out!" I yelled. But Giselle never took her foot off

the gas. "Aieee!" I screamed. The cars passed within inches of each other. I put my hand on my chest. "Oh, thank God. That was close." I giggled the near-hysterical giggle I always giggled when I survived a near-death experience. Up to now, there'd only been one other time.

I had the feeling my rate of near-death experiences might be on the upswing.

Another car approached. We were going to have a head-on collision. "Look out!" But Giselle never took her foot off the gas. "Aieee!" I screamed.

"Are you going to do that every time a car goes by?" Giselle asked.

Another car hurtled past. "Aieee!" I screamed.

"I'll take that as a yes."

"Are we going to almost get killed every time a car passes?" I asked.

"Roads are narrow here. They cut things a lot closer."

We passed motorized recliners, office chairs, bikes. Anything an enterprising local could slap a motor on was used for transportation. The big plus was that the smaller vehicles reduced the possibility of a head-on crash. Ten minutes from the airport, Giselle took a turn.

I looked at the sign on the hotel. "The Barlanadana Potentate?"

"They wanted to call it the Barlanadana Baroness, but that name was taken already."

As Giselle pulled to a stop, the sign fell off. "I thought we were going first class," I said.

"Here, this is first class." A fake pineapple tree crashed to the ground beside the car.

We walked into the foyer. Relaxed guests sat on couches sipping brightly-colored drinks. Through open glass doors toward the back of the hotel, I glimpsed turquoise ocean and white sand. Maybe it wouldn't be so bad.

Giselle and I checked in and made our way to our sixth-floor suite. The living room featured a balcony overlooking the water. Giselle continued to the bedroom while I opened the sliding glass doors and walked out to admire the view. I leaned on the deck railing, but it came off in my hand. I pinwheeled back, barely avoiding the plunge. "Aieee!" I ran into the suite, slammed the sliders shut, and locked them.

I went into the bedroom and threw myself on a bed. Two legs collapsed, and I slid to the floor. I sighed, pulled off the other legs, and threw myself back on the bed.

"Change into something cool," Giselle said.

"Why?"

"We have to be at the shooting range in thirty minutes."

Lots of the bikers back home carried weapons. But it was a machismo thing, primarily for swaggering purposes. "The *shooting* range? You mean, like, guns?"

"Yeah, I mean guns. What did you think we were going to use?"

"I guess I hadn't gotten that far," I said uncomfortably. "Tranquilizer darts?"

"Mostly those are for species that aren't shooting back."

***

Twenty-five minutes later, Giselle took a turn onto a dirt road. "I didn't see a sign for the shooting range," I said.

"This isn't exactly open to the public."

"Where does the public go?"

"Nowhere. Guns are illegal here."

"If they're illegal, how can we—"

50

"Some kind of an uh... special agreement."

"Special *illegal* agreement, you mean?"

"Technically, yes."

"In the seventies, after it was exposed that the CIA was plotting to kill people like Castro and spying on anti-war protestors and stuff, I thought they put new rules in place so the CIA wouldn't do secret, illegal things anymore."

"They did put rules in place for the CIA."

"So..."

"So they just created another agency. Where the rules don't apply."

"But I thought you worked for the CIA."

"I never said that."

"But I assumed it. And you never said I was wrong."

"I can't really be held responsible for the erroneous assumptions you make, can I, Nora?"

"You could have..." This was a rabbit hole I didn't want to head down. "So, you work for this other agency. What's the name of this one?"

"I can't tell you that."

"I'm in this up to my eyeballs, and you can't tell me the name of the agency?"

"I can't because I don't know," she said. "Since the government would disavow knowledge of any of the operations, they figured it would be easier if they just didn't name it at all. That way, anyone caught couldn't tell because they wouldn't know."

"I can't believe some administration along the way didn't ban this kind of thing."

"Well..." She glanced at me.

"There's more?"

"The agency was set up so it was virtually impossible to

trace, and it was funded covertly from the get go. So when a new administration came in after the agency was formed, the old guys kind of forgot to mention it existed."

"So the current government doesn't even know about it?"

"Hardly anyone. Since the funding was covert, the agency just kept rolling along."

"That's unbelievable."

"On the plus side, we generally don't try to assassinate foreign dictators anymore. Instead of killing them, we try to slip them something that just makes them really, really nauseous. At critical points in time, they're in the bathroom."

"And you're sure you don't work for the FBI?"

"No. Why would you think that?"

"I was sure one time when you were home you said you worked for the FBI."

"Well... Sometimes I get letters mixed up. And even though the agency doesn't have a real name, the agents gave it an unofficial name. We call it the FIB."

"You work for an agency with an acronym that spells the word 'fib'?"

"I agree it wasn't the best choice."

"What do the letters stand for?"

"I don't know. I don't know anybody who does. Like I said, the agents made it up."

"And... it's possible it's not even an acronym. It might just be a bunch of letters."

She shrugged. "Sure. It's possible." She smiled. She liked the idea.

A sudden rat-a-tat-tat of machine gun fire sounded from somewhere ahead of us. "We must be getting close," I said.

She looked at me. "We're not."

Chapter Eight

From beyond a small rise came the sound of a car engine—a roaring engine in a big hurry. We couldn't see the vehicle, but from the escalating noise I could tell it was headed our way. Giselle pulled off to the side of the road. We waited. Suddenly the car crested the hill, airborne. It sailed forward and crashed to the ground, front wheels first. The driver floored it, and a moment later the car hurtled by. Inside, two teenagers screamed in terror. Kicked-up dust followed in their wake.

"Did you see that?" I asked. "There were bullet holes in the side of the car."

"They were lucky."

"Lucky? They were shot at."

"Bullets in the side of the car are warning shots."

"They could have been killed."

"If the agency wanted to kill them, those kids would be dead now. They just don't want them to ever come back." Giselle pulled back onto the road. When we went over the hill, I saw a fence about half a mile away. The only way through was a gate topped with barbed wire where the fence crossed the road.

As we approached the gate, I pointed out an area where dirt had been disturbed. "That's where those kids turned around." We rolled to a stop on top of it. "This must be right where the shots hit them." Sweat ran down my back.

"They weren't supposed to be here," Giselle said. A second later, the gate swung open.

"How did that happen?"

"We're being watched."

I swiveled my head. "I don't see anybody."

"You don't want to see them."

"I don't?"

"The only time you see them is if they're shooting at you."

We continued a mile or so, then turned onto another unmarked dirt road. A few hundred feet down, we parked near half a dozen other vehicles. Sporadic gunfire sounded off to the left.

When we got out, Giselle went to the trunk, pulled out something, and threw it to me. "Put this on."

"Oof," I said as the weight of it thudded against my chest. "Is this what I think it is?"

"Do you think it's a bulletproof vest?"

Right. I struggled into it.

"You need to get used to the feel of it," she said.

I followed Giselle toward a dilapidated shack. Inside, a stern-faced man placed handguns, ammunition, and other gear on a table. Giselle picked up the guns and ammo.

"I've got the earmuffs," I said.

The man guffawed. "Those are ear protectors."

I could feel the heat in my face as I went red.

"Earmuffs you'd wear if you were maybe going ice skating in Schenectady. This here's a shooting range." A long volley of gunfire sounded. "In case you hadn't noticed."

"Come on," Giselle said, shaking her head at me like I was a half-wit. We headed in the direction of the gunfire. We passed behind people in various stages of loading ammunition and taking shots at targets—bull's eyes and cutouts in the shapes of humans—set up in an open field. We continued to a table at the farthest end of the range. Giselle spread out the guns and ammo.

I yawned. The lack of sleep was catching up with me. I'd hoped there'd be a Starbucks on the way. I'd have settled for a Dunkin Donuts. Instant out of a machine. But no. I'd noticed some people had thermoses. Swiping some crossed my mind, but these folks all had loaded weapons.

"This," Giselle said, picking up a gun, "is a Glock 9 millimeter semi-automatic pistol. When we get back to the hotel, there'll be one for each of us in the room. This is the gun typically used by agents."

"What do the bad guys use?"

"It can vary. But lots of times it's a Glock 9 millimeter semi-automatic pistol. They steal ours. Now, see that target?"

I looked out toward the bull's eye. She handed me the gun. It was lighter than I expected. I got into the stance she showed me and raised the gun.

"Okay," Giselle said, "line up to the target. Now, nice and steady, squeeze the—"

BLAM! The gun barrel rocketed skyward, jerking my arms up. "Geez!" I said. The recoil was so powerful I almost dropped the gun. My entire body shook from the blast. "People shoot these at each other?" The thought of actually aiming this much deadly force at another human being was sickening.

"If someone's shooting at you, you do."

Okay, I imagined *that*. That was even more sickening. I had a lot of living left to do, and if it came down to me and some guy perpetrating evil on the world, maybe I *would* shoot.

Giselle's voice came from behind me. "Get ready, aim—"

BLAM! Once again, the gun jolted my arm upward, but I kept better control this time. It was still terrifying, but a fraction less. I waited a few seconds for my heart rate to slow, then assumed the stance, aimed, and fired.

"Hold on a second," Giselle said.

I stopped and turned toward her.

"Now take a look at where you're hitting the target."

I squinted to see. "One close to the center and the other two almost off the target."

"Right. Your first shot was your best. Then you started trying to compensate for the recoil. You tightened up, and it's screwing up your aim. Try again, just don't overcompensate."

I got into position, trying to keep a little looser this time. I aimed and fired.

"Excellent," Giselle said, peering at the target.

I followed her gaze. At first I couldn't see it. Then I realized. It was dead center.

Giselle practiced with another gun, while I shot the Glock over and over again. At first some shots went wild, but as I kept at it, my consistency increased. As it did, so did my confidence. With the first blam of the gun, my exhaustion had vanished, but eventually it returned. I shot until my arms and fingers ached. I picked up a different gun and practiced with that one. After a series of five shots that all landed near the center, I turned to Giselle. "Hey, I'm getting pretty good."

"Yes, but let's talk about a couple of things related to gun safety."

"Okay," I said, yawning as I turned toward her. "I could use a break. Getting up at three in the morning is tough. I'm exhausted." I yawned again and went to scratch my backside.

"Hey!" she yelled. "Keep your finger off the—"

BLAM! "Holy shit!" I said.

"—trigger," Giselle finished.

I dropped the gun. Was my rear end still there? I turned to find out. It was, but the blast had torn the denim down to my underwear. A splotch of red seeped through.

"Like I was saying, keep your finger off the trigger unless you're shooting."

"I don't even remember squeezing the trigger."

"You startled when I yelled. That's all it takes if your finger's on the trigger. Keep your finger pressed on the side of the gun unless you're ready to shoot. And always keep control of your gun. Right about now is when a bad guy grabs the gun you just dropped and starts killing people. You might be one of them. And then again you might not."

I swallowed and nodded. If it wasn't me, it might be some innocent civilian.

I'd been quick to think I was good with a gun—then I'd almost shot my ass off. In the real world, other lives might be at stake, and someone would be shooting back. Would I be so good at hitting a target if I was hyperventilating and shaking so hard I could barely hold the gun?

"Let me see," Giselle said. She examined my rear. "Just a graze."

"Hurts like hell. But it scared me more than anything."

"You should be scared. Keeps you on your toes. You'll get into situations where you'll be terrified. That lets loose a ton of adrenaline that helps you deal with whatever it was that terrified you."

Then I might have a teensy problem. Because just talking about getting into situations that would terrify me terrified me. We walked back toward the shack, turned in the guns and leftover ammunition, and made our way to the car.

When we got to the gate, it magically opened again. A short way past, Giselle pulled over and we swapped seats so I could practice driving.

I pulled on my seat belt, then started the car. "The stick shift's on the wrong side."

"That's because the driver's on the right side."

"Geez." It was bad enough sitting on the wrong side of the car and driving on the wrong side of the road, not to mention doing it on three hours of sleep. But having to shift with my left hand? The possibility my head would explode notched upward. I gave the car a little gas and we inched forward. I gave it a little more and shifted. The car stalled.

"You shifted into fourth instead of second."

I started the car again and got it into second, then made the turn. "This doesn't look familiar," I said after about a half a mile.

"It's not."

I was momentarily confused. "Are we taking the scenic route back?"

"No. You took a wrong turn."

"Thanks a lot. Why didn't you tell me?"

"You need your senses on high alert all the time, Nora. And when you get yourself into a jam, you need to be able to figure your way out of it. Believe me, this is nothing compared to some of the jams you'll get into."

I sat up a little straighter and turned the car around. "You're not going to make this easy for me, are you, Giselle?"

"What if someone kidnapped you and blindfolded you and

brought you to another location. How would you get back?"

I gripped the wheel more tightly. "Could that happen?"

"It's better to be safe than sorry. I'm just saying pay attention. Go with what you know. And remember, you always know more than you think you know."

What the heck had I gotten myself into? I swallowed hard, then concentrated on the task. What did I know? I had to go back to where I'd taken the last turn. But how would I tell— Then I saw what I needed. The boys who'd been shot at had been speeding. The tire tracks here showed a vehicle in a hurry; they'd made a turn much wider than normal. I continued on, and in a few minutes we arrived back at the main road.

After checking for traffic, I started to pull out. A horn blared. I jammed on the brake. A Jeep swerved past, narrowly missing us. I knew immediately what I'd done. I'd forgotten about driving on the left. I'd looked the wrong way for traffic. "Crap."

"I did the same thing when I was learning."

Having nearly killed us, I took a second to refocus before looking in the correct direction and pulling out. I gained speed and successfully shifted to second. We continued on to the hotel. I occasionally forgot the actual shifting mechanism located in the center of the car and tried to shift thin air on the window side. In light traffic I regularly drifted over to the right side of the road. Once I even started around a rotary in the wrong direction and had to swerve wildly to avoid oncoming traffic. But when I made the turn into the hotel, we were in one piece. I pulled into a parking space in the lot. "I'm getting better, wouldn't you say?"

"I was thinking exactly the same thing. And you don't scream every time a car goes by."

Back in our room, we took quick showers before going down to dinner. The fried conch was like chewing pencil erasers, but maybe that's what conch was supposed to be like. Giselle seemed more interested in fancy rum drinks than food, generously offering me her leftover octopus. I opted for dessert, fresh pineapple with vanilla ice cream smothered in rum caramel sauce. By the time we trudged back to our room, it was almost eleven.

"Don't wake me. I'm sleeping in," I said, getting into my pajamas.

"We have one day before your target arrives, Nora. We have to get in as much training as possible tomorrow."

"I'm only getting one *day* of training?"

"One day for the basics."

"What's the rush?"

"Well, if you get your target *after* the coup, that wouldn't be helpful, would it?"

"*Coup*? What coup? You can't mean 'coup' as in plotting to take over the government. 'Coup' must have a different meaning down here, right? Kind of like snow has lots of different meanings to Eskimos? It's like that, right? A Barlanadana-specific kind of a meaning?"

She crawled into bed. "No, 'coup' means pretty much the same thing down here as back home. But I probably should have waited to mention that part. Let's talk about it in the morning." She pulled the covers up and put her head on the pillow. "The important thing now is to get a good night's sleep."

I stared wide-eyed at her reclining form. Oh yeah. Like that was gonna happen.

Chapter Nine

The next morning, I hovered over a sleeping Giselle. Any chance of an early start was already long gone. As soon as her eyes fluttered, I got in her face. "One *day* of training?"

"One day before he arrives. Then the rest of the training will be JIT."

"What's JIT?"

"Just in time. We work on the training right before you need it. We kind of tailor it to the specific requirements of this assignment."

"Oh." That sounded better than just one crappy day of training. We ordered room service and got ourselves organized.

"We can do this bit of training down by the pool," Giselle said.

Things were improving. This part didn't involve guns. Ten minutes later we arrived at a table poolside. The bar had been built right in the pool, where the water was a few feet deep. People in bathing suits sat on the stools, their legs dangling in the water. "What do you want to drink?" I asked Giselle as she sat down in a lounge chair.

"Whiskey."

At eleven in the morning? "You mean like with ginger ale?"

"Ginger ale? No. Straight."

I shrugged and waded toward the bar. "Okay. Whatever you—"

"Make it a double." Somewhere in a dining room to my left, a tray filled with breakables crashed to the floor. I looked back. Giselle did a full body flinch. "A triple," she yelled.

Even here, Giselle was seriously jumpy. I was getting more and more curious why. Vacationers already packed the bar. The bartender flipped his sandy-colored, surfer-dude locks out of his eyes. "What'll it be?" he asked. As I answered, a group of drunks at the other end let out a burst of laughter. The bartender put his hand behind his ear. "Come again?"

"That's one Purple Russian," I yelled. I'd heard a spy order one in a movie once. Of course, James Bond had his own signature drink. "Hold on." Maybe I should, too. "Make that a Violet Cossack." I needed my wits about me today. I'd never drink it. But now I felt more... spy-like.

"And?" he said.

"And a triple whiskey straight up."

"Giselle must be back. I thought she'd be sleeping off the triple she had for breakfast."

"For breakfast?" I asked.

"She was down earlier." He set the triple on the bar. "Now, let's see. A Violet Cossack. I'm not sure I have any huckleberries left." He moved some bottles around. "Ah. Here we go."

In his cool way, James also told them how to make the drink. "Blendered, not stirred," I said to the bartender.

"Unless you want to use your teeth as a strainer, that's really the only way to make it," he said. "All those huckleberries, ya know?"

Okay, so cool might not be my thing.

He whirled the drink and set it next to the triple. I paid him, left a twenty-dollar tip of the government's money, and made my way back toward Giselle.

Extending her arms in my direction, she made a "gimmee" motion with her fingers. She took a gulp of the drink, grimaced and waited for the heat to hit. "Ahhh," she said, settling back.

"Okay," I said. "What do I need to know?"

"Let's start with lying."

"How to or how to spot someone who is?"

"First, how to spot someone who is. The spy game is all about information. You need a way to figure out whether the info you're getting is true or false."

"Okay. What do you do?"

"What do you think you do?"

"Bring a Bible and ask people to swear on it?"

"No."

"I didn't really think so, Giselle. But aren't *you* supposed to be teaching me?"

She took another gulp of her drink. "Okay, first you try to see how they act when they're not lying. That gives you a baseline. Then while you're asking them questions, focus on when they act differently."

"So you might see two people doing the same thing. But it only indicates a lie for the one who doesn't usually do it."

"Right."

"Gotcha." I looked over at the bar. As we watched, a man with a slightly askew toupee approached two bikini-clad women. He introduced himself and sat down. We listened as they chatted. He seemed nice and relaxed.

"So," one of the women asked, "are you married?"

He crossed his arms over his chest. "No. How about you?"

The women started talking about their divorces, and he uncrossed his arms. "Have you ever been divorced?" the other woman asked him.

"Nope," he said, crossing his arms, "I don't believe in it. I'm waiting for just the right woman to spend the rest of my life with."

"Oh, that's sweet. Isn't that sweet, Sarah?" The man uncrossed his arms.

"He's married," Giselle said to me. "And it's at least his second marriage."

"How can you be so sure?"

"He's normally relaxed. But when asked if he was married and if he'd been divorced, he crossed his arms both times."

When the women left, Giselle and I took their places at the bar and started chatting with the man. After a few minutes, I asked, "So, are you married?"

He crossed his arms. "No."

He dropped his arms. "Ever been divorced?" I asked.

He crossed his arms again. "I don't believe in it. I'm waiting for just the right—"

"Howard!" A woman with an indignant stride bore down on us. "Can't you even stay away from other women on our wedding anniversary? No wonder Kathy divorced you."

"Gotta go!" Howard said. Twisting on his stool away from his wife, he extracted a gold ring from his pocket and slipped it on his left ring finger. "Nice talking to you." He hopped off the bar stool and hurried in her direction.

"Geez," I said to Giselle, "you were right." We got up to return to our table.

"Told you."

"What else?"

"Basically, keep your bullshit meter running. If something feels off, it probably is. If they try to distract you, pay attention. They could be trying to avoid something. If you ask them a question and it takes a while for them to answer, it might mean they're making something up. Stuff like that." As we sat down, she said, "Now let me ask you a question."

"What?"

"Did you really love Kenny?"

"I was going to marry him, wasn't I?"

"Excellent! It's really a lie, but you achieved it by disanswering the question."

"What do you mean?"

She snorted. "Well, you couldn't look at me. You crossed your legs and started bouncing your right one a million miles an hour. And you didn't answer my question 'yes' or 'no.' Instead, you asked me a question back."

I narrowed my eyes at her.

"It was a lie, wasn't it?" she asked.

"Well... Do you mean was my intent to deceive?"

She nodded.

"Well, in that case, yes."

"The disanswering approach works great. But you're terrible at the delivery. You're going to have to practice. Not everyone is good at it at first. Remember to use as much of the truth as possible. Makes it less likely you'll get caught."

"What else do I have to learn?"

"Let's talk about the body language that tells you how a person's responding to your spy tactics."

"I think I can figure out mad, sad and glad all by myself."

"I was thinking more like murderous, lecherous and

treacherous."

I sat up. "I'm all ears."

"Here are some of the things people will try when you've pushed them up against the wall." She ticked the items off on her fingers. "Head butts, driving your nose into your brain, a shot to the kidney, manual strangulation if it's a spur of the moment attempt on your life, pointing a loaded gun at you if they thought about killing you beforehand and brought what they needed. Any of these things are body language which tells you they're not pleased."

This was more than the frown on a happy face I'd envisioned. "So it's best not to tick them off."

"Right. In the lecherous category. Grabbing private body parts, ripping your clothes off, tying limbs to bed posts."

"Just to clarify. You mean when you'd prefer not to be grabbed, ripped and tied?"

"Yes."

Not the no I'd so hoped for. "Okay, let's have the treacherous category."

"Lying to your face, setting you up to be killed, pretending to be your friend and then stabbing you in the back."

"The stabbing you in the back. You mean that figuratively, right?"

"No," she said.

The biker dudes from Portsmouth morphed into the Brady Bunch.

"Remember," she continued, "the goal is to bring them down before any of the really bad stuff happens. But if it does, it's the signal something's not going according to plan. Sometimes you have to be inventive when things go wrong. You know, take the appropriate action."

"What's the appropriate action?"

"That depends on what's happened."

"Could you just give me an example?"

"Give me an example of what's happened."

"Never mind," I said. "What's next?"

"Surveillance."

"I can do that."

She looked at my turquoise shirt and neon orange shorts. "You do understand that surveillance means you're watching them. But they don't *know* that you're watching them. Because the *last* thing you want," she shuddered, "is them watching you and knowing you're watching them."

"What would happen if they did?"

Her eyes bugged out and she extended her arms wide out to the sides. "They'd have *questions*. And they'd make you answer them."

I leaned forward. "So what do I do?"

"Blend in. See how the other people dress and act, then do whatever you can to dress and act the same. Don't do anything to bring attention to yourself. And wherever you are, be ready with a good reason why you're there. Just in case."

"Sounds like a piece of cake."

Giselle yawned. "You should practice." She waved her hand in the general vicinity of the lobby. "Go follow somebody." Resting her head back on the chaise lounge, she closed her eyes. "Then report back to me."

"Okay," I said, glancing toward the lobby, "I'll just mosey on out there and take a look around." I stood up and took a few tentative steps. "And then," I turned back toward Giselle, "report back—" But Giselle's breathing was steady. She was already on a triple-whiskey trip to la-la land.

In the lobby, I scanned the crowd. An elderly woman who had to be in her eighties tottered toward the front door. Nah, that would be too easy. A woman with two whiny kids tugging at her dress stood near the front desk. That would be too annoying.

A woman's voice caught my attention. A blonde with the biggest beehive hairdo I'd ever seen walked from the hotel entrance toward the dining room. She wore a red cape of some thin, shimmery material, made for elegance, not warmth. Black high heels and a matching bag completed an eye-catching ensemble. "After lunch, there are some shops I want to go to—" She preceded the stocky man she was talking to into the dining room.

She would be just right. While they had lunch, I'd have time to change so I could blend in. I'd be down in the lobby in time to follow her wherever she was going.

I returned to our suite and headed for the closet. I rifled through the dresses. Giselle had said to blend in. I tried to imagine what the woman might be wearing under that glamorous red cape. Giselle had a polka dot dress that had that same feeling of elegance. Pulling off my shirt and shorts, I wiggled into the dress. Slipping on black shoes similar to the ones the woman was wearing, I turned toward the mirror. A rich, classy woman looked back.

Was I good or what? I'd fit right in.

Pulling a pair of sunglasses out of my purse, I walked to the elevator and got on. I punched the button, but nothing happened. I punched it again and waited. Nothing. These elevators seemed to have minds of their own. I waited, and when it was good and ready, it descended to the lobby.

Taking a seat on a couch with a view of the dining room, I checked my watch. One o'clock. I suddenly realized how hungry I was. Once my surveillance was in full swing, it's not like I could ask them if we could pull over to a McDonald's. On the other hand, passing out from hunger would be at odds with the whole blending-in concept.

A candy bar would get me through the afternoon. I strode across the lobby toward a shop selling sundries. On the tiled part of the lobby, my high heels created a racket. Click. Clack. Click. Clack. Everyone at the front desk turned my way. I gave a little wave and hurried on. If I went back upstairs to change shoes now, the woman might be gone by the time I got back.

Let's hope I didn't need to sneak up on them.

I bought a Snickers. Back on the couch, I took a big bite, dropping a bit of chocolate on my dress. As I tried to pick it off, I smeared it. I licked my finger and tried to wipe it off, but that jiggled the candy bar and another piece of chocolate fell on my dress. When the woman with the beehive came out of the dining room, I had two extra polka dots. While admittedly these were chocolate brown instead of black, I'd tried to make them as round as possible.

The stocky man escorted her out to a Cadillac the parking valet rolled to a stop at the entrance. As soon as the Caddie moved, I stepped outside and into a cab waiting for a fare.

"Follow that car," I said to the cabbie, pointing to the Cadillac. He turned to see if I was kidding. "Really," I yelled. He shot away from the hotel in pursuit.

Chapter Ten

We followed the Caddy into the nearby shopping district and pulled behind it when it stopped. I paid the cabbie, waited a few seconds, and got out. The beehive blonde and the man walked into a store displaying very expensive dresses and fashion accessories.

Standing near the window, I pulled a small pad from my purse and started making notes. I'd thought the woman was tall, but the beehive and the heels alone had to add up to a foot, so she was really average height. I noted her weight, hair color, what time she'd had lunch, notes on her male companion. I glanced into the window once in a while and kept writing. I could show this to Giselle so she could see how well I was doing. Suddenly the light dimmed. I thought the sun had moved behind a cloud until I looked up, directly into the eyes of the man who had driven the Cadillac. This close up, he appeared a lot bigger. In his forties, he was medium height but squat, with the physique of a linebacker heading toward paunch. He wore a dark suit that, with minor alterations, could have fit him.

"What do you think you're doing?" he asked.

Hmm. Giselle had said I should have an answer to this question. A good answer. Shopping was the obvious answer, but the truth was I hated to shop and I had no intention of shopping. But I didn't have a better answer. "Shopping," I said, crossing my arms.

"No," he said, voice heavy with sarcasm, "shopping is when you're *inside* the shop, trying on dresses and stuff."

He had a point of course.

"What you're doing, looking in the window at somebody *else* trying on dresses and stuff and making notes about it? That's not shopping. That's something else."

"Like what?" I asked with a defiant air, hands on hips. Then I crossed my arms over my chest again. Might as well do it now. I wasn't lying right this second, but I was pretty sure I was gonna be lying my ass off in a minute.

He considered the question. "Since you asked, I'd say it's more like surveillance."

I'd thought following these two would be a piece of cake. It was more like hash.

"No, I really am shopping," I said earnestly. That was a lie, but I thought my delivery had been pretty good. "It's just that I'm not very good at it. And the lady in the shop seemed like she was. So I was just watching her, seeing what she did." Truth, truth, truth. "So I could improve my shopping skills." Finishing with a lie.

Would he buy it? It was three-fifths truth.

"I thought every woman knew how to shop." His eyebrows met in the center as he puzzled this out. "Like it was genetic or something."

"I'm... I'm shopping-impaired. And I'm embarrassed enough about it, without you making fun of me." I sniffled.

"I'm sorry you feel that way." He patted me on the shoulder. "I didn't mean nothin' of the kind. It's just that, being her bodyguard and all, I gotta be on the lookout all the time."

Her *bodyguard?* It was then that I noticed the bulge under his jacket pocket. Now was not the best time to notice it. If I'd noticed it earlier, I'd be following the lady with the two annoying kids now. For that matter, shouldn't I have immediately questioned a close male friend willing to go clothes shopping? Of course he was her bodyguard! I definitely had to work on my awareness skills, with particular focus on bulging gun awareness.

"I understand." I took out a Kleenex and wiped non-existent tears from my cheeks.

"Sometimes I wonder if being a bodyguard is making me paranoid. Maybe it is. I'm gonna make it up to you though. Mrs. Tommy, she's an excellent shopper. She can help you. Hold on."

"Oh no. You don't have to—"

"Don't move." He said it in a way that didn't leave a lot of room for negotiation.

I watched through the window as he talked to Mrs. Tommy. When he pointed toward me, she peered out the window, then beckoned me in her direction.

"Shit," I whispered under my breath. Giselle had specifically said you didn't want them to notice you noticing them. And that was exactly what had happened. I smiled in the woman's direction, gave a little finger wave, and headed into the store. Mrs. Tommy had taken off her cape. My guess about what she might be wearing under that cape had been right on target. In fact, it had been *too* on target.

"Oh dear," Mrs. Tommy said in alarm as I approached, "we have the exact same dress."

This was blending in gone amuck. "Is that a bad thing?" I asked innocently.

"You were right, Lenny," she said to the bodyguard. "She

is shopping-impaired, if she doesn't know two women don't wear the exact same dress at the same time..."

"Proof positive," Lenny said.

She nodded. "I'll have to buy something to change into right now."

But then they both focused in on me. Specifically, they peered at my breasts. They moved in for a close-up. "Can I help you?" I asked, looking down at them looking at me.

"Something funny's going on with the polka dots," Lenny said. "They're not, like..."

I focused on my dress. "Equidistant?"

"Yeah. It's like some of them are moving or somethin'."

"And some of them are brown, not black," Mrs. Tommy added.

"Oh," I said, in a flash of embarrassment, "I was having a Snickers while I was waiting for you..."

"And some of the little chocolate pieces fell off onto your clothes?" Lenny asked.

"Right!"

"Happens to me all the time," he said. "That's why I always wear dark suits." He pointed to a spot on his lapel. "See, this here's from a Hershey bar. This one over here's from chocolate frosting on the cake I had for lunch. This other one's from a couple of days ago—"

"You can barely tell!" I said.

"That's what I'm saying," he said in an excited tone.

"In that case, maybe it would be better if we got *you* a new dress," Mrs. Tommy said.

"You don't have to do that," I said.

"I know I don't have to, but I want to."

"No, please don't feel—" I caught a glimpse of Lenny's face. He apparently thought it was a good idea and wanted me to reconsider. "Any particular dress you'd like me to try on?"

She eyed the rack, flipped through a few dresses, then pulled out a bright yellow number with a short flouncy skirt and a fitted halter top. She turned toward me, assessed the possibility. "This would be great on you." She glanced at the extra polka dots on the dress I wore, factoring in my tendency to wear my food in addition to my clothes. "But in a darker color." She pulled out a deep blue version. Checking the size, she said, "You're about the same size as me, aren't you? This is a ten." When I nodded, she handed me the dress. "The dressing room is over there." She pointed toward the front left of the store. As I went in, she and Lenny sat down to wait in chairs outside the dressing rooms.

I slipped out of the offending polka dot dress and into the blue one. It fit like a glove—a very revealing, very snug glove. I walked out. Mrs. Tommy smiled.

Lenny's eyebrows lifted, and he looked at my breasts again. This time, he had good reason. They were spilling out all over the top of the low-cut halter top. "That's a beautiful thing," he said.

For a bodyguard, he was a pretty nice guy.

"We'll take it," Mrs. Tommy said to the clerk, who clipped off the tag. Mrs. Tommy followed the clerk to the counter to pay, while I retrieved my purse and the polka dot dress.

When I came back out, Lenny still sat in the chair. He narrowed his eyes, perplexed.

"What?" I said.

"Remember back when you was talkin' about the Snickers incident?"

"Yes?"

"What'd you mean when you said, 'I was having a Snickers while I was waiting for you...' " He emphasized the "while I was waiting for you" part.

Oops. "Ahhh. Did I say that? Are you sure it was me? Could it have been somebody else? And if I did say it, are you sure that's what I said?"

"I'm pretty sure it was you. And I'm pretty sure that's an exact quote."

"Thanks so much for the dress," I said, backing toward the entrance. "I really have to be going now. Lovely to meet you."

"Hey," Lenny said, starting to get up from his chair.

By that time I was in full flight out the door and down the street. I took the first right off the main street and the first left after that. By now I must be in the clear. That had been close, too close. I slowed to a walk.

BLAM! A bullet whizzed by my head, catching me totally by surprise. I bolted around the next corner. I'd misjudged the bodyguard. He was only a nice guy some of the time. The rest of the time, he was a killer judging by how close the bullet had come. I flew down the street to an alley and down that to another main street. My heart pounding, I grabbed a cab—seizing hold of the back door handle of one that was moving, throwing myself in, landing directly on top of a tiny old man, who looked delighted at his good fortune.

"Oh, my sweet little chicken," he said, kissing me all over.

I scrambled off of him and the startled driver took me back to the hotel.

I found Giselle asleep on the lounge chair right where I'd left her. She stirred as I sat down, blinked, opened her eyes and said, "I'll have a triple."

"Hold on," I said. "I have to tell you about the

surveillance. Then *I'll* have a triple."

She sat up. "You went on surveillance in that?" She smacked her head.

"Of course not."

"That's a relief."

"The person I was following bought—"

"You got made!"

"A little old man tried to but I fought him off."

"I mean you got caught."

"I did not."

"Did too."

"Did not. Well, maybe I did. It's a long story. Okay yes. Good thing it was just an exercise, huh?"

She shook her head. "I'll say."

"Mrs. Tommy was pretty nice actually."

"Mrs. *Tommy*?" She jerked alert.

"Yeah, that was her name."

"Ohmigod," she said.

"What?"

"Mrs. Tommy is Tommy the Twitch's *wife*."

"Tommy the Twitch? Who's Tommy the Twitch?"

"Tommy the Twitch is your target!"

Chapter Eleven

Great. My practice surveillance had been the wife of the guy I was after and her bodyguard. What were the odds? I was starting to get the feeling the odds were stacked against me. Not exactly stacked. More like I was flat on my back looking up at Everest.

"Why didn't you tell me that?" I yelled.

"I was going to tell you about him before he arrived."

"You said he wasn't arriving until tomorrow. He's here now!"

"Tommy and his wife must have come in a day early." She pulled her purse into her lap and brought out her calendar. "Oops. No, I had the day wrong." As she plunked her bag next to her chair, a photo fell out of the side pocket.

"You had the *day* wrong?"

"That must be why Jesse isn't here yet. I must have told him the wrong day, too."

"Jesse's coming?" More good news. Giselle's sexy, devoted boyfriend would be here with her. That should give me plenty of time to think about my failed romance. I sighed, bent down to pick up the photo, and slumped back into my chair.

"Jesse's still in Washington, but he's going to join us here."

"Oh. Well, it'll be nice to see him again," I said casually. But what was that little flutter in my tummy? Why should I care that Giselle's boyfriend was coming? Was the best I could do some vicarious thrill of seeing them canoodling together? How pathetic.

I glanced at the picture Giselle had dropped. The willies wriggled up my back. In the center stood a man so evil I half-expected the paper to burst into flames. He looked like the human version of a Rottweiler with an attitude problem. But there was something else. He had a gleam in his eyes—a scary crazy gleam. "Who is this creep?"

"Hey, gimmee that." She grabbed the picture from my hand.

"Is that this Tommy guy?"

"No."

"Thank goodness. Let me see a picture of Tommy."

She rummaged in her bag. "I can't find it. I'll have to look around."

After seeing the picture of that other spawn of Satan, I didn't mind waiting. Until I had visual evidence to the contrary, I'd pretend Tommy looked like Kris Kringle. "What's next?"

"I know some of the places Tommy hangs out. Maybe we'll see him."

Back in our room, I changed into a jersey and capris. Ten minutes later, we took a right out of the hotel and strolled down the street.

"A couple of the places he goes are up this way," Giselle said. We crossed the street running in front of the hotel and walked up a side street. Ten minutes later, we stopped at our first destination. Giselle didn't see him through the window.

We headed down a cross road that led back to the street

running along the water. At that intersection, we could see a restaurant with a pier extending out over the water with tables for seaside dining. We walked a short distance to a point where we had a clear view across the water to the pier. We tucked ourselves by a tree that provided some cover. Giselle took a tiny pair of binoculars from her bag and scanned the tables. "There," she pointed, "that's Tommy. Out for a late lunch with his thugs. The table on the end of the pier."

"The three guys?"

"Yeah. He's the one facing us." She handed me the binoculars.

I could see them without the binoculars, but this let me see close up. Tommy the Twitch didn't look like Kris Kringle. But I was surprised to see he was handsome. Forties, lots of wavy dark hair with a Mediterranean tone to his skin. His eyes were wide set and his nose had a slight hook. I tried to memorize his big build and as much as I could about the way he carried himself. I didn't notice any obvious twitching. "Who are the other guys?"

"They're with him most of the time. Carlo's the string bean. Dom's the troll."

"Yeah, Dom looks like he just climbed out from under a rock." When Tommy held his hand out, Dom reached under the table and pulled out a single can attached to the piece of plastic used to hold a six-pack together. "They bring their own drinks?"

"Tommy likes Dr. Pepper," Giselle said. "You can't get that everywhere."

"Why do they call him Tommy the Twitch?"

"He... he has a medical condition."

"What kind of medical condition?"

Tommy pulled the can away from the plastic rings, then threw the plastic into the ocean.

"I don't know all the details, but—"

"Did you see that?" I asked. Giselle appeared unconcerned. "Don't you care?"

"Compared to other things he's done, that's not so bad."

"But dolphins' snouts get tangled in those rings and they starve. Someone should say something." A guy in a purple shirt from the next table got up. "Wait. I think someone is."

"Uh-oh," Giselle said.

Nothing obstructed sound as it moved across the water. We couldn't hear normal conversation, but raised voices we could make out.

Purple Shirt approached Tommy. "What do you think you're doing?"

"Doing my part to control the world's dolphin population," Tommy snarled, getting up. "What's it to you?" He pushed the man in the chest.

The man stumbled back, coming dangerously near the edge of the pier. He grabbed for the railing. "Watch it," Purple Shirt said. "I can't swim."

"Really? Maybe it's time you learned." He gave an almost imperceptible nod to Dom and Carlo. Instantly they were on either side of Purple Shirt. Each grabbed an arm and a leg, lifted, and heaved the man over the railing. He screamed as he flew through the air toward the water. "Say hello to Flipper for me," Tommy hollered. Tommy, Dom and Carlo laughed, mimicking the man's flailing and screaming.

"Geez," I said. Before this, I'd been afraid, but it had been a fear of the unknown. Now that I knew what kind of guy I was up against, the fear factor shot upward. I thrust the binoculars toward Giselle. "He'll drown." I kicked off my shoes while I unzipped my pants.

Giselle grabbed my arm. "What are you doing? Tommy will see you. You'll jeopardize the whole assignment. Let someone else help."

I took my eyes off the man for a second to glance up at the pier. Everyone sat paralyzed in terror. "No one else is going to." Shoving my pants down, I stepped out of them and took off at a run toward the land end of the pier. My lifeguard training kicked in; I couldn't just stand around and let the guy drown without trying to save him.

As I neared the pier, I glanced toward Tommy and his cohorts. They hadn't noticed me. I'd swim under the pier and stay out of sight as long as I could. I ran in. If the man went under and I didn't know exactly where, I'd never find him. I used the breaststroke so I could stay in visual contact, moving as quickly as I could. The tide was pushing him away from the pier. Purple Shirt flailed his arms, struggling to keep his head above water. I didn't have much time.

As I watched, he went under. I pushed myself to move faster, heading out from under the pier, directly toward where I'd last seen him. I dove. No luck. I came up, then dove again. There! I grabbed him, pulled him up and got to the surface, gulped air. But with every breath I took, I was painfully aware that he wasn't getting any air. Was I too late? I swam back toward the pier as fast as I could, but hauling a body made it slow going. My eyes flicked toward where Tommy and crew sat. We were still terribly exposed, but they didn't seem to notice.

People happening upon the scene gathered on the shore. Someone yelled, "She's got him." They hadn't seen the man get thrown into the water. They didn't know the danger. But if they didn't shut up, Tommy would hear and—

BLAM! From above me a shot rang out. BLAM! Another shot, this one inches from my head. Oh God! I lost my grip on the man, then clutched him again, veering away from where the bullet had entered the water. Almost to the pier. A few more strokes and I'd be under. Would Tommy or his guys follow? Would the man I'd been trying to save end up dead anyway? Would I end up fish food on the ocean floor right beside him? I just kept going as fast as I could.

Chapter Twelve

I touched ground, shaking from the strain and the fear. I scanned for shooters. No guns pointed in this direction. Relief flooded through me.

Two people carried the man across the road. Someone started mouth to mouth. Someone else wrapped a towel around me. When Purple Shirt sputtered water and started coughing, I knew he'd be okay. I ran toward the tree where Giselle still stood.

Across on the pier, Tommy and his chums chowed down, too busy to bother to kill. I pulled my pants on over my still wet undies and stepped into my shoes. As we headed down a shaded street parallel to the water, a cool breeze ruffled the trees. I shivered, as much from my first encounter with Tommy as from being wet and chilled. "I need something hot to drink."

"The hotel is a twenty-minute walk down this road. There's a place on the way."

"So tell me about this Tommy guy," I said.

"Tommy was ten when his folks moved down here from the States. His Ma's sick now with Marette's."

"What's that?"

"I'm not exactly sure. Maybe a little like Tourette's? Anyway, it features tics and out of control swearing. But on the island, they've never seen anything like it before. They can't understand the swear words, think she's speaking in some kind of tongue that's divinely inspired."

"So... the poor woman is sick. Why is this important?"

"Her version of the disease has a touch of dementia and delusions of grandeur, too. Ma fancies herself a savior of the people, kind of a female cross between Che Guevara and Castro. She's planning a coup."

"But why is the government of this tiny country so important?"

"A coup here could lead to destabilization of the entire area."

"One more nutbag amidst a sea of dictators, fascists and other assorted weirdos already in power, and it's on its way."

"Right. Especially because intelligence has shown us that Ma has her eye on other islands for her relatives to run once she takes over this one."

"How does Tommy fit in?"

"Ma has a band of rebels who believe in her cause. Even those who aren't related call her Ma. They love the idea of a coup. But she can't do it without funding. That's Tommy's part. He runs a little drug trafficking business. Ma promised that once she controlled this island and started taking over the surrounding ones, Tommy would have first dibs. If he helped her."

"Doesn't he know she's wacko?"

"We think he does."

"But she's still mom?"

Giselle nodded. "Plus, because of his connection to her, he can rake in a fortune on the drugs, and the local police won't do much to stop him. There's fear of upsetting the old-timers who believe Ma has unusual powers. And except for the Chief and those close to him, the cops are dirty. Basically, unless he's handed to them on a silver platter, Tommy can pretty much get away with anything he wants."

We came to high hedges running along the sides of the street. Not far along the hedges, a small road turned to the left. "This way," Giselle said.

As we made our way down the road, I spotted a massive stone structure with looming turrets at the four corners. "What is this place?"

"An old castle used as a hotel. Some splinter religious order runs it."

"You mean like monks and nuns? Vows of celibacy, silence, poverty, stuff like that?"

"Sort of. But the church was having trouble attracting members, so they came up with this idea for an order that appeals to folks who want a life that's a little less Spartan. They take vows of semi-silence and semi-poverty."

We continued toward the castle. "It seems so out of place here," I said.

"It was originally built in Ireland. But the people who joined the order turned out to be more narcissistic than the church expected. They said Ireland was too damp. What they wanted was a place that felt more like a vacation spot. They thought the Caribbean would be nice."

"So they had a replica built here."

"No, this is the original. The old-line members of the church thought moving here was a ridiculous idea. The church would only say yes if the monks agreed to take it apart in Ireland and put it back together here. They never thought the monks and nuns would do it."

"But they did."

"Well, sort of. They came up with a scheme where they

charged money to people who wanted to experience the life of a monk. A thousand dollars a week to dismantle the castle in Ireland and put it together here. They advertised it as a religious experience."

"People bought that?"

"They sold out. In fact, it was so popular the monks set aside a small stone building on the grounds here. It's not used for anything, they just have people disassemble and reassemble it each week. You never know where you'll find it."

A nun and a monk walked across the grounds. She was dressed in a nun's habit and he wore a monk's robe. Most of the details looked authentic, but instead of being made of heavy material that went to their feet, both outfits were thigh-high and see-through.

"What's with the outfits?"

"It's hot here. They went with short and sheer."

On the left side of the road lay a wide expanse of recently mowed lawn. "This place looks like a golf course." Suddenly I heard a whistling noise. I ducked, but not fast enough. "Ow!" I yelled as the bottom of the ball whacked the top of my head.

"It is a golf course."

"You'd think somebody would have yelled 'Fore' to let me know—"

"I told you about the vow of semi-silence," she said.

A monk appeared on the crest of a knoll, a sheepish look on his face. He saw me rubbing my head. He didn't say anything, but came close to me and made the sign of the cross, bent my head toward him, and kissed the place I'd been rubbing. He went back to his game.

I kept one eye on the sky as Giselle and I walked on. "Hey,

there's a moat and everything."

"They agreed to be true to the original design."

"That must have been a lot of work."

"Not as much as you'd think." Giselle pointed toward the rear of the castle.

I peered in that direction. "Oh. It backs up to the water."

"Right. They picked a spot on a slope. This side is on one level. Where it meets the water out back is a level down."

We walked in the front entrance. To the left of the massive foyer, a monk set up a sign on a stand. He nodded to us as he made his way to another room. " 'Welcome, Puscle Corporation,' " I read. "Wonder what that's about."

"Groups can rent out an entire wing of the castle. Off-site meetings, team building, golf tournaments, that kind of thing," Giselle said. "The agency had us all down here for a Fourth of July weekend once. Come on, here's the tearoom."

We walked through the foyer and in. Windows filled the wall facing the sea. I realized after a moment that some of the windows were actually glass doors. People sat outside at tables on a balcony overlooking the ocean.

We ordered tea and scones and took them to a balcony table. While the tea steeped, I took in the view. "Wow."

Giselle nodded. "This is called Castle Point. The most beautiful spot on the island."

Below, at sea level, a walkway led to the castle's dock. A thirty-foot catamaran motored in and tied up. The couple who'd been on board walked up a set of outside stairs and in the side entrance to the tearoom.

As Giselle and I sat and drank our tea, I noticed a plaque built into the wall of the castle. " 'Many thanks to our biggest benefactor, Mr. Massive,' " I read. I glanced at Giselle. She'd turned white. "Who's Mr. Massive?"

"How should I know?" Her face a mix of fear and fury, she sat staring at her tea. We wouldn't be chitchatting about this.

When I finished my tea, I got up and stood at the railing. Like a tourist, I continued to take in our surroundings. "Look, a labyrinth." I pointed to the land to the right of the castle.

"You mean a maze?" Giselle asked, turning to see.

"I think a maze is made of hedges. A labyrinth is a walking path, but in a circular pattern." In a level, grassy area perhaps thirty feet by thirty feet, a path formed a huge circle that spiraled inside itself until it reached the center. A monk and a nun ambled around it. But a couple stepped on, too, and silently began the trek. "Anyone can use it."

We emerged from the castle through a side door. A few stone stairs brought us to the grounds and we walked over to a wrought iron sign by the labyrinth. " 'The labyrinth is an ancient spiritual symbol,' " I read softly. " 'In quiet meditation, journey to the center of the circle. As you enter, leave your cares and troubles along the way. As you reverse direction and journey out, you will be filled with spiritual energy. May you leave suffused with serenity and joy.' "

Giselle looked skeptical.

"Wouldn't a little serenity be nice?" I whispered to Giselle. "Want to try it? It starts here." We watched another nun step onto the path. I turned at the sound of footsteps coming down the stone stairs from the castle. I grabbed Giselle. "That's him!" I hissed.

"Him who?"

"Lenny! The bodyguard. The one who shot at me!" Was he after me? He couldn't know I would be after Tommy, could he? How could he have found me, anyway? "Maybe he's here for tea," I said hopefully.

Lenny stormed in our direction, eyes intent on me.

"I don't think so," Giselle said.

It didn't take a spy to figure that out. I looked around. The labyrinth backed up to the water. Past it, the land sloped steeply upwards to a chain link fence. No way out there. Lenny was closing the distance between the castle and us. The only other option was heading toward the road. If we did that, we'd be running away from people here and increasing the chance of ending up alone with Lenny. That didn't seem like a good option, either.

"Come on!" Grabbing Giselle's arm, I stepped on to the labyrinth. I forced myself to walk slowly. Lenny took in the scene, skidding to a halt shy of the labyrinth. He crossed himself. He was religious. But I wasn't sure how far that would go. Would he just leave?

Bad news. He made no move to leave.

Worse news. He stepped onto the path.

The labyrinth was tightly coiled, which meant Giselle and I would come very close to Lenny as we made our way around the spiraling circle. I slowed but we moved inevitably nearer. When we passed side by side, he made a sudden grab for me. I did a quickstep off the path, narrowly avoiding him. The nun in front of me cast a glance backward. She didn't appear pleased.

We kept circling, reached the center, and reversed direction. In another moment I would again end up beside the bodyguard. Would a quickstep be enough this time? One more step... He grabbed for me, but as I tried to step away he seized a fistful of my shirt and yanked. Giselle grasped me by the arm and pulled me back. There was a tearing noise. He let go suddenly. I flailed my arms, struggling to keep my balance. This time the nun looked back and noticed Lenny holding a piece of my torn shirt.

She stepped off the path and darted toward him. Her oversized nametag read, "Sister Agnes Anastasia Angelina Alphonsus." In fine print below, it said, "Call me Sister Aggie!" Sister Aggie seized him by the earlobe and pinched.

"Ow!" he yelped.

Sister Aggie pointed at him. Arching her eyebrows, she pointed to the ground. She was trying to convey something to him.

He shook his head. He didn't understand. She mimed little pointy horns and then pretended to be a fire-eating dragon.

"Do I want to go to hell?" he said.

She tapped herself on the nose. He was correct.

"That's the semi-silence again. How's that work anyway?" I asked Giselle.

"They get a daily allotment of words," she whispered. "Once they reach the maximum, they have to stop talking completely. So they use words when they have to, but otherwise have developed a kind of modified Charades-type approach for getting their meaning across."

"Interesting."

Hand inside her habit, Sister Aggie pulled a pocket inside out, then raised her eyebrows.

"What's in my pocket?" he asked. When she nodded, he put his hand in one of his pants pockets. "My wallet, some change—"

She reached over and patted his bulging suit coat pocket, then glared at him.

"Oh. This pocket?" he asked, as if he didn't know already.

Hands on hips, she tapped her toe and waited. He shuffled

his feet, then pulled out a huge weapon. She mimed putting a gun to her head, a shot going off, hoisting her off her feet, and dying an agonizing death. She ended by spiraling to the ground in a heap. She looked up at him.

"Someone could get hurt?" he said.

She was on her feet now, nodding. She extended an open palm to him and waited.

"Geez, Sister."

She sucked in air.

"Gee whiz, I mean, Sister." He held onto the gun. His eyes darted to me and back to her. He started to move.

I held my breath.

But Lenny handed her the gun, which Sister Aggie tucked into a pocket. She pointed to him and next herself, then struck a pose with eyes closed, her hands folded in front of her.

"Pray for you," he said.

She shook her head.

"You'll pray for me?"

Sister Aggie dropped to her knees, reached up, and yanked him to a kneeling position.

"Pray *with* you," he said. She nodded. But as he bowed his head, he caught my eye.

From the looks of it, I wasn't going to be on his prayer list.

Chapter Thirteen

As we hurried toward the hotel, I thought back to when Giselle first asked me to take on the assignment. I'd envisioned the moment when she would hand over the check for fifty thou, I'd weep in gratitude and rush off to buy a schooner and start my school with sails.

What I hadn't pictured so clearly was people shooting at me.

I'd prefer to be upright and breathing when I got the money rather than have Giselle pin it to my cold, casket-encased body. If I wanted to increase that likelihood, I'd have to learn more about shooting back. Funny how wondering if you were going to die focused your motivation. As we entered our suite, I said, "I'm going back to the shooting range. They know about me, right?"

"I think so."

"You *think* so? They either know about me and won't shoot when I approach the gate, or they don't know and will blow me to smithereens. Could you check?" I asked, fuming. The people at the range might try to blow me up. It was also possible I would blow up all by myself.

She closed her phone. "All set. Have fun."

Learning to protect myself from a murderous bodyguard and a band of coup-crazed, drug-dealing maniacs? Yeah, that's my idea of a good time. As promised, there was a Glock for Giselle and one for me in a drawer in our room. I took mine and headed for the range. I'd done pretty well the first time at the range—for a total novice. That wouldn't be good enough if people were shooting back.

***

After strapping on my vest and picking up ammunition, I stood and watched the other shooters. A guy of medium height with a shaved head and a bulky build stood out. When he put down his weapon, I approached. "How do I get that good?"

"Nobody's as good as me," he said. "I'd be glad to help you get better though." He was generous and knew about guns. I'd overlook the ego thing. "Let's see what you got." He stepped aside and I moved into his place.

Shooting turned out to be lots more complicated than what I'd learned from Giselle. Ben talked to me about factoring in wind and weather and what to do if your target was moving. He showed me the importance of the firmness of the grip and a "nose over toes" stance. He told me exactly how to squeeze the trigger and the impact of your emotional state of mind.

The good news? I was getting a crash course in shooting from an expert. The bad news was it would take time to incorporate this flood of new information into what I was doing. Ben stayed with me while I practiced. The terrifying memory of being shot at spurred me on.

By the end of the session, I'd improved. I also knew I had lots more to learn. We walked to our cars. I was so grateful I threw my arms around Ben, thanking him from the bottom of my freaked-out little soul.

When I reached the main road, I stopped. In the distance, I saw a caravan of vehicles heading my way. All of them flew some kind of banner. As they got closer, I could see people hanging off cars, trucks, motorized Little Tykes and riding mowers, swigging rum, singing and laughing. The first few cars of the caravan passed me, banners displaying the letters RFM. I'd planned on waiting until all the vehicles passed, but a driver slowed and waved me forward. I stalled twice, but made it into the line of cars. I was now in the middle of the caravan.

People chanted and cheered. Must be a party. I rolled my window down. It took me a minute to make out the words. "Ma, ma, she's our man. If she can't do it, no one can."

Ma? They were chanting about Ma! This had to be *Tommy's* Ma. The RFM on the banners—that must mean, "Rebels for Ma." Giselle had said plans were underway for the coup. These had to be her supporters, on the way to some rally.

Up ahead, two men in military-type garb emerged from the lead car and stood in the road, gesturing to caravan vehicles to turn onto a side road running up a hill. What would happen if I tried to get by these guys? That didn't seem wise. I made the turn with the rest of the caravan.

Part way up the hill, people parked their cars and streamed down a dirt road. I pulled over, poked my head out. I'd wait until everyone was on the dirt road, then turn my car around and get away. But a guy in the crowd saw me and yanked open my door.

"Hey, she needs a tee shirt," he hollered.

Hands grabbed me out of my car. I snatched my shoulder bag at the last second. Someone pulled an RFM shirt over my head. I got sucked into the surge of people hurrying down the road. Someone shoved a bottle of rum at me. I took a big swig, passed it along, and joined in chanting with the others. Standing out seemed like a bad idea right about now. If I was noticed, I could be yelled at, detained, or tortured and killed, depending on how they felt about people crashing their party. The sweats started, sticky wet under my arms.

I glanced back at my car, sandwiched in with the others, and parked so it was headed uphill. If I had to get out fast, I was in a lot of trouble. My throat got that thick feeling, like the beginnings of strep.

We reached an open area the size of a football field. Logs served as improvised seating for some. Others had brought folding beach chairs. Lots of people simply stood.

A breeze blew a bright orange flyer in my direction. Fighting the urge to go after it, I stayed where I was, hoping another waft of air would send it tumbling close enough I could snag it. But it didn't happen. What was in that flyer?

An air of expectancy hovered over the crowd. Spontaneous bursts of chanting—"Ma! Ma! If she can't do it, no one can"—broke out every minute or so. After ten minutes, the chanting became almost continuous, then suddenly, "MA! MA! MA!" filled the air. The feeling was electric. Everyone rose to their feet amidst thundering applause.

In the field, a small woman with dark wavy hair and a slight hook to her nose ambled into the center. She looked as if she was pondering something, but really not aware of where she was. Was this the dementia Giselle had mentioned? Then suddenly, she spun around in a circle, spewing out a string of garbled swear words.

"Poopoopeepeefartfacedkakahead."

That was definitely the Marette's, the out of control swearing aspect of the disease.

"Ooooh!" the audience said, glancing in awe at one another and bowing toward Ma.

"I told you she had powers," a woman said to her companion.

"I didn't believe until I saw it myself," he said.

Ma spun again, her arms outstretched, hurling another string of expletives. "Kakaheadpoopoopeepeefartface."

"Ahhhh!" the audience said.

Couldn't people tell these were swear words? But would I have known if Giselle hadn't warned me? To them, this sounded like speaking in tongues. She was slurring her words; that was part of the disease. But they were so badly slurred, so garbled, the people here thought she'd been touched by the divine.

"I am Ma!" she screamed.

"MA! MA! MA! MA!" the audience shouted.

"I will lead you."

"MA! MA! MA! MA!"

"I will save you."

"MA! MA! MA! MA!"

"But you must help me. Coup! Coup! Coup!"

The audience picked up her chant. "Coup! Coup! Coup!"

Ma's arm jerked up above her head, in a salute-like motion. The audience saluted back. Ma did it again. The audience responded. Ma did two salutes in a row, faster than you could blink. The audience did the same. But I focused on her more closely. Ma didn't seem to be controlling her salutes. I didn't think it was divine intervention, either. This was a tic, a spastic movement associated with the disease. Ma gave them a quick three in a row. The audience did the same, but people were looking at each other now. We might be here awhile.

Tommy ran out next to Ma. He tried to hold her arm down, but it didn't work. So he held her arm up, like a politician. The audience cheered.

"Glad you could make it," Tommy yelled. "Ma's glad, too." I thought Ma looked mostly confused now, but the audience roared its approval. "We'll be ready for the coup any day now. Just waiting for a big 'donation' to put us over the top."

He'd used air quotes when he'd said "donation." Sure. Even I knew that was code for drug money. Tommy ran drugs all the time. This had to be an especially big shipment, with proceeds funding the coup.

And what the hell did "any day now" mean? I wanted to raise my hand and ask, "Could you be more specific as to date and time?" That seemed risky. But why hadn't he been more specific? What was holding the big drug deal up?

Two men hoisted Ma onto their shoulders and carried her around the field for the adoration of the frenzied audience.

These people were nuts. Revering Ma was based on a totally false assumption. But in a way, that didn't matter. What mattered was that they believed in her. And if enough people believed in her, no matter how demented their thinking, the coup could topple the government.

They thought the gods were on their side.

When Giselle had told me this, I'd thought it sounded far-fetched. Now I'd seen it for myself. It was real, and momentum was building.

I took a last look at the scene. When I did, I realized the men carrying Ma were Dom and Carlo. Tommy and those two must have picked up Ma right after lunch and headed here. The wind gusted again, and an orange flyer blew into me. I grabbed it and stuck it in my pocket.

I'd better beat feet. I didn't want to run into Tommy and team, sure. But the event was winding down, and the crowd would disperse any minute. I wanted to be ahead of the crowd, get out of here before anything went wrong.

"One last thing," Tommy yelled. "The security check. Time to show your RFM tattoo."

People started lifting up their shirts, rolling up sleeves, pulling down pants and taking off their hats, exposing the exact same RFM tattoo. I crouched down, pulled out a Sharpie marker, and scribbled "RFM" on my forehead. Would it work?

I got up. The first woman who saw it yelled, "A spy!"

Well, of course it wouldn't work, but at least I gave it the ole college try. The crowd turned in my direction. My pulse took off for Pluto, purple pressure pushing inside my skull. The nearest tree had a branch shoulder high. I boosted myself up on Gumby legs, heard an ominous crack, and as the branch splintered from the tree, I grabbed another branch and kept going, scrambling tree to tree until I got near the fringe of the crowd. I dropped hard to the ground, landed on my back, slid backward on my butt a couple of feet, sucking in breath as I absorbed the horde closing in on me. Then I flipped over and took off at a dead run, my heart way in front of me, as a roar went up from the crowd. I raced away, an adrenaline-fueled fear of dying propelling me a short distance ahead of the pack.

But I'd need more than that to get out of this in one piece.

Shoving my hand in the shoulder bag slung across my chest, I wrestled out my gun and a magazine, and shoved the ammo home. I thought back to Ben's training earlier today.

All the fine points of shooting cascaded through my brain. I heard the shouts of the crowd rushing toward me. They had to be stopped. I had to act. I had to act now. I turned. Blood burning up my veins, I fired.

The crowd shrieked and skidded to a halt.

Maybe I'd have to use all that fine point stuff another day. This time, aiming over their heads got the job done. I galloped toward my car. They'd realize pretty quickly no one was hurt. I had to get out of there as fast as I could.

My car came into view. But it was wedged in, headed the wrong way. I didn't think they'd wait for me to carefully pull out and bang a U-ee. Oh God! I didn't want to shoot anyone.

But the crowd started forward again, madder than ever, screaming in my direction. It felt like a watermelon was wedged in my throat. I neared my car, hope slithering away.

But a chicken sat on the hood. I grabbed the chicken, turned toward the crowd, shook my gun menacingly at the chicken. The crowd once again shrieked and ground to a halt.

The chicken tucked under my arm, I got in the car, pulled out of my spot, and turned around. A short ways down the road, I opened my door and freed the chicken.

The crowd surged forward as I raced away.

Chapter Fourteen

I sped down the road, only starting to breathe normally when the hotel came into sight. That had been close. If it hadn't been for that chicken, I'd be a soldier in Ma's rebel army now.

I couldn't wait to tell Giselle I'd infiltrated Ma's organization. Okay, maybe I'd been swept up in a cavalcade of her people. Was it really necessary to split hairs? I opened the door to our suite and saw Giselle on the couch. "You won't believe—"

"Where were you?" she yelled. "I told you we had a lot more to cover today."

"Don't you want to hear—"

"You're supposed to listen to me!" she squealed, waving her hands. She was breathing so fast, I thought she might start hyperventilating. She stamped her foot like a two-year-old.

I couldn't picture James Bond carrying on like this. Of course, maybe on top of everything else, Giselle was getting her period. James didn't have to contend with that, did he? I'd better go along with Giselle. If I inflamed things, I'd end up scraping her off the ceiling.

"Unless what you want to talk about is evidence you brought back to put Tommy away, maybe we should do it my way, Nora. Since I'm the trained spy."

Maybe she was right. She *was* the trained spy. The more skills I had, the better the chances that I'd be able to get the job done and remain in one piece. I said to Giselle, "What's next? If it could be something that didn't require getting shot at, that would be good."

"How about manipulation?"

"Manipulation? That sounds broad." But it didn't involve guns, so it was already an improvement. "What do you mean?"

"The act or practice of manipulating."

I beckoned for more.

"The state of being manipulated."

"Without using any form of the word 'manipulation.' "

"It's the... the art of managing things."

"Do you mean things? Or do you really mean people?"

"People mostly, actually. But things, too."

"And did you mean 'art'? That sounds so positive."

"Well, it is a skill."

"But it's the skill of being devious, isn't it?"

"That sounds so negative."

"But being sneaky, scheming, conniving, and underhanded *is* negative, isn't it?"

"You're really having a glass half empty kind of a day, aren't you, Nora? You do know that being sneaky, scheming, conniving, and underhanded might save your life someday, right?"

I swallowed. "There. I was just looking for the positive. Was that so hard? Please, go ahead."

She scowled but continued. "First and foremost is that men have two organs they think with. Your job is to get them to use the one that's not north of the neck."

I didn't like where this was going.

"Once you do that, it's amazing what they'll tell you," she said.

"Can't you just use open-ended questions to get them talking?"

"Sure, you don't want them to just be able to say 'yes' or 'no,' but with this approach you'll get more than you can imagine."

I bet. "Where are you when they're telling you this stuff? You're not talking about pillow talk, are you? Doesn't that usually come right before and after, you know..." I formed a circle with the thumb and index finger of my left hand, and poked my right index finger in and out of the circle, the international sign for—

"Sex, Nora? That's where it gets a little tricky. You've got to get them heated up, someplace private and spilling their guts, without—"

"Without doing the deed? Doesn't that really piss them off?"

"It can—"

"So what do you do then?" I asked.

"Create some impossible-to-overlook diversion and get them focused on the next time you'll meet. That way, the next time you see them, they're already simmering and primed to tell you anything you want to know."

"Doesn't a point come when they start to get suspicious about the diversions?"

"That can happen," she agreed. "That's why it's important to look for telltale bulges."

"If you helped create those telltale bulges, you probably don't have to do a lot of checking, right?" I pointed to my crotch area.

"The telltale bulges I'm talking about now are guns."

I hadn't noticed the bulging gun in Lenny's pocket the first time I saw him. That had gotten me shot at. The look on my face must have alerted her to my skyrocketing anxiety level.

"Don't worry. Everything will be fine."

Sure. That was like God telling Noah not to worry about those dark clouds.

"We're getting way ahead of ourselves," she continued. "Let's go back to basics."

"Yeah," I said. "That sounds good." I kind of liked the idea of letting myself get lulled into a false sense of security.

"Tommy loves the ladies. Cozying up will be key with him."

"I dated Kenny for the last four years. I've forgotten everything I ever knew about flirting."

"It will all come back to you. And I'll teach you a few new tricks."

"Swell."

"Hair-flipping is key." She bowed her head, then whipped her hair back. Raising her arms, she put her hands under her hair and flounced it, throwing me a sultry look.

I gave it a try.

"No," she said. "You have to arch your back, show 'em what you got."

I tried again.

"That's... a little better," Giselle said. "But I'd give it your all, Nora. If you learn to do this well, you're much more likely to get the job done while avoiding deadly altercations."

Sudden inspiration hit, perhaps connected to avoiding deadly altercations. But I was also thinking about Tommy. Without the money from the drug deal he had planned, the coup would go bust. If this was the way to get to Tommy, it could be the most important training I'd get.

Giselle went into the bedroom. When she came back out, she threw me a couple of pieces of clothing. "Here, put these on."

"What's this stuff?" I asked.

"One of those miracle bras. And a top with a plunging neckline."

"Okay." I took off my tee shirt and plain white bra and replaced them with what she'd given me. "Wow. This *is* a miracle bra. How's this thing work?"

"Who knows? But it's great, isn't it? Now try the moves again in front of the mirror."

I flipped and arched, throwing myself a sultry look.

"Much better," Giselle said. "Okay, on to eyelash batting and working your way into the personal zone."

We worked on those skills for a while. I was starting to get the hang of it. Not only that, but I suddenly realized I was actually enjoying it. *That* was a surprise. As I thought back, I couldn't remember if Kenny and I had ever flirted at all. Was I making up for lost time? "Hang on, I'm going to put on some heels."

Giselle followed me. I poked around in the closet, pulling out towering heels. She yanked a small, clingy piece of material from a hanger. "This'll go good with the top," she said.

I shimmied into a tight, fire-engine-red skirt that had slits on both sides up to my panty line. I adjusted the jet-black top over it, and slipped into the shoes. I stepped back to look into the mirror. "Wow."

Giselle laughed. "You're sizzling."

"You're telling me." I was ready for action. "Now I need a

victim."

"I have to go out—" She shoved her laptop in her shoulder bag.

"Go out? Where are you—"

"Why don't you go down to the bar and practice on someone there?"

"Yeah, it's not like someone's just going to walk in here and—"

As Giselle slung her bag over her shoulder, a knock sounded. She tiptoed out of the bedroom in the direction of the door. From where I still stood, I heard her say, "Jesse, perfect."

He must have just arrived from Washington.

"Nora's working on her flirting skills," Giselle continued. "Make yourself useful. I'll be back in an hour."

What? Wasn't there somebody else? Anybody else? He'd say "no," wouldn't he? He was Giselle's boyfriend, for crying out loud.

"Okay," he said.

"Bye," Giselle called.

"Wait," I hollered. "Where—" I walked into the living room as Jesse closed the door. He turned and saw me. He stood there for a second. Was he gaping?

I forgot about my sister, what's-her-name.

Jesse tugged at his collar and swallowed. "Hi, Nora. You look very... nice."

"Nice? That's all you can say?" My inner goddess had been activated. She knew nice didn't even begin to cover it.

"You look hot, all right? I thought it might be unprofessional to say that, but this is helping you with your skills. That's just part of the job."

I smiled. He'd said I looked hot. "Thank you." I felt

momentarily shy. But if I was going to come on to Tommy, I better practice full tilt. "Let's make this as realistic as we can. Like it's really happening." I glanced at Jesse and felt my pulse quicken. "To make the learning experience as valuable as possible."

"Hone your skills," he said, opening his arms wide.

I dialed room service. "Send up champagne and..." I thought back to romance movies I'd seen. "... and some fresh strawberries, hot fudge sauce, and whipped cream." I put down the phone and turned to Jesse. I caught him staring at my backside. "They'll be right up."

He quickly looked away. "Fine," he said, all business. "Now, anything specific you want to accomplish today?" He sat down.

"Let's see. I want to work on my manipulation skills, with a focus on hair flipping, eyelash-batting, and invading your personal space." I flipped, I batted. I walked to his chair, placed my hands on the armrests, and leaned deeply over to look closely at him. My breasts were inches from his face. "If that's all right with you," I whispered into his ear.

"Sure," he croaked. "No problem."

"With the intent of getting you so unfocused you'll tell me anything I want to know."

"That's unlikely," he said. "I'm a professional." But he was looking down my blouse.

"I'm going to do my best to learn everything I can so I'll be ready for my assignment." I was still leaning over him. "Jesse?"

"What? Oh." He looked up, then looked back down my blouse. "Those are very admirable."

"What are?"

He shook his head and looked back up. "Your goals," he

said hurriedly.

A short while later, we heard a knock. "Room service," a voice called.

The waiter wheeled in a cart. A silver bucket held a bottle of champagne. A silver dome hid the contents of a platter. I signed the bill and the waiter went on his way.

Jesse got up from the chair. "I'll pour," he offered.

I nodded as I lifted the dome from the platter. The kitchen had arranged a tray of perfectly ripe strawberries, bananas, and oranges. In the center sat two bowls. Whipped cream filled one. Thick, shiny, gooey chocolate filled the other. "Is that warm? Ooh." Jesse turned as I dunked two fingers into the fudge and sucked on them. "Mmm. You've got to taste this."

Without thinking, I dunked my fingers in again and stepped forward, moving my hand toward his mouth. Our eyes locked as he took my fingers in his mouth and sucked. He grabbed me around the wrist and kept sucking until there wasn't a chance in the world there was any chocolate left. I had to rip my eyes from his face. He was the one who was supposed to be getting unfocused, but *I* was. My mind filled with what might be best described as pure carnal lust. I gently retrieved my fingers and turned away, taking deep breaths, trying to compose myself. I heard the swish of ice as Jesse lifted the champagne from the bucket. Out of the corner of my eye, I could see the twisting motion as he pulled the cork from the bottle.

Pop! We both laughed, nervous laughter. I turned to see him tilt the bottle to pour. "Wait." His back was to me. I reached around him, one arm on either side, pressing myself against him, and plucked two strawberries from the fruit tray. I dropped one into each glass. As I started to move away, Jesse reached behind me, holding his hand on my back to keep me pressed to him. I didn't resist; it felt so good, I never wanted to stop. Jesse filled both of the glasses, waited a moment more to keep me stationary, then took his hand away from me to pick up the glasses. As he slowly turned around, I moved only enough to accommodate his rising from a bent over to a standing position. He handed me a glass of champagne. The heels made me the perfect height for him. Our faces were inches apart.

"I'm invading your personal space," I whispered.

He didn't look like he minded much. "That's good, since that was one of your goals."

I'd completely forgotten the goals. "Right. I guess I can check that one off. Thanks."

"No problem. You're doing very well."

"Do you think so?"

"Oh, believe me, I do." He raised his glass. "Here's to total training success."

I clinked his glass with mine. "You're very kind."

"Not that you can't always learn more," he said quickly.

"True," I agreed.

"In fact, I'll tell you my position..." He stopped to take a sip of champagne.

I loved thinking about Jesse in all kinds of positions. "Tell me all about your position."

"My position is that you should train really hard, Nora," he circled my waist with his free arm, "so that when you're in a real-life situation, you're ready."

"Really ready," I echoed. I was ready for anything right about then. Get a *grip*, Nora! But that made me think about what I wanted to get a grip of. Which was within reach. Knock it *off*, Nora. I took a deep breath and slowly exhaled.

It made me want to just move my lips another inch or two in his direction. Then we'd kiss. Then we'd—

STOP!

But I didn't stop. I couldn't stop. Our lips met and I wanted the kiss to go on and on and—

Stop! But the urge to stop stopped. I was all about go, go, go. Then suddenly I realized what I was doing.

"Would you like more champagne?" I said quickly, backing away from Jesse slightly. I'd forgotten I was supposed to get things to heat up, then get them to slow down, or I'd end up in bed with some muscle-bound madman who didn't understand the word no. I poured quickly. "I'm sorry. I forgot about the backing off part."

Jesse loosened his tie. "It's okay. This is a training session. Better to make mistakes like that here with me, you know what I mean?"

"I think so. Yes, better to make the mistake with you." Lord help me, I kissed him again. I was just ready to get totally lost in the bliss... I pulled back again. "I can't believe I did that again. I'm sorry. It's all my fault."

It was all my fault, wasn't it? Jesse took off his jacket and dropped it where he stood. He moved the back of his hand across the sheen on his forehead. I hurried toward the tiny refrigerator and grabbed some ice. I pressed it against my throat, trying to cool off. I went back to Jesse and opened his shirt a few buttons and held some ice on the warmth of his chest. He reached into the champagne bucket for a fistful of ice.

"Let me help," he said. He ran the ice down my throat and stopped. We locked eyes again. Then he kept going, pushing it down further and onto my breasts, until I groaned.

"Is that better?" he whispered.

"Oh yes," I said. "Oh, that's so much better."

He massaged the ice into me, but when it melted he moved his hand to my breast, using his other hand to push aside my top and then my bra.

I gasped in pleasure. Over the next three-quarters of an hour we had a very vigorous training session. I trained as hard as I could, and Jesse did his best to help me. In a training move that required me to be horizontal on the couch, I glanced at the clock. Giselle was scheduled to return soon, and I hadn't completed one of my goals. I had to get Jesse to tell me something he wasn't supposed to tell me. I'd been wondering if Giselle had lied to me about the name of the organization, and I wanted to find out. "Hey," I said. I flipped my hair and batted my eyes.

Jesse lifted his head from what he'd been doing. "What? A little to the left?"

"No. Well, not right now. I have a question." I snuggled up against him and looked into his eyes. "What does FIB stand for?"

"I'm really not supposed to say. That's secret information."

But maybe he could be talked into it. "Gee, and I trained so hard today," I pouted.

"You're right." He sighed. "But you have to promise not to tell anyone else."

"I promise," I whispered into his ear.

"FIB stands for Flat out Immobilize the Bastards."

"Oh," I said, surprised. "I'd expected something a little more businesslike."

"Some young upstart of an agent came up with the name. Said we needed one that'd show the bad guys we meant business. He's the son of one of the higher-ups. No one wanted to tell him the name stunk. That's the real reason they don't want anyone to know what it means."

"Thanks for all your help," I said a short time later, when the training session was over. "I met all my goals."

"You're welcome," he said, putting on his shoes. He stood up. "By the way, Nora. That FIB thing I told you was so secret?"

"Yeah?"

"I made that up."

I lobbed a strawberry in his direction. Surprisingly, he caught it.

"Good hands," I said begrudgingly.

"I was hoping you'd noticed."

I couldn't help laughing.

But there was a part of me that wasn't laughing. That was the part remembering that all this training had to be put to use, and soon. I'd be doing this with Tommy, a drug dealer, a killer. That wasn't funny. That was downright terrifying.

A key sounded in the lock. We turned toward the door.

Chapter Fifteen

Giselle walked into the room. "How'd the training go?"

"Okay," I said.

"Yeah, not too bad," Jesse agreed.

Giselle glanced at us and snickered. I looked down. My midriff showed from where my top had been pushed up. My skirt had shifted three inches off center. Jesse's shirttail hung out and his hair stuck up in tufts. "That was my favorite part of the training, too," she said, walking past us into the bedroom.

I pulled my top down and straightened my skirt. Didn't she mind that I was doing this with her boyfriend? Was that the corporate mentality? Anything for the sake of getting the job done? Actors and actresses performed love scenes with people who weren't their spouses, and everyone lived with it. Was it like that? Still, not to be jealous at *all*. That was kind of amazing. I didn't know if I'd be able to handle it. Of course, that was if I ever had a boyfriend I cared enough about not to want him to stray.

No wonder I was thinking like this. I'd seen proof my boyfriend had been willing to cheat on me at the first opportunity. Jesse had barely glanced at Giselle as she'd walked into the room. Was he just like the rest of them? This was business. But he'd been damned good at it. Did that mean that he did things behind Giselle's back when it *wasn't* business?

I glared at Jesse. He stopped tucking in his shirt, a confused look on his face. "What?"

"Nothing," I spat back.

Giselle walked in. She'd changed into shorts and a shirt. "Let's get some dinner."

Incredible. I'd just done this uh... training with her boyfriend, and she wanted us to go to dinner together? In some ways she was a basket case. In other ways she had nerves of steel.

I couldn't come up with a quick reason to say no. I grabbed a shawl to tame down my outfit and slipped into flat shoes. Jesse held the door and Giselle led us out. As I walked past him, he mouthed, "What?" I marched on, my head held in an imperial posture, without a glance in his direction.

Giselle made her way toward the elevator. The last thing I wanted right now was to be in a confined space with Jesse and Giselle.

"I need to stretch my legs. I'll meet you down there." I stepped into the nearby stairway before they had time to protest. I bounded down the stairs. Why was I so upset? What did I care what Jesse did or didn't do? Giselle didn't seem to be concerned. I heard the door above me open. Someone else hurrying down the stairs. Probably someone coming to kill me. My life was so miserable, who cared? I thought again about Jesse. I was thinking about him like I thought about Kenny. But was it fair to lump them together? Of course not. Kenny had been my boyfriend. Jesse was a business associate. He wasn't the problem. *I* was. My thinking was confused, as if what had just happened had been a real romantic encounter. I had to remember—it hadn't been real.

"Nora!" Jesse's voice sounded from above. So he was the one who'd been barreling after me. At the door to the main floor, he caught up. I turned to look at him. Concern on his face, he said, "What's wrong?"

"Wrong? Nothing's wrong. Let's get some dinner." I opened the door, saw Giselle up ahead. "Wait up!" I called. Jesse stood there, hands on his head. "What's wrong?" I asked.

"Wrong?" he said in an exasperated tone. "Nothing's wrong. Let's get some dinner."

***

Giselle downed a single glass of wine with dinner. After dinner though, she had three cognacs in quick succession. As she made a move to beckon the waiter again, Jesse said, "I have a couple of calls I have to make." He helped Giselle up, putting his arm around her as she stood. I tried not to wish his arm was around me. We took the elevator up, but Jesse pushed the button for five and got off there. Giselle stood leaning against the wall of the elevator and seemed okay. But once we arrived at our floor and she didn't have the wall to prop her up, she almost fell over. I put my arm around her and helped her to our room. As I opened the door, she burped in my face.

"Ewww."

I sat her in a chair in the bedroom. As she bent over to take off her shoes, she fell off. I picked her up and stuffed her back in.

"Aren't you going to meet your boyfriend later?" I asked.

"What boyfriend?" Giselle flopped onto the bed, instantly

snoring.

Giselle wasn't going to be teaching me any skills tonight. I got the flyer out of the pocket of the pants I'd worn earlier and smoothed it out. *Come One, Come All. Step Right Up. The Greatest Coup on Earth!* They definitely needed a better communications person. This sounded like Barnum and Bailey was coming to town. *Don't Like the Government? Get a New One! Support Ma. The gods will bless you for it!* That last line had an asterisk. I checked the reference. *She's Divine!* None of this seemed helpful.

At the bottom, a note said, *Send contributions to PO Box 600, ANA, Barlanadana Island.* Knowing a PO box wasn't helpful. What was ANA? A code used by people opening the mail? The name of the person who handled contributions? It wasn't part of the address, was it?

At the front desk, I asked, "Ever seen an address that had something like ANA in it?"

"Every piece of mail on the island," the clerk said.

"So what does it mean?"

"The island is broken into neighborhoods. ANA is one of them. It narrows down the destination. Like your own zip codes. Our system is superior, though."

I thought about bringing up our respective GNPs, but decided against it. "Why is that?"

"We simply took the name of the island and broke it in three, making those the neighborhood names. Barl, Ana and Dana."

I didn't give a crap about Barl and Dana. "Where's Ana?" He described the geographic area and how to get there. After thanking him, I hurried upstairs. I changed into dark pants and a loose, dark, long-sleeved shirt. I grabbed a hat and jammed it on my head.

What did I expect? A blinking neon sign, "Ma's Headquarters"? The Ana area was still a lot of ground to cover. Giselle said you know more than you think you know. Did I? Maybe so. Lots of the inland was wetland and mountains. That would force the dense part of the population to the coast. The section I needed to check had just become smaller. Now it was like a needle in a small haystack. But I had a chance for gaining an edge. I'd take it.

Giselle woke up, groggy and disheveled. "Where you going?" she asked.

"To find Ma's headquarters."

"No one goes out this late unless they're partying. I'm coming."

Chapter Sixteen

Even at nine at night, the Caribbean air felt warm. The moon was full. I got in the car on the correct side on the first try. I backed out and pulled into traffic, no problem. I might end up dead in Barlanadana, but chances were improving it wouldn't be from a fiery car crash.

Do the happy dance.

As we headed toward Ana, Giselle sucked on a coffee. I worked on my driving skills, ratcheting through the gears and getting up to high speeds as fast as possible. I took corners more and more rapidly, judging just how fast I could go without feeling I would lose control. The car was a beauty, a far cry from my truck, which I drove slowly so I didn't have far to walk to pick up pieces that fell off.

I reached Ana. The further we drove, the more densely populated it was, and the neighborhood deteriorated. Women stood on street corners wearing tight-fitting tops with plunging necklines and short shorts. They weren't waiting for the bus.

I locked the doors. "What if I got kidnapped? Sold as a sex slave?"

Giselle looked over at my drab, unisex clothes and smirked.

I unlocked the doors.

As I passed by a side street, I caught a glimpse of a man on foot. "Is that Dom?"

"You mean you really are looking for Ma's headquarters?" Giselle asked.

Both times I'd seen Dom before, it had been from a distance. Now the light was bad. Was my imagination playing tricks on me? At the next intersection, I made a last minute decision, and swerved to take a side street. People turned to look. The car I'd been so thrilled about not long ago suddenly turned to baggage. The shiny yellow vehicle stuck out like a two-ton lemon drop. I'd be better off on foot. At the first available spot, I pulled over and got out. By the time I made it to the sidewalk, Giselle had her hand on the door of the nearest night club.

"I'll have a drink with the locals, gather some intelligence," she said.

More likely she'd be losing intelligence. Whenever she had a drink, her IQ went down a few more points. I grabbed her by the collar. "You're coming with me."

I'd adjusted my shoulder bag so it draped low and in front of my hip. I could feel the weight of the gun. Would I need it? God, I hoped not. But I wanted it where I could get at it quickly if I did.

We strode in the direction the man had been going. We'd be parallel now or close to it. At the next intersection, if we took a turn and he kept going straight, he would see us if he looked this way. I was pretty sure Dom hadn't seen enough of me when I'd saved Purple Shirt to be able to recognize me. If it was Dom, I didn't want him to register my face now.

We faked interest in a corner shop window. As the man walked into the intersection, I chanced a glance. Was it him? The height, weight, and coloring seemed right, but I couldn't be sure. My doubts about his identity escalated. My doubts about the sanity in following him did too. He reached the other side of the street and disappeared into the next block. As soon as we made the turn, we had him in sight again.

He stopped at a house a few doors from the intersection and rang the bell. As he waited, he turned to look behind him. When the door opened, he stepped in. If it was Dom, who was he visiting? Were Tommy and Carlo in that house?

In front of the house stood a ten-foot-tall sculpture, illuminated by the moon and outdoor lights from adjacent houses. It resembled a totem pole, covered with ornate carvings. The street was quiet. I listened for cars.

Nothing.

Before I lost my nerve, I crept up to it, Giselle right behind me. We stood in front of the pole, peering at the intricate scrollwork and graceful symbols. I pulled out my keychain and flicked on a tiny light, which I held up to the pole. Only now could I see that some of the carvings looked a little like letters. They were almost impossible to make out amidst the flourishes and other symbols, but I continued studying it.

"Is that an 'M'?" I asked. If it was, and there were other letters, wouldn't they be of a similar size? Working my way down, I examined the area where I'd expect another letter. Again, barely discernible amidst the elaborate swirls, there seemed to be a letter. "That looks like a square-topped 'A.' Then an 'S.' A space and... Looks like an 'H' and then an 'O.' No, wait, it's a 'Q.' " I read them aloud. " 'M-A-S-H-Q.' "

"That's gibberish," Giselle said.

I gasped. "It's short for Ma's Headquarters." Ma's *secret* headquarters. Only her supporters would know to read the almost indecipherable letters.

Oh boy. We had to get out of there fast. But as I turned, I stole a look in the window. It *was* Dom. And there was Tommy the Twitch and Carlo. I moved closer. Across from them sat the woman with dark wavy hair and a slight hook to her nose I'd seen earlier. Faintly through the glass, I could hear her swearing up a storm.

Ma.

I ducked below the window, pulling Giselle with me. Tommy's voice took over. I heard words I couldn't distinguish, then I was sure I heard, "All set for tomorrow and the next day."

What did that mean?

A coup took place in one day, right? Could it mean the drug deal tomorrow, the coup the day after that? Maybe they had tee times. Maybe it meant they had office coverage. It could mean a hundred things.

"Come on," Giselle said, "let's go."

Tommy stood up. "You hear something?" An alarm went off.

Giselle and I took off. Almost to the first turn, we heard running behind us. Giselle was starting to lag already. She'd never be able to outrun whoever was after us.

"I'll go warm up the car," Giselle said.

My mind raced. I had to keep whoever was pursuing us from going after Giselle. I didn't want to use my gun. The neighborhood would be crawling with cops if I fired a shot, wouldn't it? Would Tommy go underground if that happened? I didn't want that. I ducked behind a swing set close to the sidewalk, got behind the slide. I pulled my sunglasses out and jammed them on. Whatever happened, I didn't want to be recognized. I picked up a rock, listened.

When I heard footsteps nearby, I threw it.

"Where'd he go?"

He? Whoever was speaking thought I was a guy. I hadn't dressed for a fashion show, all right? But the question was upsetting for a more important reason. Asking a question meant there was more than one of them. And more than one could mean two. Or it could mean... infinity.

For the sake of my sanity, I was going to assume two. I'd handled two before.

But never two guys who were bad for a *living*.

I peeked out. Dom and Carlo, stopped in front of the slide. They hotly discussed how they'd lost me, blaming it on each other. I crept up the slide's ladder.

They started discussing alternative plans.

I gently put my rear end down on the top of the slide.

They were getting out their phones to call for more guys to help in the search.

I slid, feet straight out, making a direct hit on the back of Dom's legs. He yelped in surprise as his knees buckled, his torso whipping forward, his head smacking into Carlo's stomach. Like dominoes, they toppled to the ground, Carlo lying spread-eagled on his back with Dom's face in his crotch.

They'd landed in front of where I sat at the bottom of the slide. I stared at Dom's butt for a second. Not having much choice, I stepped on it, swinging my other foot to the side of his prone body so I could get the hell out of there. But my foot landed near Carlo's hand. He latched on to my ankle. My adrenalin had spiked so high I kept going, dragging them as I lurched forward in a Quasimodo-like attempt to flee.

It wasn't going to work.

Dom scrambled to his feet, came up behind me, and put

his arms around me. "Hey, he's got tits!" he yelled. "Wait, I think it's a broad."

I *think*?

"It's just a broad?" Carlo said, his voice filled with disdain. He let go of my ankle, got up, and came around in front of us.

I didn't like his attitude. If I mentioned it, they'd be able to identify me later by my voice. But I felt I should make the point. Leaning back into Dom, I lifted my feet and kicked Carlo in the stomach. I'd loved to have enjoyed the look of wide-eyed amazement before he crumpled to the ground, but I was too busy rolling forward and flipping Dom over my head.

As I ran off, they were thinking up lies to tell Tommy about what had happened.

Loping toward the car, I took off my shades and hat, shoving them in my bag. Close to the car, I passed a storefront. A poster taped onto the window caught my eye. Two big letters stood out—MA. They couldn't be so brazen they advertised the coup on posters, could they? I didn't have time to read the small print. I glanced around, then ripped off the poster.

I smiled in relief when I saw the yellow car. Stopping to let a vehicle go by before crossing, I caught the eye of the driver. Was that... I was definitely getting paranoid. I'd thought that man looked like Lenny, the bodyguard.

The car passed and I crossed to mine. But suddenly the other car jerked to a stop. I turned. The window slid open.

"Hey!" the voice said.

Damn! It *was* Lenny!

Chapter Seventeen

I jammed the key in the car lock.

"Wait," he yelled. "I just want to—"

I jumped into the driver's seat and slammed the door. Where the hell was the wheel? I'd gotten in the wrong side! Clambering over the stick shift, I slipped and almost gave myself an untimely pelvic exam. Recalling I actually did need one, I made a mental note as I careened out of the space and made a tight U-turn. Lenny started to turn.

What was going on here? There was no *way* anyone could have sent him after me so fast. Leaving smoky rubber, I sped down the road. In the rearview, I saw Lenny heading after me. With only a quick glance, I pulled out into the intersection. Horns blared and cars skidded to a stop. Crap! I'd looked in the wrong direction again.

I stalled, restarted the car, and maneuvered around other vehicles. I punched the gas, but immediately had to jam on the brake as a light up ahead turned red. I checked in the rear view mirror again. Would this give Lenny a chance to catch up with me? I didn't see his car. Ha. He must be stuck on the side street. That bought me a little time. I was stuck, but he was, too.

I waited for the light to turn. "Come on. Come on." I rocked forward, willing the traffic to move. I heard a knock on the passenger side window. Lenny's face loomed in at me.

"Hey," he said, "open up. I just want to—"

"Ahhh!" I screamed. I jerked the wheel and pulled into the oncoming traffic lane. Thank goodness everyone still stopped at traffic lights. Except me, of course, in this case. I zoomed toward the intersection and around the corner, narrowly avoided a pedestrian who leaped out of my way. I kept going until I hit the end of the road. I had to choose to go right or left. I chose right. I didn't know which way led to the hotel. I just wanted to put as much distance as possible between Lenny and me. I kept going until I was miles from where I'd last seen him.

But as I drove, I started to wonder.

Why hadn't he shot at me? He'd been in his car when I'd first seen him, that was true. He'd been surprised at seeing me. He probably hadn't expected to have to use his gun while in his car. But he was a bad guy, working for Tommy, an even worse guy. When I'd seen him before, he'd had his gun in his jacket pocket. Didn't bad guys keep their guns there so they'd be easy to reach? So he should have been able to pull it out and at least point it at me. Wouldn't he at least have had it ready in case he did have the opportunity to take a shot?

Then I remembered. Sister Aggie had *taken* his gun. What if Lenny hadn't shot at me because he didn't *have* a gun? If a bad guy lost his gun, how did he get another one? Wouldn't he have to confess to Tommy that he'd lost it? Confess that he'd lost it to a *nun*. That'd be worse than a little old lady taking it. Oh, Tommy and his crowd would have a hoot with that.

So maybe he hadn't told anyone he'd lost his gun. Now he had to figure out how to get another one without going through Tommy. Wouldn't that take longer?

Lenny suddenly seemed a lot less dangerous.

***

Eventually, I realized Giselle wasn't in the car. I returned to Ana, parked in the spot I'd been in before and went into the bar. Giselle, drink in hand, limboed with the locals.

"I was just coming to rescue you," she said.

By the time I pulled into the parking lot at our hotel, Giselle was asleep. I looked at the poster I'd peeled off the window in Ana. I'd wondered how the rebels could be so brazen. But they'd been clever. The poster was about Ma, but the coup was never mentioned. Filled with the expected general crap about her powers, it could be used to generate interest in her across the island. That way, when people finally did hear about the coup, they would be primed to jump on board.

But this was odd. There was also a specific promise. *Very* specific. On two upcoming afternoons, Ma predicted business in the downtown area would be booming, and she promised it would be just a taste of the prosperity to come— for those who helped with the coup, of course.

I didn't believe in her special powers, but she'd need them to pull this off.

***

The next morning, I woke up before Giselle. I sat around watching her sleep until I realized sitting around was making me a nervous wreck. I needed to work off some of my hyper energy. Undoubtedly the day would go downhill from here.

Leaving the hotel, I took a right. The castle was less than a twenty-minute walk in this direction, but I'd seen a large park with jogging trails just before that. Dressed in running shorts and a tee shirt, I didn't have a gun with me. With what I had on, there was nowhere to hide one where it wouldn't be immediately apparent.

Bad guys wouldn't shoot at an unarmed woman, would they?

What was I thinking? Of course they would.

I continued on anyway. Cowering in the hotel would mean my muscles would atrophy and my fear would escalate. That would increase the chances of my being a victim. Lenny was the only one who really knew what I looked like anyway, and he didn't have a gun, right?

I got onto the trail and started a slow jog, then picked up the pace until I was going at a pretty good clip. I ran the section of the trail closest to the street, then took a path toward the ocean. Just before the beach, I stopped to take in the view. A perfect day, low eighties, not a cloud in the sky. People played in the surf and threw beach balls with their kids. The park sat between the castle to my left and a restaurant on the other side. Diners clustered around tables on the patio, enjoying drinks and brunch. I smiled at the scene. My eyes came to rest on a man sitting alone at a small table. I stopped smiling. Lenny.

Again.

I was getting sick and tired of running into him. He'd become a total pain in the ass and frankly, it was really starting to piss me off. I'd had it up to here with him following me and hounding me and trying to kill me. But right now, as I knew from yesterday, he didn't have a gun.

And I was far enough away from him that even if he took off in my direction as fast as his stumpy little legs could go, I'd be long gone by the time he got here. Ha! For the first time, I had the upper hand on Lenny.

I don't know what made me do it, but once I got the urge I found it irresistible. I stuck out my tongue and waggled it at him. I jumped up and down yelling, "Nyaa, nyaa, nya nya, nyaahh!" I put my thumb on my nose and wiggled my fingers. I had no idea what that meant, but I hoped it was as rude as all get-out. Even if it wasn't, I figured he'd know what my intention was, and so it was as good as rude, maybe better. I thought about giving him the finger, but by then children were watching.

I was so roiled up, I couldn't stop. "Couldn't catch me if you tried, Lenny," I hollered. I used my mouth on my hand to make a fart noise. "Leeeennnnyyy!" I taunted. Then I twirled around and wiggled my rear at him. I didn't have anything to top that, so I turned back and looked at him. He was on his feet now, his eyes bugging out. He was totally ticked off.

I put my hands on my hips. "Ha!" I yelled.

Then he took out his gun and shot at me.

"Ahhh!" I screamed, diving for cover behind the nearest tree. "Where'd you get that?"

"There's a requisitioning process. Got it this morning." He took another shot at me.

I ducked, then peeked out. "You didn't have to ask Tommy?"

"No. He has people."

What happened to the good old days when outlaws were outlaws and they didn't have people?

The adults on the beach were grabbing their kids and

scattering.

"Hey, come 'ere," Lenny yelled.

"If I was gonna come there, why wouldn't I just stay here and shoot myself?"

"You don't have a gun."

"How do you know?"

"You're not shooting back."

It would have been convenient to be able to squeeze off a round or two and make him eat his words, or even spray machine gun fire and make him dance. But of course, it would have taken a gun to do that.

And as Lenny had so astutely observed, I didn't have one.

"I just want to talk," Lenny said.

"You're shooting at me."

"Even you musta realized by now that I'm shooting wide."

"You are?"

"Oh, come on."

I could tell from the astonishment in his voice that he had been. This had never occurred to me. I wasn't used to being shot at. From my perspective, anyone aiming a gun anywhere in my direction was trying to kill me. I didn't really make the distinction between people getting close or not. "I thought you were a lousy shot."

"Thanks a lot! That's pitiful."

I'd hurt his feelings. "I didn't mean to be critical. I'm off sometimes too."

"You're a beginner. This is my profession, for crying out loud." He was clearly upset.

I thought back to the times he'd come after me. He had been off the mark. That last shot had been *way* off. "I have to admit, it doesn't make a lot of sense. I understand now it may have been intentional. But why?"

"Like I've told you a hundred times, I just want to talk."

"About what?"

"It's private."

"You can tell me."

"I want to tell you. But it's private, which means I want to tell you close up."

"Why would I believe you won't shoot at me again?"

"I've just been doing it to get your attention." He shot at me, closer this time.

"Hey!" I yelled.

"See? It got your attention, didn't it?"

Slowly but surely, I was starting to believe Lenny. What was I, a lunatic? I was going to let a guy who'd been shooting at me for days talk me into sitting down and having a drink? I needed a plan, with a strong preference for one that didn't include Margaritas on the deck.

Someone on the beach would have called the cops at the first shot. But I didn't want my last words to them to be, "I kinda thought you'd get here quicker."

I had to get away now. Behind me, on the opposite side of the park, was the castle. I'd had good luck there last time. Lenny's religious sensibilities had kept him from doing damage to me while Sister Aggie was around, and he'd actually given her his gun. Of course, now I'd pissed him off and hurt his feelings. He might not be so willing to let me go this time if I was within his reach. And I couldn't be sure Sister Aggie would be there to come to my rescue.

Zing! A bullet whizzed by my ear. "That was really close."

"You've been completely uncooperative. It's just my way of being more insistent."

"Thanks a lot!"

"And I wanted you to see that I really am a good shot

when I want to be."

"I believe you, okay?"

"So are you coming out?"

Instead of answering, I took off in the direction of the castle. I heard a noise and chanced a look back. Lenny had upended his chair in his rush to chase after me.

I ran faster, edging off the trail where bushes provided some cover. He got off another shot. This one missed by a mile. But we were moving now. Had he missed because it was lots harder to hit a moving target or because he meant to go wide? I couldn't distinguish now. His intentions weren't clear to me anymore.

A man with a gun was chasing me. I had to assume I was in mortal danger.

My best chance lay in getting to the castle. I'd have to make it up the small hill between the park and the castle. A chain link fence ran along the crest of the hill from the road to the water. If I tried to go over it, I'd end up target practice for Lenny. I was much closer to the water end. Lenny was heading straight for me. If I went along the fence to the road, Lenny could run straight across at me. The odds would shift dramatically in his favor.

I riveted my attention on the water end of the fence, which ended at a cliff above the beach; there was no land to sneak around on. If I fell, I'd drop fifty feet to the rocks below. But... if I was moving at a high enough speed when I grabbed the fence, I might be able to swing *outside* the fence, above the sheer drop and jump down on the castle side.

A wave of nausea hit me. I glanced back. Lenny was gaining. He stopped to get another shot off but it went wild and cost him a few seconds. His last two had been wide. I couldn't expect that luck to hold.

I had to make a split-second life or death choice.

Hanging above a fifty-foot drop to jagged rocks beat a bullet in the back.

I lengthened my stride. I ran as fast as I could. My timing had to be right. If I went too slow, I'd end up dangling uselessly over the rocks. If I went too fast, my grip as I swung out over the rocks to the other side wouldn't hold. In a few steps I'd be there. Now!

I grabbed the chain link fence with my left hand and hung on for dear life as I stepped off the cliff. I didn't look down as I hurtled around the end of the fence, letting go of my left hand hold as I grabbed onto the fence on the castle side with my right. I was going too fast. I slammed into the fence. "Whoof!" I felt the air go out of my lungs and I slid to the ground. I grunted as I struggled to my feet and stumbled toward the castle.

Sister Aggie appeared out of nowhere. She was running in my direction. Lenny fired again. Sister jammed her hand inside her habit, pulled out Lenny's old gun, and extended it to me. I grabbed it and tumbled to the ground, pulling her with me. I let her go and rolled, getting off one true shot.

Lenny let out a yelp and went down. Grabbing his arm, he stumbled up, staying low as he ran in the other direction.

I'd forgotten to mention to him that I was getting good with a gun, too.

Chapter Eighteen

When I got back to the room, Giselle finally woke up, and I told her what had happened.

"Nora, try not to let yourself get distracted."

"Distracted? Lenny shooting at me is a distraction?"

"I don't see any blood. You didn't get hit, right?"

"What about finding Ma's headquarters?"

"Finding the headquarters means diddley unless we can get the evidence we need. It's heavily alarmed, so it'd be hard to get a bug inside." She made a call. "It's easy to get one outside, but that's not as good. Might as well try it though."

"What about hearing Tommy say 'All set for tomorrow and the next day'? Something big might be about to happen."

"Maybe. Or it could mean they have dinner reservations." She stretched. "Look, it's important you keep focused on the training. I'm going to show you some nifty spyware."

"I hope it includes a nifty supersonic force field able to repel bullets."

"Get me a drink if you want me to show you this stuff."

"Aren't you supposed to be showing me this stuff? Why do I have to wangle everything out of you?"

"Just get me—"

I'd go someplace and get a bottle. Then I wouldn't have

to head downstairs or call room service every time Giselle wanted a drink. Which was a lot. I hopped on the elevator and pushed the button. It started moving right away, but in slow motion. What was it with these elevators? Ten minutes later, I'd made it to the lobby. Amongst all the shops in the area, there had to be one that sold booze. The one I found even sold the brand Giselle liked. Jameson.

I returned to our room. Giselle sat cross-legged on the bed, smiling happily when I handed her the glass. She took a few sips. "Ahhh. Okay, now get that bag."

I fetched the bag and she spread its contents on the bed. One of the devices looked like a pregnant armadillo. She blitzed through the pile of gadgets, picking each one up as she talked about it. "This one's used to do surveillance on cars. This one's used to do surveillance on buildings. This one's used to do surveillance on people. This one's used to blow up cars. This one's used to blow up buildings."

"Is there one to blow up people?"

"That's kind of a freebie."

"A freebie?"

"If you blow up a car, you blow up the people. Same for a building."

I nodded. "Of course."

As she sped through the other devices, I said, "Wait. You're going too fast."

"If you want to be a spy, you have to be a fast learner." She picked up one of the gizmos. "I'll show you how to install this baby." Climbing off the bed, she pulled on shorts and a shirt.

"Is that one of the surveillance devices or one of the blow-up devices?"

"Car surveillance," she said in an exasperated tone.

"Weren't you listening?"

I followed her toward the door. "One one thousand, " I muttered. Well, I was the one who'd wanted easy money. And okay, maybe a teensy weensy part of me had wanted some excitement in my life. Just another thing in life that was better in the theoretical.

In the lobby, Giselle turned toward the garage. She found a quiet spot and stopped beside a car. "Now you see it," she said, holding the device in the palm of her open hand, ducking down for a few seconds and popping back up, "now you don't."

"It's that easy, huh?"

"Oh sure," she said, "after a little practice."

Back up in the room, I looked at the devices strewn on the bed. "Did we go over this one?" I pointed to a device shaped like a little can of shaving cream.

"That's a flash bang."

"That sounds like a good one."

"Works like a grenade. You pull out that ring hanging off it and heave it. There's a blinding flash and a really loud noise."

"No massive explosion?" Not having to duck assorted body and building parts sailing through the air would be a plus.

"Right."

"That's nice," I said.

"If you want a distraction, yeah. But if you want to blow stuff up, use the other ones."

"I have a few more questions."

"I have someplace to go," Giselle said, disappearing into the bathroom. A minute later she reappeared, wearing her bathing suit and carrying a towel. "Why don't you practice?"

I stared down at the devices. "I'm not sure I—" The door closed behind her as she left.

"Practice. Okay. Sure. I can do that." I piled the devices back into the little bag. Had Giselle always been this annoying? I headed down to the lobby and into the hallway to the garage. Did she know you dramatically increased your chances of drowning if you drank before swimming? Gee, what a shame she was gone already and I couldn't remind her. I wondered who would get her car if she—

But there she was. Not at the pool, but in the Internet café, huddled in a corner. I stepped to the side of the window. We had Internet access in the room, so she must be doing something she didn't want me to know about. Her fingers flew over the keyboard, and as they did the look on her face changed from concern to fear to sheer terror. This must have something to do with why she was so jumpy. But there was no way I could read what was on the screen. She'd positioned herself so she could see everyone who came in, and no one could get behind her.

I continued to the garage. Ducking between two cars, I spread the contents of the bag on the pavement. Examining the devices, I tried to remember what each did. "This one you stick under a car if you want to know where it's going. This one you stick under a car if you want to blow it up. This one you stick in your ear if you want to listen to a conversation." I thought back to Giselle speeding through the lesson, then leaving me to fend for myself. "You have to be a fast learner," I said, mimicking her.

But then I looked at the devices again and wasn't sure. "Or is *this* the one you stick in your ear and *this* one you stick under a car. I'm pretty sure this is the one that blows up. So I probably don't want to stick that in my ear."

As I put a small, round device down, it rolled under a car. Getting on my knees, I stuck my hand under the car, but it was just out of reach. Since this could be one of the blow-up devices, I couldn't leave it where it was. I sighed and lay flat on the dirty pavement, snaking my way on my belly toward the device. Finally I snagged it and started backing out.

As I was about to clear the bottom of the car, I felt someone looming above me. I jerked up with a start, smacking my head on hard metal. "Ow."

"Hi," Jesse said. "Lose something?"

I straightened up and jammed my hands on my hips, filled with bad attitude. "Yeah, I lost something. I lost my marbles. I must have lost all of them to even be thinking about trying to do this." Then my attitude crumbled and I started to softly cry. "I'm having so much trouble. I'll never learn to be a spy. Just another thing Giselle is better at than I am."

"Whoa. Whoa. Whoa. Come here, Nora." He leaned back against a car and extended his arms. He pulled me into a hug, which I tried not to really, really like. Rubbing my back, he said, "Don't be so hard on yourself. It takes time is all." He rested his cheek on my head.

"Not according to Giselle."

"I've gotta go back to Washington again, but maybe I can teach you a few things."

"Great," I said, reluctantly leaving his arms. "When do you go back?"

"Ever since I got promoted to management, it seems like every other day. Lots of meetings and lots of paperwork, the two biggest timewasters in the history of work."

"Doesn't sound like much fun."

He waved it off. "This next trip'll be a quickie. I leave at dawn tomorrow, but I'll be back here by the afternoon."

I squatted back down to the task at hand. "I guess you know pretty quickly who the fast learners are."

"How?"

"The ones who don't blow themselves up."

He laughed. "Good one." He kept laughing.

"It's not that funny."

"Well, we all blow ourselves up from time to time, Nora."

I stared at him, aghast. "I'd prefer not to, thank you very much." I focused on the gadgets again. "If I can help it." My hands sweated as I weighed the options and tried to decide which gadget to use. Finally I made my choice and moved to slip it under the car.

"Uh." I peered up. Jesse was shaking his head ever so slightly.

"I know that," I said. "I just wanted to see if you were paying attention." I picked up another, glancing up at him. He smiled and nodded. On the fourth try, my hands covered in grime, I slipped the device into place.

There. I'd done it. I let myself feel a little surge of satisfaction.

Of course, if I ever had to put a device in place in a hurry, I was totally screwed.

Chapter Nineteen

Giselle and I sat in the hotel restaurant finishing an early lunch. The waitress refilled my large tumbler of iced coffee as Giselle answered a call on her cell phone. I sipped as I watched my sister. Her side of the conversation consisted of occasional monosyllabic responses.

"Let's go," she said as she hung up.

"Where?" I said, sitting up.

"One of the guys bugged Tommy. Outside Ma's headquarters."

"You don't look excited."

"It can be kind of boring. Hurry up."

"Hold on." I slurped down the rest of the iced coffee. "I want to be able to stay awake."

"Gee," Giselle said, "I wouldn't have done that if I were you."

"Why?"

"Now you're going to have to pee."

"They must have bathrooms at the office."

"We're going to be in a van," she said, "for a long time."

"Hold on. Let me run to the—"

A van pulled up outside. "We gotta go."

"*I* gotta go."

"We both do. Come on." She stood up.

"No, I mean I really, *really*—"

The people at the next table looked up. Giselle gave them a fake smile before turning to me. Barely moving her lips, she said, "The longer the van sits there, the better the chances are someone will remember it." She threw money on the table and strode toward the front door. I had no choice but to follow.

Giselle opened the rear door of the windowless black vehicle enough for us to slip in. A driver sat in the front section. Toward the rear, someone sat at an array of computer devices. Giselle took the seat to his left and I grabbed the other as the van started to move.

"What's up, Louie?" she asked him.

"Equipment's working fine. Good luck." As the van slowed, Louie eased open the rear door and disappeared.

"Here're your earmuffs," Giselle said. She burst out laughing.

"Very funny," I said, putting the headphones on.

The van moved to a new location and stopped. Hours later, nothing had happened. "Giselle," I whispered, "my bladder is going to explode. Couldn't I just run up the street? There's gotta be a restaurant with a bathroom I could use."

"I told you you'd be sorry you drank that coffee."

Hands on my hips, I said, "You told me after I drank it."

"James Bond doesn't run up the street to find a bathroom."

"James Bond can pee into a potted plant." I crossed my legs. "Please, Giselle." With a sudden flash of insight, I realized the brilliance of Depends adult undergarments.

"So you can get shot at again?"

I shut up. Suddenly voices came across the line. I pressed the headphones to my ears.

"Dom, it's me."

"What's up, Tommy?"

"Just called to see how you're doing. You get that root canal done?"

"Yeah, I'm all set. You need anything?"

"No. I had a job. But I got Buddy working it."

"What's the job?"

"You know the cruise ship down at the dock?"

"The big one there? Queen something or other."

"The *Queen Bee*. I played poker with the captain yesterday. I think he was cheating."

"That's not very nice."

"Yeah, so we're gonna blow the boat up. Teach him a lesson."

I looked at Giselle in alarm.

"Serves him right," said Dom. "The whole thing going down?"

"Nah, just blowing a hole in the side. I'm not sure the guy was cheating. That'll show him in case he was."

"When's that gonna happen?"

"I think they had a bomb ready to go. Might have it on the boat already. Real soon anyway."

"Hope that wasn't inconvenient, havin' to get Buddy, boss."

"Hey, don't worry about it. You gotta take care of your teeth." They disconnected.

Giselle immediately dialed a number. "There's a bomb threat. Get everybody off the *Queen Bee*." She finished her call and hung up.

"Aren't there hundreds of people on that ship?" I asked.

"Probably close to a thousand."

The van started to move. "What's happening?"

"The driver will take us down to the dock."

"He was listening? He heard that whole thing about my exploding bladder?"

"Of course. He's wired in. I thought you knew."

"How would I know? Did you think I was a spy for Bob's Bikes? I was an administrative assistant. We don't do surveillance. I was so bored, I almost told you about my recurring yeast infection."

"I'm still listening," the driver hollered from the front.

I glared at Giselle, although that last part really hadn't been her fault.

A few minutes later, the van slowed. We slipped out the back of the vehicle into an alley. I followed Giselle to the end where we could see across the dock to the *Queen Bee*. The evacuation was underway, people hurrying to get off. Police herded the passengers away from the ship. Most headed for the shops.

We watched to see if anyone attempted to get on the boat instead of off. Everyone we saw boarding was police or fire or emergency services. We didn't notice anything suspicious.

But if the bomb had already been planted, it could go off any time. How many innocent people would croak? It gave me the willies. We had no way of knowing how big the bomb was or its location.

In front of a store, I spied a potted plant. If James Bond could... But then I noticed a hotel a couple of doors beyond it. I ran to it and peed with a glee not normally associated with urination. When I returned, all remained quiet. Eventually the bomb-sniffing dogs and the emergency personnel departed.

"It's been four hours since you called the bomb threat in,"

I said. "Maybe we headed them off. Couldn't put the bomb on the boat with all the police around."

"Maybe."

Or maybe the bomb was on there and hadn't been found.

"What's up for tomorrow?" I asked.

"More surveillance."

But as each hour ticked by, I worried. We needed info about the drug deal and the coup. Would we get it tomorrow? Would we get it before it was too late?

***

The next morning, I got up early, went down to the restaurant, and drank two cups of coffee. By the time Giselle joined me, I'd peed until my bladder was bone dry. I picked up the carafe. "Coffee?"

"I'll have a little."

I filled her cup to the brim. We ate breakfast and waited. A van appeared, but this one was blue and had a different company name. "How many of these do you have?"

"One. We paint it whenever we need it and change the sign."

Once again, we drove to the listening location and waited for hours. Finally, again in the middle of the afternoon, we heard voices on the line.

"Buddy, it's Tommy. Hey, what the heck happened?"

"Oh geesh. Sorry about that, boss. I didn't know someone else used that big bomb already. We had plenty of small ones, but to do the job right, we needed a big one."

"You couldn't call and let me know?"

"It slipped my mind, I was so busy gettin' a new one. Couldn't get it until today."

142

"Probably just as well anyway, 'cause I told you the wrong boat."

"I coulda blown up the wrong boat?"

"Yeah," Tommy said. They laughed. I looked at Giselle, shocked.

"That woulda been a royal fuck-up, huh?" Buddy said.

"Hey, things happen. Anyway, it's not the *Queen Bee*. It's the *Sea Queen*."

"Now I understand how you coulda been confused. Two names so similar."

"Tell me about it."

"Same deal?"

"Use the big bomb and a small one too," Tommy said. "I'm pissed off I almost had you blow up the wrong boat."

"You got it." They disconnected.

Giselle sat back and sighed.

"What's wrong? Aren't you going to make the call?"

"They're playing us."

"What do you mean?"

"They know we're listening."

"They're jerking us around? You mean there was no poker game, no cheating captain?"

"Nope."

"What makes you say that?"

"Most of the time when you listen to these conversations, you get nothing. Routine stuff. They were saying too much."

"It seemed odd they were talking about blowing up ships instead of concentrating on the coup. Almost as if..." I pulled the poster out of my purse. "I got this the day we found the headquarters. It says Ma predicts business will be booming on two afternoons—today and yesterday. I thought it was nuts. But they're *using* us. Both days the bomb scares happened late afternoon, when everyone is typically getting back *on* the boat. They wanted us to get people back *off.* Then everyone goes into the shops—and Ma's prediction of prosperity becomes true."

"Word spreads and creates more followers," Giselle said.

"We can't be sure there's no bomb. And too many lives are at stake to take a chance."

She nodded as she made the call for the evacuation. We made our way to the dock again and watched as the passengers evacuated and the dogs searched for a bomb.

"What if we hadn't planted the bug?" I wondered.

"Without the bug, one of them picks up the phone and calls in a bomb threat. When they figured out they were bugged, they just tricked us into calling it in. The evacuation happens either way. Bet they got a charge out of making us look like idiots."

I sighed, watching men and women arm in arm helping each other off the ship. They thought they were in danger and were worried about each other. For some people, love is grand.

Jesse flitted to mind. I'd thought in the garage for just a second that he'd seemed interested in me. But he'd had last night to make a move, and that hadn't happened. He had to know I was free and clear. No ring on my finger made it pretty obvious.

The last of the passengers disembarked. Once again, nothing.

We headed back to the hotel. I asked, "So, what does this all mean?"

"We need a bug they don't know about, one that picks up everything they say."

"Great."

"Not really. That phone tap could go anyplace along the circuit."

"Even outside the house."

"Sure, that's what made it so easy. And somebody else did that."

"But?"

"This is a lot harder. It means getting close in person."

"Who's gonna do that?"

She didn't say anything. But she was looking at me.

Chapter Twenty

We jumped out of the van as close as we could get to the hotel and made our way through a crowd of people. A sign read "Chicken Appreciation Day." People and chickens in matching outfits partied along the street.

"Hold on." I stopped to buy a turkey dog from a vendor. "So someone has to get close to Tommy? How close? This guy is dangerous. He threatened to blow up a whole bunch of people because he thought a guy *might* have cheated him in poker."

"Take it easy. We come up with a plan, ease you into it."

"Oh. Step by step, I get closer to Tommy."

"Exactly," she said. "You don't just rush in all willy-nilly."

I would still end up face to face with Tommy, but somehow it didn't seem as dangerous this way. I liked that.

Jesse walked out the hotel entrance, looking at the locals and their chickens, now doing a weird chicken dance. "So what are you up to?" he asked.

"I'm telling Nora a little more about how we do things," Giselle said.

People held their chickens up to us for adoration. We tickled them under their beaks, talked baby talk to them. I kissed every chicken just to be on the safe side.

We huddled in the middle of the crowd. "What's Nora working on?" Jesse asked Giselle.

"Tommy," Giselle said.

"Giselle said it'll be easy," I said.

Jesse's eyebrows shot up. "You told her Tommy the Twitch is an *easy* assignment?"

Giselle scratched her head, looked away. "No. I said, 'Not every assignment is tough.' "

"Right," I said, fully alert now, "so..."

"I didn't say *this* one wasn't tough. I said *some* of them aren't tough. This one... Well, yeah, this one would be considered a little tough. But I've seen tougher."

"Sure," Jesse said, putting his hands on his hips, "the Russian mafia that time they had the nuclear weapons and the missile launchers."

"See?" Giselle said.

"We sent our most experienced guys on that, and they had military backup," Jesse yelled. "Tommy the Twitch. And the deadly duo, Dom and Carlo, are never far away. You should be ashamed."

I stared in disbelief at Giselle.

"She told you why they call him Tommy the Twitch, right?" he asked me.

"Some medical condition. I figured an eye twitch, maybe restless leg syndrome or—"

"A *trigger* finger twitch. Half his victims, he didn't even mean to kill."

"His finger twitched," I said softly.

"Yeah," Jesse said, giving me a long look. "What does your fiancé think about all this? Isn't he worried about you?"

I stopped. "My fiancé? What fiancé?"

"That Kenny guy. He was bragging Thanksgiving night

he was going to propose."

"He did, but—"

Jesse's cell phone rang. He kept his gaze on me while he answered it. "Yes. No. Yes. No. Yes. No. Damn." Long pause. "Okay," he said, annoyed. He hung up. "I have to fly back to Washington. Again. This time for a *planning* meeting. This isn't even the actual meeting. This is the *pre*-meeting meeting. Then we'll have the actual meeting. Then they'll schedule a *post*-meeting meeting to talk about what we discussed in the meeting." He ran his fingers through his hair in exasperation, then narrowed his eyes at me. "Don't do anything until I get back. Nothing," he said to me, wagging a finger. "I'll be back tomorrow and we'll sort this out." He scanned the street. "There's the car." He started towards it.

"Already?" I said to Giselle. "He just hung up the phone. How could there be—"

Jesse thought I was still involved with Kenny. Did that explain why he hadn't made a move on me, or was I still just hoping for interest that wasn't there and never would be? I wished he hadn't had to leave. Come to think of it, how had he even been able to leave? "Hey, this island's so tiny. I thought planes only flew in and out once in a while."

"Right. But he's going on a 'copter. The agency uses them for high priority stuff. They'll have him in Washington in a few hours."

"What are we going to do now? Start on this plan?"

"Well... I happen to know Tommy's going to be at a party tonight."

"So there's really no planning?"

"Umm. This is more an example of short-term planning."

My anxiety shot through the roof. "What about the

easing into it, going step by step?"

"This is more the 'expect the unexpected' rule. We didn't get to that part of the training yet. It's just that I know how important the money is to you, that's all."

"Right. It's all about what's good for me." How many times had I fallen for that one? "You're my big sister. You're supposed to look out for me. Aren't you?"

"I do, but—"

"You do?" I yelled. "Remember that time you gave me a bouillon cube?"

"Yeah?"

"You *told* me it was a caramel. I ate it."

"I can expl—"

"You said you didn't know. But you did know, didn't you?" I was fuming. "And that time you got all the neighborhood kids to come over, then told me there were ants in my pants. I danced around like Michael Jackson in drag that day, while everyone laughed at me. But I never did have ants in my pants, did I?"

"Okay, I admit—"

"Remember that time you tried to get me to whitewash the fence?" She looked perplexed. "Wait, maybe that was in *Tom Sawyer*. But there were other times."

"You always blamed me for everything."

"It was always your fault!"

"You're not considering the upside—"

"Upside? What upside?"

"You were the first one in our neighborhood to learn break dancing. I always thought that ants-in-the-pants thing helped get you started. You already knew a lot of the moves and—"

"Ah!" I threw up my hands in disbelief. I'd seen through

Giselle and she knew it. But still... Tommy was the key. If I didn't stop him soon, would I be able to stop him at all? Was I already too late? I thought about how badly I wanted to start my school-on-a-schooner. If I could pull this off...

I turned away, thinking, then gyrated wildly, barely avoiding stepping on a chicken.

"What would I have to do?" I asked.

"Get him to take you to his place. Plant a listening device and get him talking to find out what he's up to. We'll be able to get what we need to put him away. I guarantee I'll be right here in case you need to call."

I heard myself ask, "Where's the party?"

Chapter Twenty-One

An hour later, I'd showered and stuffed myself into the blue halter top dress Mrs. Tommy had bought for me. Luckily it was only the top that fit tight. The skirt had a flirty little flounce, the better to run wildly from the scene of my impending death should the need arise. I felt a little guilty about wearing it. It seemed rude to seduce the woman's husband in a dress she paid for. On the other hand, who knew his taste better than his wife? She was a nice lady. I hoped she wouldn't be swept up in the dragnet when we rounded up Tommy and his gang.

Barefoot in front of the mirror in the bedroom, I considered my footwear options. Sneakers would be my best bet if I had to make a run for it, but even ones in a matching color definitely wouldn't go with the dress. I stepped into pointy-toed three-inch spikes. If they slowed me down enough for someone to catch me, the heels *and* the toes were as good as daggers. I stood in front of the mirror to get the full effect. I'd caked on a lot of makeup, and what can I say?

I looked hot.

Too bad Jesse wasn't here. It would have been nice to get Jesse's assessment of how I looked for the job, on a professional level, of course.

I went into the living room to ask Giselle a few more questions about the devices, but I found her asleep on the couch. From the level of Jameson left in the bottle, more likely she'd passed out.

I positioned her cell phone on the table next to her. If I did need to call her later, she'd be in better shape if I let her sleep now. She'd said to use code names if I called. That way she'd know immediately I was in trouble.

I spread out the devices. Okay, concentrate. But try as I might, I couldn't remember the details Giselle had sped through. How was I going to— "Eenie meenie miney mo, catch a gadget by the toe, if it blows up let it go, eeney meeney miney mo." I picked up the device I was pointing to. Wasn't that the flash bang? That would be a good choice. Save the blow up devices for when I had a little more experience. I also picked up a small, round disk like the one Giselle had practiced with in the garage. That definitely was a bug. I put both items in my bag.

A few minutes later, I walked into the Tropical Paradise Hotel and approached the concierge desk. "Could you tell me where the Twitch party is?"

He scanned down the list. "I don't see a Twitch party."

Oops. That wasn't the name *Tommy* called himself. That was the name the spies called him! "I'm sorry. I meant the Tommy party."

"Ah, yes," he said. "Down the hall, last door on the left."

As I walked in that direction, I remembered what Giselle had taught me. I sashayed my ass off to the door and right on in. As I headed across the room, I glanced around for

Lenny and Mrs. Tommy. I breathed a sigh of relief. From what I could see, neither had attended.

At the bar, I ordered a Violet Cossack. The bartender started moving bottles around, nonplussed. "Do you know the recipe?" I asked.

"Yeah, but we don't get much call for drinks with huckleberries. If you don't mind waiting while I run to the kitchen? It'll just take a minute."

"No problem." As he disappeared though a swinging door, three men approached. If I hadn't been wearing really nice heels, I would have thrown up on my shoes. Tommy, Dom and Carlo. Dom and Carlo wouldn't recognize me from when we'd had our fight, would they?

A major benefit of wearing a dark, sleeveless dress was that it hid my instantaneous, massive pit stains. I hoped my choice of perfume would make the sweat springing from every pore smell musky.

"Where's the freakin' bartender?" Tommy said.

"Tommy," Dom whispered, nodding in my direction, "there's a lady present."

Tommy turned. "Oh," he said, smiling, "and a lovely one at that."

For a cold-blooded killer, he could be quite charming.

"Sorry about my mouth," he said.

"That's okay," I replied, gazing at his lips. "Your mouth is fine." I slowly moved my tongue across my lower lip. I was way out of practice with this flirting stuff. Did this look seductive? Or like I was out of Chap Stick?

But when he looked back, a sexy smile started across his face.

"And by the way..." I said.

"Yes?" he said.

"The freakin' bartender ran to the kitchen."

Tommy gave me a full smile now, and a bad-boy twinkle lit up his eyes. He turned and faced me head on. "Now why'd he do that?" He took a step in my direction.

"He needed hhh-huckleberries," I said in a breathy voice. I took a step toward him.

"And why did he need hhh-huckleberries?" He was inches away.

"To make me a Violet Cossack." I closed the gap a fraction more.

He was up against me now. "Oh," Tommy said, "you like the hard stuff."

And no question about it, Tommy had hard stuff. This was what I was supposed to want to happen, right? I just was surprised it was happening so darn fast.

"Yeah," I said. "I definitely like the hard stuff. What do you like?"

"I liked it when the hard stuff and the sweet get mixed together. Know what I mean?"

He thrust his hard toward my sweet, pinning me against the bar. "Oh, I definitely do." My lips were a hairsbreadth from his. As he closed his eyes, I slid away and skirted behind the bar. "You mean like a pina colada or a daiquiri. I think a Manhattan would also fall into that category, as would a Cosmopolitan, a Mai Tai, and a Caribbean Breeze," I said, counting on my fingers. "What'll it be?"

Surprise crossed his face, and he laughed. "Let's see—"

"I think I can guess." I looked him up and down. "A *Man*-hattan," I said. Lucky I picked up occasional bartending jobs back in Portsmouth. As I mixed up the drink, I flipped my hair, throwing him a sultry glance. Oh yeah, Tommy liked that. As I slid the drink toward him, the bartender returned.

"Sorry about the wait," he said in a quavering voice to Tommy.

Tommy stared at him for a couple of seconds. "Don't let it happen again."

The bartender turned pasty. "No, sir."

"And hurry up with her drink."

This was the part that wasn't so charming.

"Yes, sir," the bartender said. His hands shook as he mixed ingredients.

Dom approached Tommy and they whispered for a moment. As Tommy's attention returned to the bar, the bartender poured the drink into a glass and slid it my way.

"It's not purple," Tommy said.

The bartender froze. He'd been so nervous, he'd forgotten to add the huckleberries.

I'd seen Tommy's deadly reaction when people got on his nerves. One of the longest seconds of my life passed. "Well," I said, "if you hadn't been so busy talking to your friends, you'd know I asked him to hold the huckleberries."

"I thought he just went to *get* the huckleberries?" His voice held a tinge of disbelief. He was looking for a lie, and he'd found one.

Fear turned to terror. I felt sure the bartender would disappear if Tommy decided he should. And if he thought I was up to something, I'd be among the missing, too.

"A few minutes ago, I didn't care if my teeth were stained purple," I said, pinning Tommy against the bar this time. The bartender wiped sweat from his forehead.

"Oh," Tommy said, "but now you do."

"Oh yeah." I fixed a lip lock on him designed to make him forget all about lies and bartenders. It seemed to have the desired effect. When we pulled apart, his eyes were glassy.

Giselle had said to pump him for information. If he had his way, he was going to be the one doing the pumping. And it wasn't going to be for informational purposes.

"Wanna see something?" Tommy asked.

Uh-oh. I was afraid I knew what he wanted me to see. He couldn't take me to dinner first? "What?" I blurted out.

"My boat."

I'd heard it called cock, prick, dick, woody... but I'd never heard it called "my boat." If he'd said kayak or canoe, then at least the shape would be close. And just the word "boat." How big was this thing anyway?

"It's right down at the pier," he said.

How could his dick be down at the pier if he was standing here with— "Oh!" He meant a real boat! Relief coursed through me. "Yeah," I said, "I'd like that." I liked it a lot considering the other possibilities.

I'd been hoping Tommy would take me where he lived. That way I could plant a bug. Instead he was taking me to a boat. Not what I'd hoped, but at least I could try to get him talking. Maybe I'd find out something useful.

On the other hand, maybe I'd get killed. I sucked down my drink like I was Giselle. I tried not to gag. Definitely not as good without the huckleberries. I hoped to be able to try it again with the huckleberries sometime in the future.

If I had a future.

Tommy kept his eye on me while he swigged his drink. As soon as he finished it, he slapped the glass down and grabbed my hand. "Let's go."

Chapter Twenty-Two

A few minutes later we stepped onto a main pier from which dozens of smaller piers jutted. We passed boats where the lights showed people sitting and having drinks. We continued to an area where all the boats were dark.

"Which one?" I asked.

Tommy pointed to a boat that had to be forty feet long. I walked up close to it. Shiny black and, for a cabin cruiser, sleek-lined. Above deck, built-in benches and a table aft for those along for the ride. Just fore of that, you stepped up to a midship cockpit area where the captain piloted the boat. To the right of the wheel, a set of stairs led below to the living quarters. Tommy stepped onto the boat and extended his hand to me.

I took it and hopped on board. He pulled me into an embrace. When he kissed me this time, I wasn't quite as enthusiastic. I wasn't trying to save someone's life.

Except maybe my own.

"Can I get a tour?" I asked.

"Oh." He gave me a sly look. "Ohhh."

Crap! He thought that was code for, "I want to see the bedroom."

But when we descended into the living quarters, he seemed to enjoy showing me around. Here was something we had in common. We loved boats. "Custom made to combine speed and luxury. Faster than any other boat like it," he said. "Makes it back and forth to Florida in no time flat. Operating at night is no problem. Dark color makes it practically invisible."

Hello! This was the boat they used for moving drugs to the States. I'd hoped he would take me where he lived. Instead, he'd taken me where he did *business*. This was so much better. I could plant a bug here, and we'd record Tommy speaking with people directly involved in running the drugs. I wanted to plant the bug and get the heck out.

"Could I freshen up?" I asked.

Oh, he liked the sound of that. Did he think I had a negligee in my purse? Would have been tough to fit that in what with all the spy devices already in there.

He pointed. "Use the head off the master bedroom."

As I walked through the bedroom, I thought I heard a noise. I glanced around. Must be my imagination in overdrive. I continued into a bathroom bigger than the one in my winter rental. That of course was back when I had an apartment, which I didn't anymore, thanks to Giselle. But what was important right now was that the counter was big enough to spread out the devices. I needed the bugging device handy so I could install it. And I wanted to be sure I was familiar with the flash bang in case I needed to use it. I dug them out of my bag and placed them carefully on the counter. I had to hurry so Tommy wouldn't think anything funny was going on.

But as I picked up the flash bang, my mind went blank. What had Giselle said about it? How long did I need to hold it before I threw it? She'd told me it wasn't designed as an explosive, yet something that could cause that much of a flash and that loud of a bang wasn't the kind of thing you wanted to be holding when it went off. Wait. I could call her. I dialed her number. I let it ring past any possibility she would pick up. Maybe she was in the bathroom. Leaving a message would be worse than useless. I could picture it. Tommy beside me when she called me back. "Oh, hi Giselle. Thanks for returning my call. Now tell me a little more about this flash bang thingie." I shoved it back in the bag, then put the tiny bugging device deep in my cleavage where it would be easily accessible when I was ready to plant it.

Now, how exactly was I going to manage that?

I opened the door and hurried through the bedroom to rejoin Tommy. Again, I heard a noise. This time I was sure of it. I looked toward a closet and caught a glimpse of a face as the door quickly closed. I gasped and stood rooted to the spot. The door opened a tiny bit again. Lenny peered out. "Shhh," he implored, putting a finger to his lips.

I spun around and left the room. What was going on? Would Lenny shoot me in the back? After all, the last time we'd seen each other, I'd shot *him*. Why was a bodyguard who worked for Tommy in his closet? And why was he so concerned that I be quiet? He'd been after me for so long, why didn't he just come out and grab me? But if he was simply after me, he wouldn't be in the closet, would he? How could he have known I would end up here on the boat in the first place? The only part that made sense to me was the "Shhh" part. No way was I going to mention to Tommy that someone was hiding in his bedroom closet.

When I got back to Tommy, he had his phone to his ear. He signaled me to wait a minute, so I wandered back up to the cockpit. As soon as I was out of his sight, I made for the starboard side. The boat was made primarily of fiberglass, like mine. And like mine, little storage pockets had been cut out of the fiberglass on both sides. I plucked the device from my cleavage. "Now you see it," I murmured, attaching it to the roof of the storage pocket, "now you—" But the device dropped to the bottom of the pocket. "Now you still do." I grabbed it. When I'd practiced this in the garage, it had taken me four tries to get it in place. Tommy would be off the phone in seconds. "Now you see it," I said quickly, "now you don't." I stooped down to see if it was secure. Tommy appeared behind me.

"Whatcha doing?"

Another second-long eternity went by. "I was just admiring the economical use of space. Everywhere you look, the available space is used as well as it possibly could be." Actually, I was waiting for the device to drop and my body to be flung overboard.

"Yeah, boats are cool, aren't they? Like floating RVs."

Yeah, yeah. Miracle of miracles, the device stayed put. Now that I'd once again narrowly avoided disaster, I had to move on to figuring out how I was going to deal with the next problem. How could I get him talking?

He clicked his phone shut and put it in his pocket. "Come on. Let's go below."

I followed him. I needed an open-ended question to start him blabbing. How about... "When did you decide to live a life of crime?" No, that might give him a lot to chat about, but he *could* say, "1998," and that would be the end of it. And I needed something not quite so in-your-face. What about, "So, what do you do?" That was better, and definitely open-ended, but so overused.

Opening a cupboard, he took out a bottle of scotch. He poured two drinks and handed me one. Rummaging in the cupboard again, he grabbed salsa and chips.

"Mmmm," I said, cramming my mouth full of salsa and chips. "Thith ith delithious." On one hand I was starving, but on the other I hoped he'd find the sight of me chomping away disgusting and unattractive. "Sorry for being such a pig."

"I like a woman with big appetites," he said. He downed his drink. "So whaddya say we hop in the—"

"So what do you do?" All right, the question was trite. But it beat the heck out of Tommy jumping my bones.

His voice dropped to a whisper. "Don't tell no one, but we smuggle drugs."

I choked on my chips. I thought I'd have to work a lot harder at getting him to talk. I thought I'd have to look closely at how he acted to figure out truth from lies. But he was just blurting it all out. Did Tommy feel so immune from the law he could be completely open about what he did?

Of course, if he planned on having sex with me and then feeding me to the sharks, that might also account for it.

I smacked him on the shoulder. "Get out! Drugs! How exciting."

"But we have a strict code," he continued. "We only sell to adults."

"Really. I never heard of—"

"Oh sure. We check IDs and everything. And we only sell it for medicinal purposes."

"That's not so bad then, is it?"

He laughed. "I'm joking wit' you. Hey, if some twelve-year-old wants to buy a little crack, why should I stand in the way? Long as someone's got the dough, that's all I care about. I respect the free enterprise system, so I make sure I have enough for all. I'm anti-discrimination, know what I mean?" He elbowed me.

"So to make sure you have enough for all, how much do you carry on a trip?"

"Usually about fifty kilos. But I got a huge deal coming up. This'll be a hundred."

"A hundred *kilos*?" That was more than two hundred pounds. I didn't know a lot about drugs, but my guess was that had to be worth eight or ten million dollars. This had to be the big deal to finance the coup. It hadn't gone; I wasn't too late.

"Yeah. That's why I'm so excited about the boat, see what I mean? You wouldn't believe all the hidey-holes. And we made little secret compartments inside the hidey-holes. Anybody on the boat who didn't know where we hid it wouldn't even know it was there," he said. "And see here, we store it in these bags so it stays nice and dry." He reached into a compartment and up, pulling out a filled bag. "I keep a couple for showing customers and training new guys. Makes it more realistic like."

"Can I touch it?" I asked.

"You can touch anything you want, honey." With a smirk, he handed me the bag.

I bounced it in my hand. Cocaine. How many lives would that much coke destroy?

He tucked it away, then proudly showed me the operation in detail. He sounded like he expected the drug dealers' awards committee to drop by and pin a gold star on him any minute.

"Must be nice to have all that money. What do you do with it?"

His eyes got hard and he clammed up. "Enough business. I can think of something to do that's more fun than talking."

A loud whistling noise sounded from the stern of the boat. A thunderous boom and a flash of light followed. Was someone shooting at us? I ran to Tommy. "What's that?"

"Some hotel gimmick. The anniversary of something-or-other, so they're doing this big fireworks display."

"Oh." Since there had to be a lot of people who wanted Tommy dead, I felt relieved no one was shooting at him. Normally, I wouldn't have strong feelings about it one way or the other. But right now I was with him. We stepped above deck to get a better look.

Fireworks exploded in the sky, the last one a rapid series of brilliant blue and red flashes.

Tommy's phone rang again. "What?" he barked. He listened, then turned away from me. "Frisk her?" he whispered. "That's your job, Dom." He listened again. "Okay, you're right. I said you couldn't come. All right, all right. I'll do it myself. And I'll check her bag. It could spoil the mood, though, know what I mean?"

Tommy was going to frisk me and go through my bag? That would be right before he killed me.

Chapter Twenty-Three

The fireworks continued. Tommy was having trouble hearing Dom. As he headed below deck, I heard snatches of the conversation, "moonlight cruise... any problem...."

If he looked in my purse, it would be tough to explain why a nice girl like me carried a flash bang around. I had seconds to act. I opened my bag and grabbed the device. I could tell Tommy was getting ready to end his call. How had Giselle said this thing worked? I had to pull the ring, but in war movies, grenades had lag time, right? Would it blow up in my hand? Fingers trembling, I pulled the ring. But as I did, I noticed lettering. A one and a half second delay! With a grunt, I heaved it into the air as far from the boat as I could. I ducked for cover in the corner and stuck my fingers in my ears.

BOOM! A blinding flash lit the sky and a huge percussion rocked the boat.

A second flash occurred, this one in my mind. I'd just replayed the bits of Tommy's conversation I'd overheard and put the pieces together. Dom had told him to take me on a moonlight cruise. If I was any trouble, Tommy would get rid of me out there. I punched the speed dial number on my phone. I had to get a hold of Giselle. I remembered her instruction to use code names. But w*hat* code names? For future reference, I made a mental note to think up code names before getting in a tight spot. "Sitting Bull!" I said into the phone. "This is Sitting Duck!" Where was she? Why didn't she answer? "Giselle! Help!" I said desperately.

Tommy suddenly appeared, saw me hiding in the corner.

"That last firecracker was a loud one," I said. I started to get up from my squatting position, slowly putting my phone away.

"Hey, come here. It's just fireworks." He helped me to a standing position. "Let's go back downstairs." He moved to the side to let me precede him. I stepped below and kept walking. He stopped, and I turned to face him. "Who were you talking to up there?" he asked.

"Talking to?"

"Yeah, up there when you were just talking. Using code names."

"Oh, up there? Well... Did you ever have an imaginary friend when you were a kid?"

"Sure. Doesn't everybody?"

"Right. And most people give them up when they get older. When they can distinguish between the real and the imaginary."

"I'm with you so far."

He was going to buy this? I felt a little more confident. "But I have a minor mental condition. The chief symptom is a need to keep my imaginary friends. I have imaginary Indian friends. Sitting Bull. Sitting Duck. Pocahontas. It doesn't hurt anybody, and it's comforting to me. You know how some people believe they have a guardian angel?"

"Yeah."

"It's kind of like that."

"That's a total load of crap."

I thought about my earlier assessment that he was buying it. This was definitely an area I'd have to work on. In the meantime, I'd try another tack. "Are you a religious man, Tommy?"

"You mean do I believe in God? Sure."

"You know how you'll hear people exclaim, 'Lord help me!' when they're upset? I belong to a small religious group, and our leader's name is Giselle. So I exclaim, 'Giselle help me!' instead."

He considered it. "That's also a total load of crap," he said, removing a gun from the drawer near where he'd stopped. "Which is kind of too bad, because you and me, we were about to have a really good time."

This was a small upside. Thinking about what he considered a really good time made my skin scamper.

He continued, "Now, usually when someone is talking in secret and using code names to get backup assistance, it's a very bad thing for a drug dealer. I'm comforted by the fact that apparently no one was listening to you. You're all alone, here with me, on this big boat, too far away for anybody to hear you if, for example, you screamed."

He screwed a device onto the end of his gun. I'd flunked Spy Devices 101, but I recognized a silencer when I saw one. I'd seen no evidence of the twitching Tommy was supposedly known for. It would be hard for him to miss in these tight quarters. I looked wildly around for exits. Tommy blocked the only one I could see.

"Don't get excited," Tommy said. "Right now, I just want

to talk."

"Sure," I said, hands on my hips, nodding at the gun.

"No, really." But he shot at me.

"Then why are you shooting?" I yelled. And this close, how the hell had he *missed*?

"I got a condition. I twitch!"

"You were fine a minute ago!"

"It only happens when I'm feeling severely stressed."

Giselle had forgotten to mention this important little fact to me. "Crap!"

"Like now." Another shot rang out. "I mean, I'm not saying I won't kill you later, but right now, I really just want to talk."

I was used to bobbing and weaving to avoid the guys grabbing at me at Biker Bob's. This was like that, only deadly. Worst of all, bullets ricocheted if they hit metal. I had to dodge them once, then hope they didn't get me when careening off a piece of metal back in my direction.

Tommy kept twitching and firing and I continued dodging. I'd just finished a nicely executed arabesque, an almost impossible task in a boat, when suddenly there was silence. Tommy was bent over. Oh no. He must be reloading!

I ran toward him. He blocked the aisle. Smashing into the table on my right, sending scotch and salsa flying, I hit him with all my body weight, knocking him off balance. I scrambled by and ran above deck but he was close behind. Instantly I realized jumping on the pier would just make his job easier. I stopped and turned to face him. He took another shot. I hadn't been prepared for it. I lifted my arm and hunched over in a protective gesture, waiting for the next shot, the one that would kill me. But I heard a splash, then silence. I looked toward Tommy. He was bent over again.

Reloading already? I ran toward him, leaped on a seat, and got him in a headlock.

"Ow!" he said. "The pain."

"You big baby. It can't hurt that much."

"No. I'm shot."

"I don't even have a gun," I said. "Oh. A ricochet?"

"Maybe. But..."

"But what?"

"I twitch so bad, I mighta shot myself. And the gun ended up in the water."

For a second, I felt bad for Tommy the Twitch. "Must be tough being a bad guy. Wondering all the time if you're going to shoot yourself." I rubbed his back like he was a little boy.

"Not really. Usually Dom and Carlo are with me. I tell them who to kill and they do it."

I stopped rubbing his back.

"I'm getting a little woozy," he said. "I can't stand the sight of blood."

Tommy had both hands pressed against his right thigh a few inches above his knee. He had chunky blood? Did he have a rare coagulation disease or—

"I spilled salsa on you!" I said.

"But there's blood, too." He perched on one of the cushioned benches.

Most of it was salsa, but a little blood dribbled around his fingers and onto the floor. I didn't know a lot about boo-boos, but I guessed it was just a graze. Of course, he was a man, so I knew he'd expect me to make a big fuss about it. "Oh my. You did hurt yourself, didn't you? Hold on." Below deck, I found a tee shirt, duct tape, and a boat knife.

While I was there, I grabbed the bag of drugs Tommy

had shown me and tucked it in my underpants. Hey, I didn't have a lot of options. I was lucky the dress wasn't a sheath.

Above deck again, I cut a square from the tee shirt. "Lift your hands up for a second." As Tommy did, he turned his head away, his eyes squeezed shut. I tucked a folded piece of tee shirt under his hands. "Now keep your hands firmly pressed on the wound."

He was bent at the waist, forearms on his thighs. "Don't worry. I don't want to see it."

Quickly unrolling the duct tape, I looped it over his hands and under his legs.

"Hey!" He struggled, but it was too late. I kept going, duct taping around again and again. I'd heard the military used duct tape as a quick fix on equipment in the field. I had no worries it would break.

"Get up," I said, jerking him by the back of his shirt. He got to his feet. I applied more duct tape, working my way up his forearms until they were attached to his thighs. I slipped the roll onto my wrist like a big bangle bracelet. "Let's go." Tommy was bent at the waist and could only move his legs from the knees down. When he shuffled forward, he banged into the side of the boat. "Over here," I said, standing near the step connecting the boat to the pier.

"Where?" he asked.

"Here."

"As soon as you stop talking, I don't know where you are anymore."

I hummed the *Jeopardy* tune.

"I hate that show," Tommy said.

"Maybe a song would be better. Umm...." I cleared my throat. "A my name is Annie," I sang, "my husband's name is Al, we live in Alabama and we sell apples. B my name is

Bar—"

Tommy shuffled toward me. "Okay, I'm here."

"B my name is Barbara, my husband's name is Bill—"

"I'm already in pain. You're just making it worse. You have a terrible voice."

"It's not like I had a chance to warm up or anything."

"I'm just sayin'. Keep your day job as a spy. Even though you're crummy at that, too."

"You're duct taped into submission," I said, indignant.

"You had help. I shot myself."

"Yeah, I almost forgot to thank you," I said sarcastically. "I guess I'd have been dead in the water if it wasn't for you." My stomach turned. Maybe sarcasm wasn't warranted, since I probably *would* have ended up dead in the water if Tommy hadn't shot himself.

I jumped onto the pier. "Time to go."

Tommy stood looking down at the boat deck where he stood, his duct-taped legs, and the pier. That was pretty much his range of vision, duct taped in half like that. "I'll fall," he said.

"You won't fall. It's a tiny jump."

"I can hardly move my legs. I'm telling you, I'm gonna fall."

"Just try it."

"If I try it, I'll fall!"

I hopped back on the boat. "Watch," I said. Moving my legs as little as I could, I jumped to the pier. "See how easy it is? And *I* did it in high heels."

"Your legs aren't duct taped," he whined. "And you moved them a little."

"Hardly at all. Trust me. You'll be fine."

He made a movement. It took me a moment to realize that

was what a shrug looked like when someone was duct taped up like that.

"Okay. Here goes." He jumped onto the pier and fell on his face. "Ow! I told you."

"I knew you were going to fall. There wasn't really any alternative though, was there? Did you expect me to carry you? You've had a few too many cannoli for that."

"You—"

"I'll be glad to help you up, though." We struggled to get him to his feet.

I walked him back to Giselle. Actually, I walked, he waddled. Just before we went into the hotel, I realized he was in the perfect position for a headlock, which would make a much more dramatic entrance. I put my arms around his head. "Would you mind acting like you're struggling a little?"

"No, I'm not going to—"

"I'll do it for you if our situations are ever reversed."

"Oh, all right."

As we walked into the hotel, I saw Giselle by the pool. Obviously tipsy, she was trying to focus on her laptop screen.

Would she run screaming from the room when she saw I had Tommy in tow?

Chapter Twenty-Four

Giselle's jaw dropped when she saw us. Before she freaked out, I removed the roll of duct tape from my wrist and taped Tommy to a chaise lounge. Then I pulled the drugs out from under my skirt and taped them inside Tommy's shirt, to his hairy chest.

"That's really gonna smart when they rip it off," he said.

After explaining to Giselle what had happened, I handed the waitress Giselle's glass of booze and asked her to bring caffeinated soda. Giselle would tell the cops the story and Tommy would land in jail.

I had other things to do. Heading back to the boat topped the list. First, I got my gun.

As I neared the boat, I drew my gun and crept forward. Through a porthole, the first thing I saw was a beehive. Mrs. Tommy sat at the table having a drink with Lenny. That was unfortunate. He would have told her about seeing me with her husband. I waited until a motorboat loud enough to mask my movement buzzed by, then stepped on board. Kneeling by the steps that led below deck, I pointed my gun at them.

I wasn't quite sure what to say. I settled for, "Hi."

Their heads turned in my direction. Lenny started to move. "Uh uh," I warned. He stopped, and I moved the few steps down into the boat. "I have a lot of questions to ask you."

"Shoot," he said. He glanced down at a four-inch square bandage on his upper arm, apparently from when I *had* shot him. "Do over," he said quickly.

"Sure," I said. "I have a lot of questions to ask you," I repeated.

"Questions? Ask away."

"Why do you keep following me and trying to kill me?"

"I told you already," Lenny said. "I only want to talk to you."

"That's what Tommy said. Right before he shot at me a whole bunch of times."

"I'm telling you the truth," he said, hands open in the air. "I aim to maim."

"What? You say that like it's a good thing."

"No! I mean when I do have to shoot, which I'm not going to do to you, I hardly ever shoot to kill. I aim to maim, that's my motto. Killing is so... kinda barbaric. Maiming is more humanitarian. Look, it's even on my business card." He moved his hand toward his pocket.

"Hey!" I said.

"Take it easy. I'm not going for my gun."

"Keep your hands up. I'll get the business card."

"But—"

"But nothing," I said, shaking the gun in his direction. I kept the gun trained on him and got up close. I realized I was going to have a problem.

"See, that's what I was trying to tell you."

"Shut up." I quickly moved my hand toward his pocket, then changed my mind and started to take it back. But Lenny grabbed my arm.

"It's too dangerous, see?" He let go and I scuttled backward, once again training the gun on him. "Will you let me help you now? Just listen for a second."

"Okay, but hurry up."

"You get too close to me and I can overpower you. But if you train your gun on Mrs. Tommy, then you got some leverage."

"Oh." I smiled. "Makes sense."

"Sure. Try that," he said. "If it's okay with you, Mrs. Tommy."

"Of course. I'm glad to help."

I trained my gun on Mrs. Tommy and walked in Lenny's direction.

"Just one thing," he said.

I stopped. "What?"

"You gotta be careful. If you get some bad guy who's on the insensitive side, he might not care if you blast the brains out of the other guy. But in this case, I won't make any sudden moves. I care a lot about Mrs. Tommy and don't want her brains splattered all over the boat."

"Thank you, Lenny," she said sweetly. He reddened slightly and she smiled demurely.

I made my way up to him and put my hand in his pocket.

"Hee hee," he said, squirming away.

"Stay still." I tried again.

"Ha, ha, ha. I can't help it. It's one of those automatic responses. Like the gag reflex."

"Or blinking," Mrs. Tommy said, blinking.

"Yeah," Lenny said, "or when they hit you with that itty

bitty hammer in the knee and you kick the doctor in the groin. I tried to tell him not to stand so close, but he—"

"Just give me your wallet."

He tossed it. I juggled the gun and the wallet, but dropped the gun. Lenny leaped across the room and landed on Mrs. Tommy. We hit the deck. BOOM!

"Hey!" Lenny hollered. "In the case of an object being thrown to you when your hand is otherwise occupied in holding a gun, allow the object to land and *then* retrieve said object."

"Got it," I yelled.

"Unless the object being thrown is or might be an object with explosive potential."

"How come you sound like you're quoting from a training manual?"

"I am."

"You get training?"

"From what I can tell, it's better training than you got." I rose to my feet. Lenny remained on top of Mrs. Tommy. "Are you sure you're all right?" he said to her softly.

"I think so."

He moved his hands up and down her body. "I don't feel any broken bones."

"Thank you for checking so thoroughly," Mrs. Tommy said.

"My pleasure." He lifted himself off and, kneeling by her side, extended a hand to her. He was humming "Getting to Know You." She took his hand, batted her eyelashes, and got to her knees. She made no movement to get up. They gazed into each other's eyes.

"Ahem," I said.

Lenny glanced at me, then turned back to Mrs. Tommy.

"Here," he said, "let me help you." As he stood, he circled her waist with his hands and lifted her to a standing position.

All key body parts were touching. "Thank you," she said breathily.

He sighed. They turned toward me. I was definitely starting to feel like a third wheel.

I flipped open the wallet and removed a card. Gold letters on a blue background. I read it out loud. " 'My claim to fame, I aim to maim. Call Lenny Lentini.' This is very nice."

"Did you notice it rhymes and everything? Mrs. Tommy helped me with that." They beamed at each other.

"Excellent job." I put down my gun. I didn't think I'd be needing it. "So I don't get it. Why did you keep coming after me?"

"I admit I was after you, but I wasn't trying to hurt you."

"You almost killed me the first time you shot at me."

"Oh. I was trying to kill you that time."

"I thought you just said—"

"But only because I thought then you might be trying to hurt Mrs. Tommy. I'd kill anyone who tried to hurt her."

"You are the sweetest man, Lenny, I do declare," Mrs. Tommy said.

"I never was after Mrs. Tommy," I said. "There's more to the story than I can tell—"

"More than that you're a spy?" Lenny said.

"Oh," I said. "No. That's pretty much it. How did you know?"

"Spies are always coming after Tommy. I keep hoping one of them kills him before..."

"Go ahead," I said, steeling myself.

"Before Tommy kills them."

"I wish you hadn't said that."

"You told me to go ahead!"

"I know. I know. I know," I said.

"Anyway, me and Mrs. Tommy finally put two and two together and realized you were after Tommy, not her. We'd already taken a liking to you from the shopping expedition. We noticed you seemed to be in a little trouble and might benefit from our help. I must have been up and down this island a hundred times looking for you."

"So that was why I kept running into you."

He nodded. "Like when I was shooting at you in the park, it was because I wanted to talk to you about this."

"Couldn't you have just hollered 'Hey, you!'?"

"If memory serves, I did try that but you wouldn't listen. For a guy with a gun, takin' a couple of shots just seems like the obvious next step in tryin' to get someone's attention."

"I would have thought you'd be on Tommy's side," I said.

They laughed. "Oh no, dear," Mrs. Tommy said. "We hate his guts."

"He's been um... disrespectful to Mrs. Tommy's femininity, so to speak—"

"He screws anything with breasts and a—"

"—so we've taken a disliking to him."

"So you know I'm out to get him?" I asked. "And you don't have a problem with that?"

"On the contrary," Mrs. Tommy said. "We'd like to render assistance."

"I just turned him over to the police," I said.

"His lawyers will have him out in no time," Lenny said. "You saw the name of the boat, didn't you?"

"No."

"The *Greasy Palm*. The police tend to let him be because of Ma's supposed special powers, but he spreads money around so they won't change their minds. Not all the police are corrupt, of course. But you're going to have to pin something big on him and make it stick."

"Oh. In that case, I guess I could use some help." I couldn't plan on help from Giselle or Jesse. I'd known Giselle wouldn't be much help. I'd hoped for more from Jesse. Instead, he kept taking off. And I suddenly realized that he'd probably made up what he'd said about not knowing I wasn't engaged. After all, I wasn't wearing a ring. "Funny, I hadn't thought help would be coming from you two."

"Who better? We know his friends, his routines." Lenny stopped abruptly, listening. Voice dropping to a hurried whisper, he said, "For instance, I know Dom's and Carlo's voices."

I heard people moving down the pier. We ran into the bedroom closet. What must have been spacious for Lenny and would have been semi-comfy for two was sardine city for three. We waited. We heard their footsteps as they descended into the living quarters.

"Tommy and that dame left already," Dom said.

"We waited too long," Carlo said.

"I didn't want to come down here too soon. Tommy's noisy when he—"

"Yeah," Carlo said, "I'm surprised we couldn't hear her screams from the hotel."

They snickered. "Maybe it's just as well. That last time..."

"Yeah. Not all the screams from that last girl sounded like she was enjoying herself."

I almost lost my salsa and chips.

"Let's get outta here, Carlo. He'll call us when he wants us."

We stayed where we were until we heard their footsteps

fade. We popped out of the closet and went to the table. Lenny poured drinks all around.

"So, as I was saying," Lenny said, "we could help you."

"I'd take his advice, dear. It's really a miracle Tommy didn't kill you already."

"I'd love the help. I didn't get the best training. They gave me the accelerated version."

"Government training's never as good as ours," Lenny said. "We always have the advantage. More money, better equipment. We don't obey the law. Stuff like that. Government spies generally stink the joint out."

"That's not very encouraging," I said.

"And now that Tommy knows about you, he'll mobilize as soon as he gets out of jail. If he has to tangle with you again, you're as good as gone."

I felt the color drain out of my face.

"You won't live to be... How old are you?"

"Lenny, you mustn't ever ask a woman her age," Mrs. Tommy said.

"Okay," Lenny said. "You won't live to next week."

I stared at him silently, then finally croaked out, "You really think it's that bad?"

"Oh, they'll pull out all the stops to prevent you from getting in the way now. Unless we help you learn more about how he operates. So you stop him—"

"—before he stops me."

"Exactly. Mrs. Tommy and I will talk to some people, find out the latest. Then let's get together tomorrow morning."

"Great," I said. "I can't thank you enough."

"Don't worry about it. You're doing us a favor, too. Assuming you can pull it off."

"I have just one more question," I said to Lenny.

"What?"

"When I came down here with Tommy, why were you in the closet?"

"I didn't expect Tommy to use the boat tonight. We didn't want him to see us."

"You were *both* in there?"

They nodded.

"So you thought since he wouldn't be using it, it would be nice if the two of you did."

"Right."

"But Tommy might not be too happy if he knew what you were using it *for*?"

They nodded, embarrassed. Lenny was a lot more than her bodyguard.

"Ohhh." But when they gazed at each other, I could see they really cared. "That's so cute. I'm very happy for you."

"Thank you, dear," Mrs. Tommy said.

"So have you filed for divorce?" I asked her. They looked at me like I was crazy. "What?" I said.

"Divorce is expensive," Mrs. Tommy said. "Bullets are cheap."

"He'd kill you instead of give you a divorce?"

"After I married Tommy, I heard his first wife went missing the day she went to a divorce lawyer. She was last seen on the boat with Dom and Carlo. No one ever heard from her again."

"That sounds like a bunch of gossip. She probably just took off. Who told you that?"

"Dom and Carlo."

"Oh."

"Anyway," Lenny said, "we'll find out as much as we can before tomorrow. He's going to act fast. You're going to have to act faster."

I got up to leave. They got up too. "You're not staying on the boat?" I asked.

"If Dom or Carlo stops by again, it could get back to Tommy we were here together overnight. That wouldn't be good," Lenny said.

"Right," said Mrs. Tommy, "he'd kill us both."

Chapter Twenty-Five

The next morning, I was up before Giselle. Lenny and Mrs. T needed time to make calls, so we weren't meeting until eleven. I turned on the television. The show *All My Chickens* was just beginning. It was pretty good, but I only had time to catch the first half before heading off to rendezvous with them at an out-of-the-way café.

I wore sunglasses and a hat and arrived early, standing in an alley across the street, observing people entering and exiting. Lenny and Mrs. T arrived, both in sunglasses. Mrs. T had a scarf on, but hiding that towering beehive? Not a chance. I waited another few minutes, scanning the street for unusual activity. No signs that they'd been followed. I felt like a regular Miss Marple, a regular Jessica Fletcher... well, any sleuth would do, as long as it was one who didn't end up dead in a ditch.

Walking in, I saw them in a booth, grim expressions on their faces. I slipped into the seat across from them. "What?" I asked.

"He's out already," Lenny said.

"He just got in!"

"His cop friends were on duty when Tommy was brought in," Lenny said.

"When did he get out?"

"Sometime last night."

"We were on the boat last night," I said.

"It's very upsetting," Mrs. T said. "We could have been killed."

That *would* have been upsetting. I wondered how close we'd come. "How the hell could he possibly have gotten out so soon? He had that big bag of cocaine on him."

"The evidence was 'misplaced.' And all the cops were acting funny, talking really fast and sniffing."

"You're saying the evidence was misplaced as in used? The cops just divvied it up?"

"Looks that way."

"Well, that's a handy little solution, isn't it? The cops wanted to let him go anyway. They got to party, too." I hadn't anticipated this.

"You would have thought at least some of the honest ones would've been on duty. He got lucky, that's all. I found out something else," Lenny said. "Tommy scheduled a mega-shipment. He figured he could give the coup a big push with the proceeds."

"I knew about that."

"Here's the good part. He couldn't handle that big of a job by himself. Needed a partner to help with the financing. He hooked up with some big money guy, a terrorist into funding coups worldwide. The partner's been having legal troubles so he never came down here, just set the whole thing up from the States. The shipment was supposed to go out this morning."

I smiled. "I stopped a big drug operation just in time. That's pretty good."

"Not everyone's as happy about it as you. You messed up a multi-million-dollar deal. The partner in the States found out the stuff's not on its way. He thinks he's getting screwed. If it doesn't happen real soon, he's gonna have Tommy killed."

I admit it was a selfish concern, but if someone else killed Tommy, would I still get the fifty thousand dollars? I didn't think so. "So Tommy will get things moving ASAP, right?"

"We think this will be highly motivational to Tommy."

"Maybe he got up early and loaded the boat this morning."

"Tommy has never in his life gotten up before eleven," Mrs. T said.

"And Dom and Carlo work out in the morning, so not much goes on then," Lenny said.

"So I can get him when he's loading the boat," I said quickly.

"Better yet," Lenny said, "catch him at the warehouse. That's where he stores the stuff before he ships it. Just wait there. When you see him arrive with Dom and Carlo, call it in as an anonymous tip. You don't want to be connected to it. If you tell the cops it's a hundred kilos, they'll have to come. With that much stuff, even Tommy won't get away with it this time. Here's the address." He pushed a piece of paper across the table to me.

"I don't know how to thank you." I pocketed the paper and hugged them both.

"Hey, it works for us," Lenny said. "You get him behind bars. We're taking the boat for a few days."

"A little R&R?"

"If that means romantic romp," Mrs. T said, gazing at Lenny, "then yes."

"We're turning off cell phones and radios, all the electronics. It's gonna be just us," Lenny said. He smooched her on the cheek.

I thought about what I was about to do. "What if something goes wrong?"

"What could go wrong?" they asked.

***

After parking on a side street, I hurried toward the warehouse. I'd thought about telling Giselle, but discarded the idea right away. There wasn't time, and I didn't think she'd be any help anyway. If Jesse had been around... But he wasn't. I was on my own.

I'd have to talk to Giselle about this later, of course, since that was the only way I'd get the fifty thou. I'd call the tip in anonymously to the police, but I'd let Giselle know it was my doing loud and clear. After the fact would be soon enough.

The warehouse was set off the main road. A paved driveway led down a slight incline to the parking lot. To the right stood the warehouse and on the left, a thicket of shrubs and vines. I hoped it wasn't thorny, because that was my cover. Elbowing my way in, I positioned myself directly across from the three pull-up doors big enough to accommodate good-sized vehicles. I scanned the building. The trucks they used to move the stuff would have to pass through those doors. Covered by the foliage, I hunkered down and waited. After half an hour, I went from hunkering to sitting. Thirty minutes later, I went from sitting to leaning back. I hoped they'd come soon. Lying down wasn't an option in the middle of this much vegetation. I tried not to think about the island's abundant lizard life.

But as time went on, I started to wonder. Had something gone wrong?

Then I heard the sound of an engine. A car turned from the main road and moved toward the warehouse. I dialed the police, informing them they'd find massive amounts of illegal drugs when they arrived, and that they'd better make it quick. The car slid to a stop in front of the warehouse doors. I'd expected them to arrive in a truck. That must mean the other vehicles were in the garage. Tommy, Dom and Carlo got out of the car. Dom bent down and yanked up on the handle of the middle door. It slid open. Odd. Still no trucks in sight.

Police sirens sounded. A few seconds later, others joined in. Would Tommy, Dom and Carlo jump in the car and take off? But they seemed strangely unconcerned. Tommy walked into the garage and disappeared off to the right.

The first of the police cars rocketed from the main road down the incline to the warehouse. Others quickly followed, screeching to a stop as Tommy walked out of the building. He now had a jacket hanging from his right hand. The officers leaped out of the cars, got into firing position, guns pointed at the threesome. Tommy's cop buddies worked a different shift; these guys definitely weren't giving off friendly vibes. Still no reaction from Tommy though. Could Tommy really believe he had friends—maybe in higher places—who could save him from this much trouble?

The officer in charge barked questions. Tommy held out his coat. "I just came back to get my jacket." In indignant tones, he told them they had no right to harass a legitimate businessman.

The other officers kept their guns trained on Tommy while the charge officer lifted the doors on the other two bays and walked into the garage. My stomach fell out. Even with all three doors open, I couldn't see any trucks. But still, they would find the stuff, right? I watched the officer walk around the inside of the building. When he came out, he shook Tommy's hand. "Sorry, we got a bad tip. Apologize for the inconvenience."

"No problem," Tommy said.

I stared at the unfolding scene in total disbelief. These hadn't been the corrupt cops. This hadn't been a joke to them. Still, something had just gone very wrong. But what?

The cops holstered their weapons, got into their cruisers, and took off. Tommy and the boys started laughing before the police cleared the end of the driveway. Dom opened the trunk of the car and pulled beer from a cooler. "Can you believe those idiots?" he said.

Tommy turned serious. "Good thing we moved the stuff last night when I got out."

Shit! The stuff was already on the boat. It must have happened right after Lenny, Mrs. Tommy and I left.

"Now we gotta hurry up and find that damned captain before I get killed."

"It's not his fault, boss. He made other plans when he found out you were in jail. Even you didn't think you'd be out that fast."

"I know. We just gotta find him and get him on his way. Nobody else knows that route. Anybody else tries it and the whole shipment could end up at the bottom of the ocean."

So they had a crucial guy missing. Someone with specialized knowledge of the waters. They had to find him before Tommy's pissed-off partner got hold of Tommy.

"We're trying, boss. All we know is he said something about a relative's kid getting bar mitzvahed on one of the other islands. I'm sure he wouldn't have turned off his phone if he knew someone was trying to kill you."

"Yeah, I know. Let's go talk to some more of his friends. See if we can find out anything else." They got in the car and motored away.

Now what? How was I supposed to get Tommy now?

With an awful start, I realized the people who had tried to help me were in terrible danger. Lenny and Mrs. T would have left port for their romantic getaway. They'd turned off the electronics. I had no way to warn them. Tommy had said the drugs were hidden when they were loaded on the boat. Lenny and Mrs. T would have no idea the drugs were aboard.

They were missing other critical information. Tommy hadn't landed back in jail as they'd expected. As soon as he figured out the boat was missing, he'd start searching for it.

And when he found Lenny and Mrs. T together, he was going to kill them.

Chapter Twenty-Six

I returned to the hotel, and found Giselle in the room. She hadn't eaten, so I had lunch delivered. I didn't tell her about the events of the morning. I was concerned about how she would react if she found out Tommy had already been sprung. "Heard from Jesse?" I asked.

"Nope. Maureen tries to keep him around as much as she can. She doesn't like it when he's away."

All this time I'd thought it was business causing Jesse to go to Washington so often. Business had to be a part of it—he'd mentioned all those meetings—but there was also this Maureen who liked him so much. He probably had a girl in every port.

As concerned as I was about Lenny and Mrs. Tommy, I had no way of figuring out where they were. They didn't want Tommy to find out about their relationship, so they wouldn't have told anyone else about their impromptu trip. Tommy hired a captain to take the boat to the States, so parts of that journey had to be difficult. That implied there could be limitations on where Lenny and Mrs. T would head, but still left a lot of possibilities. My only consolation was that once Tommy figured out his boat was missing, he wouldn't know where to look for them either. It was a big ocean. I hoped Lenny and Mrs. T had headed someplace very private.

So private Tommy wouldn't find them and blow their brains out.

I thought back to the plan to capture Tommy at the warehouse. It hadn't been a bad little plan. Except for the dismal failure part. But now I had nothing. The extent of my plan right now was waiting to see if Tommy's partner killed him.

Giselle walked out of the bedroom, said she was heading down to the pool. But I could see the outline of her laptop in her shoulder bag. Giselle hadn't been as happy as I thought she'd be about Tommy's capture the night before. What was she searching for on the Internet? Why was she so terrified of what she was finding? Was it related to Tommy? Or was it something else entirely? Why was she hiding it even from me?

I had to find something to do, too, before the anxiety made *me* resort to drugs and alcohol. I'd get a paper at the little store downstairs. But I went via the Internet café. Yes, there was Giselle, holed up in the corner. What the hell was she doing?

I took the paper to the lobby and read it cover to cover. If I'd hoped to get some big insight into the coup and how to stop it, I was sadly mistaken. The big news today was the pineapple festival. The picture showed the pineapple queen, a tiny woman staggering under the weight of a three-foot-tall crown in the shape of the top of a pineapple.

I'd wasted hours and accomplished nothing today. I went

to the room. Giselle was in the shower. Sitting in the living room, I listened to the water running. Giselle's shoulder bag sat on a table near the couch. I stood up quickly and moved to the table, pulling the laptop from her bag and opening it up. The last web site she'd visited was a search engine. I clicked on it. Would it have stored a list of her recent searches? I typed in "A." Yes, a list of two searches she'd made, both beginning with the letter "A," appeared. Nothing frightening about either.

I kept going, entering different letters. She'd been researching getting out of jail, sentence reductions, release for good behavior, those types of things. Why would she be interested in that? If Tommy went to jail, he wouldn't be getting out for quite a while. Sure, he'd been lucky that first time—getting out because his cop friends let him out, but she didn't even know about that, so why would she be—

The water in the bathroom stopped. I quickly closed the laptop and slipped it in her bag.

By seven o'clock, Giselle had had a couple of drinks and lay snoozing on the bed. I'd hoped my getting Tommy behind bars would make her feel better, enough better that she'd stop drinking herself into oblivion. It wasn't working. If only I'd had more time on her laptop... She'd thrown her shoulder bag on the bed next to her, and the laptop was in it. With her arm draped over the bag, I knew I couldn't get the laptop out without waking her. I hadn't had a chance to see much of what she'd been looking at, but what I had seen didn't seem like the kind of thing that would cause the terror she felt. What had I missed?

We hadn't heard from Jesse. He'd said he would be back today. The truth was I was dying to see him. With nothing that I could do about the situation at hand, the idea of seeing him blossomed in importance. No bullets flying gave me time to think about how much I missed him. I shouldn't be thinking of him at all. Okay, I wouldn't.

But suddenly I wanted breath mints. Not breath mints in case I ran into Jesse, because even if I did run into Jesse, who cared?—just breath mints because they were good to have. You never knew when you might need one for yourself or want to offer one to a friend. The fact that I never carried breath mints didn't change my mind. They must have breath mints down in the little shop off the lobby, where, if you were going to see anybody, it would be there. Not that I was planning on seeing anybody, or hoping to for that matter, but for people who were meeting each other, that's where they met.

The doors of the elevator opened onto the lobby. Rock music blasted from down the hall. I could feel the floor vibrating from here. Some dance event in the ballroom by the bar. As I crossed the lobby toward the shop, I glanced around. No one I knew. It's not like I was looking for Jesse. On the other hand, he and Giselle were the only two people I knew at the hotel, and I knew where Giselle was.

I reminded myself I was here to get breath mints and entered the shop. After selecting a peppermint roll, and also a spearmint, I walked to the counter to pay. While waiting for my change, movement out the window toward the lobby caught my attention. Was that Jesse? I stood still. He turned slightly. It *was* Jesse. But I wasn't going to think about Jesse, was I? No.

Well, all right, maybe I was, a little. After all, there he was. Back from Washington.

Where he had a girlfriend. He might have them stashed all over the globe. So *what* he had girlfriends? It's not like he was married. Hey, if you're going to think about him, how about showing a little spunk, Nora? Was I going to take this lying down?

That was the problem. I did want to take it lying down. Lying down, standing up, off a trapeze device hanging from the ceiling, as long as it was with Jesse. Still, if he was involved with other people... Was this like putting "total humiliation" on my to-do list?

I probably should at least say hello. It would be rude not to say hello. But would he read something into my saying hello? Maybe I should wait for him to say hello. That meant he'd have to see me through the window or when I went through the lobby. I'd just wait for him to—

He turned in the other direction and started for the elevator. "Keep the change," I yelled to the cashier, running out.

"You gave me a twenty," she hollered.

"Jesse!" He turned. I couldn't gauge his reaction. Was he happy to see me? Indifferent? Wishing I'd never been born?

"Hi," he said.

"I wanted to... I wanted to... offer you a breath mint." I dug into the little bag and pulled out the mints. "Peppermint or spearmint?"

"Spearmint."

"I had a feeling you'd be a spearmint kind of a guy."

"Really. That's funny. I had a feeling you'd be a peppermint person."

I popped a peppermint into my mouth and looked up at him. "How odd." We stood there smiling at each other. How odd? How romantic was more like it! We knew without telling each other what kind of breath mints the other person liked. That meant something, didn't it? I mean, not everyone would peg me for a peppermint person, but he'd known right away.

"How's Giselle?" he asked.

"About the same."

We both knew that meant she'd ingested too much of something mind-altering.

"I think it's time to have a talk about her," he said. "Come on, I'll buy you a drink."

The dividing wall between the bar and the ballroom had been taken down to create a single large room for some dance event. We walked into the bar end, ordered drinks, then found a table. The band was on a break.

"Jesse," I said, "before we talk about Giselle, I have to tell you something."

"What?" He looked at me and I got lost in those beautiful— "Nora?" He shook my arm gently.

"Oh. Right. I brought in Tommy last night."

"You could have been killed. Are you all right?"

"I'm fine. The problem is, they let him right back out."

That wasn't the whole story but would suffice for now. I wanted time to sort through possible scenarios before telling Jesse more.

"I wished you'd waited," Jesse said.

"Giselle doesn't know he's back out. Maybe we should worry about her first."

He nodded. "Was your sister this much of a party animal when she was younger?"

I shook my head. "What you're seeing Giselle do? That's not partying. I think she's trying to lose consciousness. Something so bad has happened, or is about to happen, she's trying to drown out every waking moment."

The band returned. The sound system made it seem like

they were right next to us. We turned our chairs directly toward each other. It was still hard to hear. We bent forward until our noses almost touched.

"You think so?" he asked.

"Yes," I said.

The band picked up the beat. People joined those already on the dance floor. The noise reached a deafening level. We leaned forward more. His lips grazed my ear as he said, "You don't just think she's turned into a wild woman?"

"No," I said.

"What?"

I pressed my lips softly against his ear. "Definitely not. She was never like that when we were younger. She's terrified of something."

He jerked his head back, looked at me intently, and said, "I have to do this, Nora." Then he kissed me. At first I was so surprised, I didn't join in. But hey, what the heck. If he was overcome with desire for me, I could go with that. I was so glad I did. For a kiss I hadn't seen coming, it was a doozy that went on and on and blissfully on. Finally, he pulled back.

"Sorry about that," he said.

"Sorry? Why sorry?"

"Tommy the Twitch's guys just went by. I was afraid they'd see you."

I turned to see a dark-haired guy in a lime green shirt laughing with a bunch of his friends as they left the bar. Where were— But then I saw Dom and Carlo not far behind them. So Jesse hadn't been taken by the moment. It hadn't been a real kiss at all.

I was a fool.

What did internal bleeding feel like? It must feel the way I felt right then. "I have to go to the ladies' room," I said without looking at him.

Ten minutes later, I wiped the last of the tears away. I didn't have the heart to go back.

Chapter
Twenty-Seven

I got on the elevator and hit the button. Nothing. I jabbed it again. No luck. I turned around, then whirled, stabbing it five times in a row. Not even a tremor. I was bashing the button when Jesse walked in.

"Where'd you go?" he asked.

"Obviously, I'm going upstairs," I said coldly. Was that a hurt look in his eyes? I dropped the arctic tone. "I thought I'd better check on Giselle." We waited for the elevator to be ready. "You know, the more I find out about Tommy, the more I realize how dangerous he is. I thought it would help that she thinks he's in jail now. Maybe it's just taking her a while to wind down. I mean, no wonder she's been so jumpy. She might be okay now."

"I don't think it's just Tommy. Gotta be something else." He thought about it. "I'm guessing the jitters won't just go away."

Giselle backed into the elevator. She had her gun in her hand and was focused totally on what was in front of her. She must have finally sensed us behind her. She whirled.

Jesse and I dove for the corners of the elevator as she fired. "You're right!" I said. "She is still a little jumpy."

"Giselle!" Jesse and I yelled together. "It's us."

"How could you sneak up on me like that?" she screamed back.

Jesse and I glanced at each other. "We were in here already," Jesse said.

"Oh," Giselle said.

"You're not going to shoot anymore, are you?" he asked.

"I don't think so," she said.

I looked up from my corner. Giselle stood with the gun hanging limply.

I stood up slowly and gently removed the gun from her hand. I had a bottle of water in my bag. I opened it and handed it to her. She was shaking so hard, most of it sloshed on her shirt when she tried to drink it.

"Giselle," I said, "talk to me. The police took Tommy to jail. Doesn't that make you feel better?" Of course I knew he was out, but she didn't.

She turned away.

Jesse tried. "Are you worried someone even more deadly will be coming down here because Tommy's operation was disrupted?"

"No. Nora disrupted the operation. They'd be coming after her."

Coming after *me*? "Oh," I said. I have to confess I hadn't thought about it in exactly that way. Tommy and his guys, sure. I got that. But someone even more deadly, coming in from another country? No, I'd missed that.

Jesse sighed. "If you won't tell us, we can't help." We stood there, silent for a few moments. "Oh, Giselle, before I forget," he said. "When I was in Washington, I found out some news you'll be interested in."

When Giselle didn't respond, I said, "What's the news?" I hit the elevator button again.

"That guy you put away on your last assignment? Mr. Massive is getting out."

"Mr. Massive?" I asked. The elevator doors closed.

"He used to be called Mr. Big, but he thought that was overused. Plus he wanted to be bigger than the other Mr. Bigs. He considered Colonel Colossal but decided—and I think he was right—that would be going too far. So he settled on Mr. Massive," Jesse said. "They're letting him out early for bad behavior."

"For *bad* behavior?" I asked. The elevator lurched up a few feet, then stopped.

"He's so obnoxious, they can't stand having him around. He'll be out late today." Jesse looked at his watch. "Might be out already."

Giselle started hyperventilating.

Jesse stared at Giselle. "What's wrong?"

Her eyes wide, between gasps she said, "I-thought-he-was-going-away-for-good."

"No, he pulled all kinds of strings to get out. In jail, just about everyone's obnoxious, so convincing them you're so obnoxious they should let you out isn't easy. Funny. A lot of his friends are there, and in the past he's been pretty happy to stick around. He can run most of his operation from inside anyway. But it seems important to him—very important—to get out quickly." He narrowed his eyes at Giselle. "Almost as if he has something he personally wants to do."

"Yeah," Giselle said, "maybe he does."

"Anything you want to tell us, Giselle?" Jesse asked.

"I... I kind of... borrowed a lot of money from him."

"When you say 'borrowed'—"

"All right, 'stole' might be a better word—"

"When you say 'a lot'—"

"Close to a million."

"He's an international terrorist. You did pay him back, right?"

"I *meant* to."

Jesse slapped his forehead.

"I didn't think it would matter. I thought he was going away for good. But I've been following his case, searching for anything I could find on the Internet. When I saw a couple of weeks ago he might get out, I couldn't believe it. I was hoping the parole board would stop it."

Jesse was wide-eyed with alarm.

"There's more," Giselle said.

"More?" Jesse said.

"Sometimes I have such a big mouth. I wish I hadn't said what I said."

"What did you say?" Jesse asked her.

"I called him Mr. Teeny Weenie."

Jesse slapped himself on the forehead again.

"Mr. Massive, you're teeny weenie," I mused. "What's wrong with that? He was overweight. He slimmed down."

"He wasn't overweight," Jesse said, his face going red.

Mr. Massive, you're teeny weenie. "Ohhh." I'd figured out what Giselle meant. "*Ohhh.*" I'd figured out why Mr. Massive might want to see Giselle again. She'd ripped him off. Worse, she'd questioned his manhood. He wanted to make her pay for that.

"He was restrained at the time. And, like I said, I thought he was going away."

"But now," I said, "now he's coming to gitcha."

Chapter Twenty-Eight

So this was what all Giselle's frantic logging onto the web was about. Not Tommy getting out of jail, but Mr. Massive.

Jesse's phone rang. He turned around to talk, his finger in his ear so he could hear.

"We'll get the best guys," I said to Giselle. "And air support."

"This isn't the agency's problem. They had nothing to do with it, and they won't fix it," Giselle hissed, glancing toward Jesse's back. "But I'll pay you ten thousand dollars."

"You royally ticked this guy off and you're going to pay me ten grand to risk my life? No way!" I said.

"Fifty! It's all I have left." She shrugged. "It's Mr. Massive's money anyway."

"What if we go to the police?"

"Then the agency will know, they'll fire me, and I won't pay you the fifty thousand."

At this point I didn't care if Giselle lost her job, but the family would be devastated. I thought about the concern on my dad's face when he'd pleaded with me to keep an eye on her, when he'd said, "She's acting... a little funny." If by "funny" he meant totally off her rocker, I'd have to agree with him. Who in her right mind steals a million dollars from a terrorist?

"Just to be clear. This fifty thousand you'd pay me is in *addition* to the fifty thousand dollars from the agency for bringing in Tommy, right?" I wouldn't even need a loan to buy a schooner and start my sailing school.

She nodded.

"All right. I'll do it."

Jesse hung up, turned to face us. "I have to go back to Washington."

"Now?" I said. "You just got here."

Giselle put on a brave front for Jesse. "We'll be fine," she said. "Mr. Massive's just getting out. And he doesn't know where we are."

"I'll see if I can get help while I'm there." He looked up.

Giselle and I gave him ten fingers and boosted him out of the top of the immobile elevator. Jesse reached down for Giselle. I pushed her from below. Then they managed to pull me up. We stood on top of the elevator.

He faced me. "Remember the last time I had to go to Washington, and I said don't do anything until I get back?"

"Yes," I said.

"Do you think this time you could follow instructions?"

"Sure. Sure, I could." I *could*, but of course I wouldn't.

"I'll be back as soon as I can." He cast a worried glance in my direction and then disappeared down the hall.

"Come on," Giselle said. "I need a drink."

"*I* need a drink. If you want help, what you need is to tell me a whole lot more about what's going on."

We went to the hotel bar on the beach. I went up to the

bartender and ordered our drinks.

"Gotta be in the contest to drink," he said, nodding his head toward the beach. Outdoor lights illuminated people all over the sand. I looked up to see a sign. There was a sand sculpture contest going on. I glanced toward Giselle. She dropped to her knees in the sand, frantically forming shapes. The bartender gave me the drinks. I grabbed them and kneeled beside Giselle.

I started working on a sand castle. "So spill it. You must have faced a lot of bad guys in your career," I said. "Is he that much worse than the others?"

"Mr. Massive was my first assignment."

I blinked a few times, struggling to understand. "What are you talking about? You've been in the agency for years."

"Right." She sighed. "But not as an agent."

"What about all those stories you told? The running-around-the-globe-keeping-the-world-safe-from-bad-guys stories."

"Those were things other agents did."

"But they... they seemed so real."

"I've always had a good memory. And I was always a good liar. I'd just listen to their stories when a bunch of us would go out after work."

"And feed it back to the family when you came home?"

"I'd embellish a little, but basically, yeah."

I stared in fascination as Giselle feverishly worked the sand, but the impact of what she was telling me was also starting to sink in. "What about all my training?"

"Of course I have almost no real experience. Lots of your training is from what I remember about my own training."

"That's a relief," I said, exhaling. "I thought for a minute you were going to tell me that was fake, too. That none of my training had any foundation whatsoever—"

"Well..."

Grabbing her by the arm, I yelled, " 'Well...'?"

"I had to make up a bunch of it to fill in some of the blanks." Giselle had been using her foot to try to nudge her bag out of sight. I saw a magazine fall out of it.

"Gimme that," I said, snatching it. It opened to a dog-eared page. I looked at the article, titled "Liar Liar Pants on Fire." I read from it. " 'Watch your man squirm. His body language tells the tale of whether or not he's chasing somebody else's tail.' " I flipped it closed. "*MOAN* magazine? Tell me you didn't use this as the basis for what you taught me about lying."

"I kinda did. I couldn't remember everything they taught me in the training." She shrugged. "I'm a natural liar, so I wouldn't have paid much attention anyway. Even if I had, when I'm under a lot of stress, my memory falls off."

"What do you mean?"

"I was freaked out by what I was getting into, and that got in the way of my concentration when I was in training. And then there were the drugs."

"The drugs?"

"I started taking them early on. I didn't realize until later how much they screw up your ability to remember things."

"So, the stuff you rushed through on the devices?"

"I couldn't really recall all the details. I thought if I went fast you might not notice."

"So some of what you taught me might not be exactly true?" I punched my sand castle.

"Maybe even a lot."

"A *lot*?"

"I'm just not sure, okay? I've been under a lot of stress."

"I could have blown myself up!"

"Don't forget, you could have blown someone else up too."

I stopped. "But why? Why all the lies?"

"You think my life growing up was easy? I was under a ton of pressure. I had to learn to lie and cheat. How else could I meet the expectations of the family? I was the oldest, the one who had to live out the entire family's dreams! No wonder I'm a nervous wreck. I wanted to be a CPA! Coming from a family of bookkeepers, that seemed like success to me. But was that enough? Oh no. Not by a long shot. So I took the job with the agency. Even the agency needs people to do administrative stuff and bookkeeping. The family assumed I was a spy."

"So you started telling the stories."

"I'd just substitute my name for the name of the agent. Everyone was so desperate to live my life vicariously they swallowed it whole."

"What about all the postcards we got from those foreign countries?"

"I told the spies someone in the family was a philatelist."

"How could you do such a thing? I've heard rumors that Uncle George *might* be, but it's never been proven."

"A philatelist is a stamp collector."

"Oh. Oh!"

"Yeah. So I'd give agents the postcards I'd already written out and they'd send them when they got to whatever foreign country they were going to."

"So that's why the messages were so boring. I always wondered why you'd think we'd care about the gross national product and unemployment rates."

"I couldn't exactly say, 'Wish you were here.' I told them my stamp-collecting nephew was doing a school project to learn about all the countries of the world. Everything I wrote, I found on the Internet. The souvenirs I brought home I got on the Internet, too."

"No wonder you're so stressed out. Your life is a total lie."

"You're not helping, Nora." She slugged back her drink.

I slugged back mine. "You haven't exactly helped me! Now my life is in danger."

"I know. I'm a total screw-up. Which is weird."

"Weird why?"

"The life I wanted was so simple. I wanted to stay in Portsmouth, have a family and a regular job. Join a bowling league, vacation in the White Mountains. But there were so many expectations. So much pressure. And not just from mom and dad. The whole family."

"I had no idea it was so hard on you. They never cared enough about me to have expectations."

"They cared enough about you *not* to try to run your life! You know what Aunt Deirdre said at Thanksgiving? 'Next time we see you, you'll probably be wearing a mink coat and driving a Ferrari.' "

"I'm sure she only meant it as a possibility. Maybe a suggestion."

"Like hell. From the time I was twelve, people were making demands in the form of suggestions. Now someone mentions something like Aunt Deirdre did, I'm already thinking about how to make it happen."

"Dad and mom don't do that."

"They don't do it *now*."

I thought back. "You're right. They used to do it all the time."

"When I told them not to screw up your life like they did mine, they realized they needed to let me live my own life, too. But by then it was too late. Once you've heard demands veiled as suggestions for so many years, it's hard to stop. You're on automatic."

"I never thought about it that way. So I get the part about the secret life. But that doesn't explain why you ripped off Mr. Massive."

"The agency paid me next to nothing to do my admin job. I needed lots of money to look like I was a successful spy, so I got more credit cards. Then I started to take out loans. It wasn't long before I was buried in debt. I'd done a great job for the agency, so when I tried to convince my boss to let me be a spy, he said yes. But the skills that made me good at the administrative stuff were useless for a spy. After the Mr. Massive assignment, I knew I didn't have what it takes. But I still had that mountain of debt. When I thought Mr. Massive was going away forever, it looked like my chance. So I 'borrowed' some of his money to pay off all the bills."

"Maybe you're not as bad a spy as you think. It takes skill to steal that much money."

"It was right there in a bottom dresser drawer in his bedroom. Enough cash to solve all my problems. Then I heard he might be getting out... I knew he'd come for me." She was trembling again.

"You're sure you're not cut out to be a spy? It's not a learning curve kind of a thing?"

"Look." She rummaged in her purse, pulled out a piece of paper, and handed it to me. I could see right away it was a kind of report card on the progress she'd made in training. I searched for something positive to say. "In the classroom you did pretty well."

"But I fell apart in the field. I was good at the theoretical but stunk at the practical."

"How'd you catch Mr. Massive if you were so bad?"

"I got lucky. His bodyguards screwed up, took the same lunch hour. Mr. Massive didn't even know he was on his own."

"So when you saw me at Bob's Bikes and Boats back home, you thought..."

"Yeah, I saw you handling all the bikers and I thought you could, you know..."

"Save the day?"

"Yeah, kinda."

"Holy shit."

"The agency had sunk so much time into my training, they didn't want to let me go back to admin so quickly. They thought I'd improve. But I'll never get better. I will only be a huge disappointment to the agency and the family and... and get myself killed." Giselle started to sob.

I put my arms around her and hugged her tight. As angry as I was that my sister had gotten me into this mess, I finally understood what life had been like for her. It gave me a totally new perspective. I held on to her until she stopped crying.

But any ideas I had of Jesse caring for me evaporated. Giselle was sure the agency wouldn't help. Jesse's promise to "see what I can do" was a lie. Worst of all, he'd known that Giselle was a novice, and he hadn't told me.

If he'd cared one iota, how could he leave me in such danger?

As we got up, I looked at Giselle's completed sand sculpture. In intricate detail, she'd created a cemetery complete with Nora and Giselle headstones.

Chapter Twenty-Nine

Back in the room, Giselle finally wiped away her tears. I needed time to think. It was also ten o'clock, and I was ravenous. "Could you get us some dinner?" I waited for a vehement no.

"Okay." She got up and disappeared into the bedroom.

Had she given up all hope? Was she just going to let whatever happened, happen?

A few minutes later a woman with long black hair, a hat and sunglasses entered the room. Since she'd come from the direction of the bedroom, I realized it was Giselle in disguise. "I'll be back in a little while," she said.

She'd known there might be a time Mr. Massive would come after her. She had a disguise all ready. Hey, if it made her feel better about going out, great.

I had no idea what Mr. Massive's plan would be. But I had to do some thinking about ours. Giselle had said planning was better than rushing in all willy-nilly. I didn't think project planning would be my strong suit. All that... planning. But I'd have to try. Hmm.

I sat for a while thinking about how to start. Maybe I was more of a willy-nilly person.

I'd do better if I had a sample. Looking across at Giselle's briefcase, I wondered if she'd mind if I...

Tiptoeing over, I rifled through folders labeled "TOP SECRET" and "SUPER SECRET" in official lettering. There was even one marked "SUPER DUPER SECRET" in Giselle's script. I fought the urge to look in it, and after a few seconds of dramatic internal battling between right and wrong, I opened it. Aha. A project plan—just what I needed.

Things should go more easily now that I had a model. This was a project she'd needed to accomplish in just a couple of days, right before we came on the trip. I hadn't even known she was working on an assignment when she was home. Must be something simple. I started to scan the activities. " 'One,' " I read, " 'pretend to be interested in Nora's life.' "

"Huh?" I read it again. " 'Pretend to be interested in Nora's life.' " I read on to step two. " 'Lose Nora's crappy job.' " I thought back to when Giselle came to see me at Biker Bob's. She'd known my boss would be showing up. " 'Three. Change Nora's crappy look to more Giselle-like.' " I remembered how odd it had seemed that her hairdresser had been waiting for me.

I thought back. Right after I'd so neatly handled Hulk, Giselle sat there typing away on her little computer, making calls on her cell phone. Right under my nose, she'd been formulating this plan. Planning to piss off Bob so I'd lose my job, calling her hairdresser because changing my look to sexy was crucial to having me take on the Tommy assignment.

She'd set me up.

My sympathy for her evaporated. I'd been had pure and simple, and I was pissed. I couldn't wait for my dear sister to return. We needed to have a little chat, she and I.

I read on. " 'Four. Get rid of Nora's crappy boyfriend.' "

I froze. What did she mean by "get rid of"? "Get rid of" could mean dump, right? But Giselle was a spy. When she said "get rid of," did it mean what I was afraid it meant?

I heard the key in the door. Giselle walked in and put a bag of food on the table. I stared at her. Who was she? I felt like I was seeing her for the first time. All right, she did have a disguise on. But it wasn't because of that. Later, I'd deal with the fact that she was a thoughtless, conniving bitch. I'd start by throttling her skinny little neck first chance I got. But right now, I was worried—terrified—about Kenny, even if he was a two-timing bastard.

"Giselle," I said.

She reacted to a new, no-nonsense tone that surprised even me. She turned. "What?"

I held up the project plan.

"You looked in my briefcase? How dare you—"

"Shut up, Giselle." She did. "When you wrote, 'Get rid of my boyfriend…' " I could hardly say the words.

"What?"

"You know, did you mean dump him or—" I acted out the rat-tat-tat of machine gun fire, being hit in the chest and croaking.

"Oh." Giselle started taking food out of the plastic bag. "Hey, I got Chinese."

As I watched her, alarm bells clanged in my head. "Well?"

"What?" Giselle asked, preoccupied with the food.

"Did you kill Kenny?"

"Kilkenny is a town in Ireland, Nora. Did you know that?

I've actually been there. It's quite nice, unlike its name. A little medieval town with a—"

"Ohmigod! You're disanswering the question. So you did kill him?" I gasped.

"No, of course not."

I breathed a sigh of relief.

"How could I have? I've been here with you."

I gave her a laser look. "Did you or anyone you know or ever have known or ever will know kill Kenny or set into motion any set of events or circumstances that would cause harm to come to Kenny?"

"Ahh..."

I sucked in my breath.

"I'm just playing with you. The answer is no."

A feeling of relief flooded through me.

"I mean, something may have happened to Kenny. Just not anything I did."

"What?"

"I'm just saying there are car accidents, flood, fire, famine, random acts of violence. Pestilence. I can't be held responsible for everything."

I shook my head. "Pestilence?" I muttered as I dug my phone out and hit Kenny's speed dial number. I didn't want to talk; I'd disconnect as soon as he answered. I heard the first ring.

"What are you doing?" Giselle yelled.

"I'm calling Kenny to make sure he's not dead." I heard the second ring.

"That's ridiculous. The only possible problem could be if someone tailed me when I was home. There was that tail on the way to the airport, but Kenny wasn't with us then. Otherwise, I was careful. If I hadn't been... Well, then, for example, someone might torture Kenny to find out where I am. Even then, he might still be alive."

"But then... they'd know where you are." I heard the receiver click on the other end.

She grabbed the phone out of my hand. "Okay, I heard his voice. Happy now?"

But she dropped onto the couch, color draining from her face.

"So what did he say?" I asked.

"Say?"

"What did Kenny say?"

"He said, 'Help.' "

"He said, 'Help'?" I felt the color drain out of *my* face.

"Do you think they got to him?" Giselle asked.

"Does he usually answer the phone, 'Help'?"

"No."

"Then of course they got to him!" I shouted. "Wait. How did they even connect him to you?"

"I dropped by to see him the night before we left."

"You dropped by to see Kenny?"

"I don't know that many people in town anymore. He's an old friend. When I saw him, I told him I'd drop by."

"When did you see him?"

"When he was directing traffic. Don't you remember? He asked me over for dinner?"

"What? You seduced my fiancé so I'd break up with him and then went to see him later? You didn't tell him you were coming here, did you?"

"He asked me. He was concerned." She sat stunned. "I didn't want him to worry. And I... I didn't think anyone was tailing me." She looked at me. "See? I am a crummy spy."

"Shit." I dialed Kenny's best friend on the force and asked

him to get to Kenny's ASAP.

I thought back to when we'd been in Portsmouth. It wasn't just the person after us on the way to the airport. What about all the men in lime green shirts? As I put the pieces together, I realized it had been *one* man—one man who didn't change his shirt very often. He'd tailed Giselle in Portsmouth, seen her with Kenny at the construction site. Seeing her with a cop might have slowed him down. Why risk coming after her when she's with a cop? Then he'd lost her when he'd been in the accident near the airport. He must have ended up in the hospital for a couple of days. But when he'd gotten out, he'd known Kenny was a local cop, knew how to find him and—with Mr. Massive's release so soon— he was desperate enough to tangle with a cop. So he could get back on Giselle's trail.

"Ohmigod," Giselle whispered. "Ohmigod. Ohmigod. Ohmigod."

I flashed on Tommy. Hell! Was he in the middle of the drug deal right now? Would the coup come right after that? I couldn't do anything about it right now. I had more immediate problems. "We need a plan. We *really* need a plan."

"I don't have a plan. But I do have a stop-gap measure."

"A stop-gap measure. That would be good. What's the stop-gap measure?"

"Did you notice I have on a disguise?"

"Of course I—"

"When I went out to get the food, I stopped at the front desk."

"And?"

"And I rented a room."

Had she gone over the edge? "We have a room."

"No. They'll find this room. I rented another room on this floor under a different name."

"Where they won't find us."

We ran into the bedroom, flinging clothes haphazardly into suitcases and jamming them shut. Sleeves, pant legs and underwear hung out the sides. We hightailed it down the hall and around the corner to the new room and tossed the bags in. Back in the original room, we grabbed armfuls of hangers from the closet and again flew down the hall. The second we crossed the threshold, we dropped everything on the floor, dashing back down the hall for the rest of our stuff. We picked up the trail of bras and shoes we'd dropped along the way. After throwing the Chinese food back in its bag and shoving our toiletries and miscellaneous other items into smaller bags, we made the third trip to the new room. I'd slung the bag of food over my arm. I flung it on a table. Everything else we once again dropped on the floor just inside the door. We had to go back and get our purses and the guns and check we hadn't missed anything.

In our original room, Giselle pocketed her gun. "Almost forgot something," she said. She laid her purse carefully on the table. As she walked into the bedroom, a five by seven picture dropped out of the side pocket of her bag.

I picked it up. This was the same picture Giselle had dropped the day after we arrived. Once again I looked at a face full of malevolence and madness, on the brink of berserk. Giselle appeared from the bedroom, a bottle in her hand. "Mr. Massive?" I held up the picture.

She nodded, then gulped whiskey from the upended bottle.

The edges were frayed and the photo wrinkled. I could only imagine how many times she'd taken this out and stared at it in terror. The expression on the man's face was so cold and crazy it made me shiver.

I stopped. This guy did look tough, but was he smart? I mean, he wasn't drooling on himself, but from what I could tell, he listed way toward the brawn side of the brawn/brain scale. I could do a million bicep curls and never have the strength he had. He could squash my head like a walnut, but he'd have to catch me first. In terms of speed and flexibility, I'd win big time.

And I liked to think I was lots farther to the right on the brain scale.

Of course, Mr. Massive and his guys had guns, probably the best. That meant most deadly. It wasn't like this was going to be some road race and I could just sprint ahead of them and disappear. I couldn't run faster than a speeding bullet. And if they did catch me...

My bubble of optimism went poof.

In the picture, the corners of Mr. Massive's mouth turned up slightly. I shuddered when I realized he was smiling. This was his friendly look.

Something in the picture caught my eye. Peering more closely, the picture just inches from my face, I squinted. Yes, I was right. Mr. Massive did have just the tiniest bit of drool coming down his chin.

But the closer view had uncovered something else, something worse. For the first time, I focused on a man standing slightly behind Mr. Massive. With a jolt, I realized he was the dark-haired, stocky man in the lime green shirt I'd seen leaving the bar with his friends when I'd been downstairs having a drink with Jesse.

Mr. Massive might be getting out tomorrow. His guys were already here.

Chapter Thirty

The blood pounded in my temples. How long would it take Mr. Massive to get here? How many of his flunkies had already arrived? Mr. Massive had plans for what he wanted to do to Giselle. His people could find her and have her ready for him. I felt sick.

How close were they? If they'd found Kenny and made him talk, then they knew we were on the island. How many hotels would they have to search? Were the men I saw in the bar in this hotel because they were staying here?

Or because *we* were?

Once they knew we were in the hotel... Tracking us to this specific room? Throw enough money around, and someone would fold. Getting another room under a different name might slow them down for a little while.

But I had to get Giselle out of this one now.

She'd seen my reaction. She guzzled more whiskey. "What's wrong?" she said.

"They're here," I whispered.

"No." She backed toward the bedroom, then stopped. She chugged the rest of the whiskey and threw the bottle to the side. It crashed against the wall. She ran into the bedroom. I dashed after her. Fully clothed, she got under the covers and curled up in a fetal position.

"Giselle." I shook her. "We have to get out of here." She didn't move. I threw off the covers and pulled her to a sitting position. "Here we go." I started moving her legs so they'd dangle over the side of the bed, but she flopped back down. Leaning over, I whispered in her ear. "They're coming to kill you."

She sat bolt upright, smacking me hard in the chin with her head.

"Ow." At least she'd snapped out of it. We moved into the living room. My hand shook as I retrieved my Glock from a drawer and pounded in the magazine. "Okay, quietly," I whispered. But she was hyperventilating again, with a very audible wheeze as she breathed in and as she exhaled.

Being quiet wasn't an option.

I poked my head into the hall and glanced both ways. We stepped out and headed away from the elevator, toward the new room. As we neared the end of the hall, the elevator doors slid open. Giselle looked back and hesitated.

"Don't stop," I said, pulling her. But she was frozen in fear. Her wheezing increased. I followed the direction of her eyes.

Two jumbo-sized men in dark jackets accelerated in our direction. I yanked Giselle's arm and she finally sprang into motion. If we went to our new room now, they'd see us going in. We ran for the stairs. I pushed the door open and we bounded down. Within seconds I heard the door open again and felt pounding footsteps behind us. A shot rang out, the sound of the ricocheting bullet reverberating off the walls.

Their bigness was a disadvantage here. Plus, I knew the building. They'd assume we'd try to escape out the front door. Instead, at the floor above the lobby, I grabbed Giselle, opened the door, and we silently stepped in. I guided the door closed to avoid the slam that would give us away. As we took off down the hallway, I heard footsteps running down the stairwell. They'd fallen for it; they were continuing to the lobby. Giselle and I dashed to the stairs at the opposite end of the floor and up to six. Panting, we exited the stairwell and made our way to our new room. As soon as we got in, I bolted the door behind us.

I shoved aside the bag of food on the table and stood there panting for breath. "Shit."

"What?" Giselle asked.

"The Chinese is cold."

After we ate the congealed food, Giselle went into the bedroom. I sat back to think.

I was desperate for shuteye, and it wasn't just because it was late. The last few days were catching up with me. I hadn't been sleeping well. Extreme stress did that to me.

I hoped we'd be safe for a few hours. If we were lucky, they thought we'd fled. But at some point, they'd figure out we were still here. Shots fired would have been called in to the police. Cops were lax here, but this was a tourist hotel so the police would respond. Cops crawling all over the place would slow them down. But eventually the police would leave, and Mr. Massive's guys would be back.

In the bedroom, Giselle was already out, aided by additional alcohol she'd sucked down. I'd bought a bottle—the one she'd smashed against the wall in the old room—but I'd made the mistake of telling her about the shop, and at some point she'd bought more. I flopped on the other bed and fell into a troubled sleep. Sometime later, I awoke with a start. I'd heard a noise. I grabbed my gun.

I glanced over at the other bed. My God. Giselle was gone. Had they come and... But wait. I'd heard something hit the floor. No carpet to muffle the sound. The bathroom.

Gun pointed in the air, I moved soundlessly toward the slightly ajar door. Easing it open with my foot, I peered in.

Giselle. She was on her hands and knees, picking up pills and shoving them in her mouth. I kicked at them. "Stop that! You'll get us both killed."

"I'm as good as dead already."

"I'd prefer not to be. How many of those have you taken?"

"Enough so I won't wake up until a week from Sunday, I hope." She chugged whiskey from a bottle to wash them down.

"You've got to throw up, Giselle. You've got to get them out of your system."

"No."

"Yes." Her open toiletries bag sat on the counter. I dug through it. "They must give you spies ipecac in case you're poisoned."

"Ha! I used that up a long time ago."

I hurled the bag, scattering the contents. "Then stick your finger down your throat."

"I'm not sticking my finger down my throat. That's so... so... unladylike."

"You did it all the time in high school."

"You knew about that?"

"Everyone knew about it."

"I'm still not going to do it."

"Yes, you are."

"Make me."

"Why didn't I think of that? Come here."

"You're going to stick *your* finger down *my* throat?"

"I'm trying to be inventive."

She shrugged. "It's actually not the worst idea I ever

heard."

"Get over here then."

"No."

"You said it was a good idea!"

"I meant strictly from the inventiveness standpoint!"

I got her in a headlock.

"If you do it, I'll bite you," she said.

I hesitated.

"You didn't think about that, did you?"

"Well, no. I have to admit I didn't." Hmm. "All I really want to do is trigger your gag reflex. I'll use a toothbrush!" I said.

"That won't work either."

"Why?"

"I took a bunch of other pills before you woke up. It's too late to get me to throw up. I'll strangle on my own vomit," she said triumphantly.

"That's a real victory all right, Giselle," I said. "Besides that, you're a liar. You probably didn't even take any other pills."

Giselle slid to the floor in an unconscious heap.

"Okay, so you weren't lying for once," I said to her inanimate form. That was all it was, wasn't it? Giselle was unconscious. She wasn't... She couldn't really...

I dropped to my knees, frantically grabbing the open containers, speed-reading the labels. Vitamins. C, E, A—she had half the alphabet here. There were only two bottles that weren't vitamins. One was laxatives; that would serve her right. The other was an over-the-counter sleeping pill. That could be trouble. But I pawed through the pills for the distinctive-colored capsules, counting them up.

She'd only taken two.

There were containers with the covers still on. I picked those up—stronger pills to make you sleep, pills to make you relax—these could have hurt her but they were empty. She'd used them up before. She might have wanted to knock herself into next week, but she hadn't taken anything that would.

From the looks of how much remained in the bottle of hooch, she'd consumed enough alcohol to stop a water buffalo. That combined with the two sleeping pills would put her out for a long time, but she'd live through it. I watched her chest moving up and down. She was already snoring. She'd be okay.

At least the pills wouldn't kill her. I slumped onto the toilet seat. How could I possibly get us out of this mess? Giselle would be dead weight. Maybe she was right. Maybe we were both goners already.

My eyes drifted from Giselle to toiletries scattered on the floor. Was that her hair dye?

I sat up. What if they thought I was Giselle? With my hair cut, we resembled each other *except* for our hair color. The people searching for her had probably never seen her in person. They'd miss the telltale signs that differentiated us. Could they be fooled?

I wasn't sure. But I had to try.

I crawled to the bottle and unscrewed the top. Suddenly I felt a whack on the side. Giselle's unconscious body had tipped over. The bottle slipped through my fingers, hit the floor. No! The contents splashed out. I grabbed it, righted it and peered in. Would I have enough now?

I got up carefully and placed the bottle on the counter. Bending down, I righted Giselle, propping her in the corner. She snored through the whole thing.

An hour later, I looked into the mirror. A blonde Giselle look-alike gazed back.

I dragged Giselle into the other room. For my plan to work, she had to be out of sight. I looked around, pulled her toward the bed, lay her down, and rolled her under. Now I had to time things so the bad guys saw me at the exact time and place they expected to see Giselle. They'd come after me and she'd be safe.

Me? I'd be in doo-doo up to my derriere.

Chapter Thirty-One

I was wide-awake with worry. How would they come for us? And when? I pictured a huge ticking time bomb, but I couldn't see the clock.

It was what happened *then* that I could control. Or at least I hoped I could. I had a plan. Would it work? There was no way to be sure.

I checked on Giselle. Still out. It was after midnight. I banked on nothing happening overnight, but I slept with my gun beside me.

When a slight noise awakened me in the morning, I looked out the peep hole. Room service arriving at the room across the hall. Half an hour later, the jangle of silverware and glasses alerted me that the remains of breakfast sat in the hall for room service to retrieve.

When the meal had been delivered, I'd focused on the outfit worn by the room service waiter. Simple black pants with a white shirt, and a small, white towel slung over one arm. With the other arm, the waiter had balanced the tray on one hand high above his head. The outfit I could pull off.

The tray balancing would be a little trickier. I dressed, slicking my hair back and going without makeup, both things Giselle would never do. Then I watched out the peephole for a few seconds. All quiet.

I darted across the hall, grabbed the tray, and brought it back to my room. I'd eaten hardly any dinner. I lifted the silver cover off the plate. My neighbors would never make it into the clean-plate club. I scarfed down leftover eggs Benedict in a creamy if cold Hollandaise, washing it down with the orange juice. I broke the blueberry muffin in two. Opening the carafe, I poured cream directly into it and chugged coffee, pausing occasionally to cram another chunk of muffin in my mouth.

If this wasn't an occasion for stress eating, I didn't know what was. I feared for my life and for Giselle's. I'd have eaten anything in sight.

Fortified, I got up and replaced the silver top over the plate. I hoisted the tray above my head and practiced walking around the room until I felt comfortable. I had to leave the room. Guests didn't notice service people. I needed to be invisible like they were.

I stuck the gun in my pants, positioning the towel over my arm to hide it from view. Opening the door, I marched out and down the hallway with an air of confidence I had to fake. Feeling exposed, I hit the elevator button and waited. After what seemed like a very long time, the bell dinged. The door slid open.

I almost choked when I saw the group of six dark-suited men. Quickly moving to the side and hoisting the tray higher, I hid my face from view as they exited. Jamming my finger on the button, I prayed they wouldn't turn around.

They were already on our floor. There were six! And even

as goons go, they were ginormous. They'd moved more quickly than I'd expected and with more manpower. My plan might still work, but I'd have to speed up. On the ground floor, I walked down the hallway that led in the direction of the dock. I set the tray down in front of a random room. It had served its purpose. I pushed open the door to the outside.

I headed for the jet ski rental area on the dock. A young man sat, eyes closed, taking a siesta. I read his nametag. "Excuse me, Dwayne," I said. "I'd like to rent four jet skis."

Dwayne looked at me. I hadn't taken into account that he might be wondering why a waitress would be renting anything.

"Are you wondering why I'm dressed as a waitress?"

"No. If you were wearing a string bikini, then I'd care. Otherwise..." He shrugged. "You said you wanted four jet skis, right?" He glanced around. "You renting them for later?"

"Oh! I'll be coming back with my friends shortly."

"What size? The big or the small?"

A group of eight was just returning to the dock on the large jet skis.

"The small," I said.

"How long do you want them? There's a tropical storm brewing. They don't think it's going to head this way, but you never know."

"An hour will be plenty."

"You should be okay then."

"We'll be back soon. I know they'll be very excited when they find out what I have in store for them."

Dwayne unlocked the jet skis. "I'll get them gassed up for you. Just be careful. They're a little tippy."

Glancing at one of the jet skis, I saw the manufacturer

name—in foreign characters. Back home we had laws about safety. Down here, I was guessing they didn't. I started wondering just how tippy these things might be.

I hustled back to the hotel. At the doorway, I stopped, used my key to open the door, then positioned a pen on the floor to keep the door open a fraction of an inch.

I hurried down the hall and up to the sixth floor. As I passed a room a few doors away from ours, I heard noise—annoyed voices and things being thrown around. Mr. Massive's men must be checking room to room. I sped by. Back in our suite, I knelt down by the bed and checked Giselle. Still snoring, no signs of puke. Good.

I stripped off the waiter uniform. After drying my hair, I styled it to look like Giselle's and applied her makeup. I pulled on casual but loose clothing Giselle had brought. I wavered about putting on my bulletproof vest. I'd be safer, but it would slow me down. I heard noise. They'd arrived in the room next to ours.

I hurried to finish getting ready. They wouldn't be in the next room much longer. I opened the door to the hall a tiny bit and listened. The throwing noises stopped, and the voices suddenly sounded louder. They'd opened the door to the hall.

I took a deep breath and stepped out, turning to face them directly.

"It's her!" one of them shouted.

I took off, making it around the corner and into the stairway. Stairs ran seven to a set down to a landing, then seven more, then the landing at the next floor. By grabbing the banister, I could leap from the edge of one landing to the landing below, take two steps to make the turn and leap again down to the next landing. These guys after me were strong but not limber.

I had the advantage now.

I heard them above me. They entered the stairwell but didn't bother to shoot. I was too far ahead. I made it to the ground floor and bounded down the hallway toward the back of the building. Now a shot rang out. Sprinting to the end of the hall, I blasted through the door. They'd gain on me as we neared the dock.

As we approached the rental area, Dwayne stood up, a look of alarm on his face. "I told you they'd be excited," I said. Another shot rang out. Dwayne dove into the water.

I ran to the first jet ski, threw my leg up and mounted it. In Portsmouth, I'd ridden these things more than most kids ride bikes. I kicked it to life and took off at full throttle, rocketing away from the shore.

I wanted them to come after me.

When I glanced behind me, I saw them move toward the unchained jet skis. With six of them and three skis, they figured out it was two men each. Their huge size suddenly wasn't such a plus, but it wasn't long before they headed over the water toward me.

One of them got off a shot, then another. A bullet caught me in the side. Screaming in pain, I lurched to the right and almost toppled into the water. I jerked myself in the other direction and scrambled to an upright position.

If I hadn't worn the bulletproof vest, I'd be dead now.

I looked back. The three jet skis had started out fast, and the initial propulsion had helped keep them upright. But as soon as they slowed to aim, the jet skis started to sway and, with the weight from two oversized men... I heard yelling. The jet skis toppled like dominoes.

Dwayne was right. These jet skis were tippy.

I circled back to the dock, climbed off the jet ski, and stood for a moment watching the guys flounder in the water. They were soaked to the skin, and I hoped their guns were in the ocean. I figured at least some of them couldn't swim, so hopefully they'd be shaken up, too. I started down the dock toward the hotel. The bastards had been shooting at me, but I still didn't want to be responsible for their deaths. By now, someone must have called the police, who'd come round them up.

"That's her!" someone shouted.

I turned. From where I stood near the shore end of the dock, I saw Dwayne on the beach, twenty feet away, pointing at me and talking to a cop. The cop looked at the guys in the water, but glanced at me and waved me over.

"I don't even know those guys." Hell. One of them had reached a jet ski.

"Sure," the cop said. "I want to talk to you anyway." He crooked his finger, signaling me toward him.

I hesitated. One of the guys had been trying to get on a jet ski and had just managed to mount it. He'd help his friends, wouldn't he?

"Go, Joey, go!" one of his buddies yelled to him.

No! Joey headed toward shore.

The cop had started a slow walk in my direction.

I changed my stance slightly so I'd be ready to flee. The cop noticed and picked up his pace. He headed for the end of the pier to block my exit.

Joey neared land.

"Help!" A chorus of voices sounded from the water. The guys who couldn't swim struggled to keep afloat.

"They're going to drown!" I yelled at the cop. "You've got to help them. They're my friends."

"I thought you said you didn't know them," he said.

"Well, they're somebody's friends," I said, "and they're definitely going to drown."

He wavered. "I still want to talk to you. Stay right there."

"I will."

He dashed for a large hard-bottomed dinghy Dwayne pointed to—the hotel's emergency boat. The cop jumped in and roared away.

Surely he didn't expect me to wait all day, and it had been close to fifteen seconds already. Joey hit land. I took off toward the hotel.

I pulled the door open and kicked the pen out of the way, then rushed down the hall. Behind me, I heard Joey pounding on the locked door. He'd have to use the front entrance.

I didn't want to be in the elevator and run into Joey. He knew what floor I'd been on, and he'd head back there. I opened the door to the stairwell. Coming down, the bulletproof vest had actually given me momentum as I sailed between landings. But going up those stairs with that extra weight—I'd be taking it one step at a time.

And while the vest had kept me from dying, it hadn't kept me from being hurt. I felt like I'd been hit in the side by a truck. That would slow me down some more. I was gasping for breath by the time I made it to the third floor. If he'd caught the elevator just right, Joey could be in the room already. That spurred me on. By the time I made it to six, I was exhausted. I gave myself a few seconds for my breathing to calm, took my gun out, then opened the door to the hall. Clear. I hurried down the hall, my back to the wall, moving sideways, glancing both ways as I went. I got to the room and went in.

Instantly I knelt to feel the rug. It was wet. Joey had been here. I listened. Silence.

I hurried to the bed. Stooping down, I lifted the ruffle. Giselle was gone.

Chapter Thirty-Two

I sank onto the bed. I'd screwed up. Now Giselle was in deadly danger. I choked back a sob. I'd have plenty of time to cry later.

At her funeral.

Stop it! Colliding thoughts scurried around in my skull. On the verge of panic, I took a deep breath. *Knock off the whiney-baby whimpering.* There was no one to rescue us. There was only me. Now think!

Giselle had said to go with what you know.

I knew if Giselle was unconscious, getting her back to Mr. Massive would be difficult. If Joey had to carry her, wouldn't he go back to his friends for help?

I ripped off my shirt and the bulletproof vest. I saw where the vest had been impacted by the bullet. Terrifying how close I'd come to death. Another couple of inches... But all I'd have is an enormous bruise.

If I opted for the protection of the vest now instead of speed, it might cost Giselle her life. I couldn't let it slow me down. Yanking on a tee shirt, I ran for the stairs and headed for the ground floor. Seconds later, I peered through the glass door toward the dock.

Joey wasn't there. Dealing with Giselle must have slowed him way down. I was still banking on him showing up. All I could do now was wait.

The police officer had plucked the drowning guys from the water and was touching back on shore. But as the cop stepped out of the dinghy, the others scrambled out, overpowered him, and started beating him. Grabbing line from the dinghy, they tied him up. He'd rescued them, but he was still a cop. Laughing, they heaved him into the bottom of the boat and pushed the dinghy out to sea.

This was the way they treated someone who saved their lives. I shivered as I thought about what they would do to someone who pissed off their boss.

Someone like Giselle.

Suddenly, hands circled my shoulders from behind. I ducked and pitched left, hit the floor and rolled, gun at the ready, my finger on the trigger.

"It's me!" said a startled voice.

"JMJ and all the saints," I hissed. "I almost killed you."

"I noticed that," Jesse said. "It's amazing how much you've learned already."

"Oh thanks," I said. "You noticed that roll and ready-to-shoot thing I did?"

"That was pretty good."

Then I remembered I'd almost shot him. "What were you thinking, sneaking up on me like that?" I hollered.

"I thought you were Giselle, you'd be too woozy to react. The blonde hair confused me."

"Do you like it?" I asked, fluffing it a little.

"Actually, I prefer your natural color."

"Sweet of you to say that. Anyway, Mr. Massive's men already arrived, and that was part of my plan. Make them think I was her. Which worked pretty well at first. I did get them to come after me. On jet skis."

"Nice going."

"That was before things went to hell. There were six of them, and one of them circled back here before I could. He got Giselle."

"Ohmigod. They got her? What are you doing about it?"

"You're a guy. Aren't you going to swoop in and rescue your girlfriend?"

"She's not my girlfriend."

"Thanksgiving you were all over her!"

"Mostly holding her up. Sometimes keeping her from doing something dumb. I'm not her boyfriend. I'm her handler."

Her *handler?* It was like the piece in a jigsaw puzzle that finally lets you see the picture. So many things finally made sense. "Hey, I could use a handler. Could you handle me? I'd like to be handled by you. I'd like it a lot." Suddenly I looked away. I felt myself go red as I realized just how much I'd like to be handled by Jesse.

Had a sweet, goofy grin crossed his face for a second? Had he just looked interested in me? Or was it wishful thinking?

"I'll see what I can do. But the word on the Massive situation is it's not our business."

"Oh, that's the word from your girlfriend Maureen?"

"She's not my girlfriend either. What is it with this girlfriend—"

"You certainly seem to spend a lot of time with her."

"That's right, I do. She's my boss. And when she refused to send help and I told her I was coming back here to do what

I could, she threatened to fire me."

"But you came back anyway?"

"Yes."

"Like a friend helps a friend?"

"It's a little more than that!" he said.

"Why'd you act like you didn't care?"

"I thought you were engaged."

"That's a line. Hello! No ring." I waggled my left hand in the air.

"I figured you were having it sized."

So he *had* been thinking about it. "Oh."

Jesse and I locked eyes.

A shout came from outside. "Joey!" All Massive's men looked to the left.

Joey was there? He was outside our range of vision. I opened the door a fraction. Oh God! There was Giselle, slung over Joey's shoulder.

I heard sirens. Someone must have seen the beating of the cop and called more police.

Joey trotted toward the dock, Giselle's body bouncing limply across his shoulder. Had he killed her already?

But no. Mr. Massive would want Giselle to himself for a while at least. He might want to talk to her about the money, but that would probably be after they discussed her "Mr. Teeny Weenie" comment. Then, I had no doubt, he'd kill her, or one of these guys would.

Through my fear, I bristled. Not if I could help it.

Joey reached the dock. "You got the wrong one, Joey," one of the guys said.

"No, you nitwit. I got the right one. The one on the jet ski was a fake."

As Jesse and I peered out the glass door, I asked, "What

exactly will they do to Giselle?"

"First, they'll try to get her to talk."

"When you say 'try,' you don't mean ask sternly, do you?"

"Not exactly. They'll use knowledge accumulated over the years in ways to be persuasive."

"What about killing her?"

"Well, sure," he said, "but not until after the usual torture and talk."

We kept watching. The six guys argued about the plan.

"Hey, by the way?" I said. "Why didn't you tell me she was still in training?"

"Confidentiality. There are strict agency rules."

"I could have been killed!"

"That's not against agency rules."

"What?"

"Not all the rules make sense, Nora." He shrugged. "It's the government."

I looked back out. "I can't believe they're headed to the pier again."

Jesse gestured in the direction of the sirens. "Their other option is to walk into the arms of the cops."

"But if they get on the jet skis, they'll end up in the water, just like before."

But one of them pointed his gun toward the water. Dwayne arose, quaking, from where he'd been submerged. He pulled a key out of a tiny pocket in his swim trunks and hurried to where the rest of the jet skis were locked up. Joey pointed to the larger, more stable jet skis I'd seen being returned by guests earlier today. He forced the youngster to unlock them all—more than enough for each of Mr. Massive's guys to have his own.

"Once they get on those jet skis, we could lose them. We'll

never see Giselle again." I couldn't let that happen. "Cover me," I yelled.

"No!" Jesse grabbed my arm in a vice-like grip, but I wrenched free, shoved the door open, and ran. The bad guys caught the movement and turned.

"It's the other girl!" Joey shouted.

I heard two shots immediately. Jesse's shots. Then a scream from their side. He'd hit at least one. But others raised their guns toward me. BOOM! BOOM! BOOM! The blasts came in rapid succession. I twirled to the left and right. I managed to avoid the first and second. But the third one caught me in the left arm.

"Nora!" I heard the shrill terror in Jesse's voice. With a jolt I knew. That was what terror sounded like when someone you cared about was in danger.

The force of the bullet blew me to the right, but I rolled with it and landed near the water. More gunfire sounded. I couldn't tell if it was coming from Jesse or the bad guys. I jumped in and ducked underwater, coming up between a kayak and a motorized dinghy. Part of my brain registered red in the water. Blood. My blood. But my legs and my shooting arm worked. That was all that mattered now.

Some of the guys looked for Jesse and me. I moved to the other side of the dinghy, out of view. The other guys hovered near Joey, focused on Giselle and getting her to Mr. Massive.

"I found her," Joey said. "Finders keepers. I'll just sling her over in front of me on the jet ski and take her to him."

Didn't he realize her face would go into the water? She'd drown!

"That won't work," one of them said.

"Sure it will. You just want some of the finders' fee, but you're not getting any. I'll buy you guys a drink though."

When he laughed, they all stepped away. If he wasn't willing to share, they weren't going to help him. But Giselle was unconscious. If they didn't help him and he lost his grip on her while on the jet ski—

I untied the dinghy and, pulling it soundlessly through the water, moved in their direction. Behind me, I felt the water swirl. I jerked my head back. Jesse! He kissed me hard and fast, then let me go. He realized instantly what I was doing.

"I'll cover you," he said. I heard the quaver in his voice— terrified for me, yet knowing there was no alternative.

Submerged to just below my nose, I inched my way toward Joey. Standing knee deep in the water, he lifted Giselle down from his shoulder. His arm encircled her waist. She hung like a rag doll, the top of her head in the water, her hair floating like seaweed. He tried to mount the jet ski, struggling to lift his leg up and over while maintaining control of Giselle. The jet ski started to tip. He quickly put his leg back down. He tried again. The jet ski started to tilt again, but he kept moving his leg. The jet ski rolled suddenly and, in a last ditch effort to regain control of it, he let go of Giselle.

I grabbed her hair, yanking her head out of the water. I pulled her toward me. Jesse hung on to her while I scrambled into the boat. I jerked her in as he shoved her up and backed away to cover me. I ripped the cord and the engine sprang to life. As I gunned the throttle, a shot rang out but went wide. I lurched wildly to the right as I turned the dinghy sharply, churning through the water to get us behind a pier.

More shots pierced the air. I heard yelling and the sounds of a struggle. I looked back.

I had Giselle. But now... Oh my God. Now they had Jesse.

Chapter Thirty-Three

I felt as if I'd been kicked in the gut. I could hardly breathe, barely think. At that moment I hated Giselle, loathed her in a way I'd never even known possible. If they killed Jesse because of her, I'd... I looked down at her, still unconscious.

"I hate you. I hate you, I hate you, I hate you," I screamed. "I'd like to roll you out of the boat and leave you to drown. I'd like to hand you over to Mr. Massive, and give him sharp metal instruments, and laugh while he tortures you. I'd like to dress up in a cheerleader's outfit and cheer him on. I'd like to—"

"I wouldn't blame you if you did."

"Ahhh," I screamed. Giselle had been unconscious so long, it was like the waking of the dead. "You scared the crap out of me."

She sat up, pushing wet hair away from her eyes. "Anything happen while I was gone?"

"Aside from me pretending to be you," I hollered, "you getting kidnapped, me getting shot, Jesse and me getting you back, and the bad guys kidnapping Jesse, not much!"

"They had me?"

"Yes, they had you, and they were getting ready to bring you back to Mr. Massive and serve you up on a silver platter."

"See? That's why I wanted to be unconscious. What a relief I slept through that."

"Unfortunately for me, I was conscious and busy trying to save your butt."

"You should have taken some of the pills."

"Then they'd be torturing you right now!" I said, fuming.

"Oh right," she said, rapping her head with her knuckles. "Don't do drugs, Nora. They mess up your brain."

"Save your advice, unless you've got any to help get Jesse back."

"If I..."

"What?"

"Never mind."

"What?" I screamed.

"If I come up with any ideas, we'll have to go after Jesse right now. That might mean heading toward Mr. Massive, and I don't want to do that."

"Oh, we're doing that anyway." I'd hidden us behind a pier. The bad guys were so busy arguing about what to do next they hadn't even heard the noise I was making. But when sirens sounded, much closer this time, Joey's voice rose above the others. He was taking charge.

"Hey, Nora. We gotta run. But we got your boyfriend," Joey yelled. "And we're willing to trade for your useless friend, if she ain't dead yet." They laughed at his joke. "Keep in touch."

Suddenly everything changed. Getting away would have been easy in comparison. Now we had to follow them and figure out how to get Jesse back.

They headed out on the jet skis, seven of them. All of the bad guys had worn suit jackets. But the only jacketless person now looked larger than Jesse. Joey must have forced Jesse to put on one of the jackets. Picking off a couple of the guys to try to even the odds wasn't going to work. Unless we were a lot closer, shooting anyone would mean the risk of shooting Jesse.

I took a second to assess the dinghy. About twelve-feet long, thick rubber with a rigid fiberglass bottom. With a forty-horsepower motor, this thing would whale, but at full throttle, the bow would go up. Since you operated the boat from the throttle attached to the motor at the back, that would make it tough to see what was ahead. Worse, we'd capsize if the bow rose high enough. The big plus—extreme maneuverability.

While I let them get slightly ahead, I listened to the sound of the jet skis. It was a high-pitched whine, similar to a motorcycle. I couldn't hear their voices, but I'd know their location. I took off after them. When they disappeared for a moment behind an anchored boat, I still could tell where they were.

"Did you hear what they said about me being your useless friend?" Giselle said. "That kind of hurt."

I said nothing.

"Nora?"

"What?"

"You wouldn't really trade me for Jesse, would you?"

I didn't respond. I wasn't even sure I knew the answer.

I felt a change in the temperature. Looking toward land, I saw leaves swirling on the trees. Dwayne had mentioned a tropical storm. Had it changed course? I scanned the sky, searching for signs of a storm. We had them all. The sky was darkening like the rapid onset of dusk. Clouds scudded across the skies. At home I would have turned back immediately.

"I... I want to help," Giselle said.

Giselle had been worse than useless. She'd put innocent bystanders, Jesse, herself and me in peril. I didn't think she was going to be of any assistance, but talking out loud sometimes helped me think. At least she could listen. "Okay," I said. "Here's what we got. We have a boat, which is faster than the jet skis and very maneuverable."

"The jet skis are maneuverable, too."

"Right."

"And this thing," she said, patting the side of the dinghy, "can be punctured."

"Let's take a minute to discuss the meaning of 'help,' Giselle."

"But you have more gas," she said. "Or to be more precise, this engine holds more gas than the engine of the typical jet ski."

"More gas. *That's* helpful." Giselle's brain cells were starting to fire. I'd been wondering if she'd killed off too many for that to ever happen again.

Anchored boats dotted the water. Slipping behind them whenever I could allowed us to get nearer to the jet skis. I wanted to keep them guessing about where we were. "The dinghies would be kept gassed up for emergencies. But they gas up the jet skis right before they're taken out. The ones Joey made Dwayne unlock... They wouldn't have gassed them up," I said. "Shhh." I held up my hand for silence.

"What?" she whispered.

"The sound of the jet skis just got fainter." As I edged out from behind a catamaran, we looked toward the jet skis. We saw people gesturing. *Alarmed* gesturing. It was hard to tell in the dim light, but... "Giselle, see if you can count the jet skis."

"Hard to be sure," she said. "One, two... There're six."

"One went down."

"He ran out of gas!"

We high fived. "But what if it was Jesse?" I said. We stopped celebrating to watch. The jet skis maneuvered around in a small area. They must be picking up the guy in the water. If it was Jesse who'd fallen in, would they let him drown? Then I realized they'd save him. He was their bait. Once again we heard the sound of the jet skis moving forward.

"They doubled up on one of the jet skis."

At least we now had confirmation Jesse was still alive. We continued following. "Giselle! The doubling up was a problem for them before. These jet skis are larger, but they're still too small for two really big guys."

"Uh huh," she said, waiting.

"Jesse is the only one who's not really big. That means he's got to be on the jet ski where they doubled up."

"You're right. Okay, that's really good. Now we can pick off some of these guys."

It *was* good. "Wait." I grabbed her arm. "They're heading toward land."

"They must be worried the other jet skis will run out of gas."

"Unless they're close to their destination and heading to shore anyway."

"That wouldn't be good," she said. "Once they get where they're going and move inside, getting Jesse back will be much more difficult."

I sped up, but veered across open water to the right of where they headed. "If I come in from north of where they land, we might be able to surprise them." I darted behind boat after boat, trying to keep from view. But what if I overshot the mark? We'd lose crucial time.

"I think I know where they're going," Giselle said. "This stretch of shore is pretty much restaurants and private property. Except the castle."

"The castle? Mr. Massive and his whole gang? They'd need something private like a house or an apartment—"

"Groups can book an entire wing. They'd have complete privacy."

"And Mr. Massive is a benefactor. They'd get the discount rate." If she was right, I'd gone too far. I started to alter course. Suddenly they turned, too, and headed directly for the castle. "Hang on!" I shouted. I hit the throttle. Giselle lurched backward. My hand shot out to steady her. She grabbed it and hung on.

"Hurry, Nora," she yelled. "I don't want Jesse to die because of me."

We heard a scream. Oh God! I knew that voice. Jesse! I pushed the boat to full throttle. We raced across the water, thudding along the waves. Could they see us? Neither of us cared. Giselle knew she'd put Jesse's life on the line. And now I knew I cared enough to risk my life to save him.

The storm broke. The winds roared to life and the rain pelted down. The waves increased to a wind-blown chop of four feet. I bounded towards them, the boat slamming down again and again. The bow rose to a perilous angle. We could capsize at any moment.

What was happening at the castle? The din of the motor,

the rain and the darkness made it impossible to know. Hang on, Jesse! A bolt of lightning arced across the sky, the flash illuminating the shore.

Turning the throttle to the lowest position, I slowed as we neared land. From a balcony jutting out above the water, Mr. Massive looked down. Someone behind him turned on an outdoor spotlight. The awful scene on the beach below came into focus. Six guys fought Jesse by hand, as if in some throwback to the days of the Coliseum. Mr. Massive jumped on the balcony railing, totally exposed to the fury of the storm.

I understood Giselle's terror now. Mr. Massive was a madman.

"I knew you'd come," he shrieked to me. "Want your boyfriend? You'll have to trade."

"Stop them," I screamed. But his men kept punching Jesse, kicking him, taking turns holding him, hurting him.

"Not until I have what I want," he shouted, pointing to Giselle.

I shifted my position, moving away from Giselle. I had my gun ready, under my shirt. I raised it, pointing it at Giselle's head.

"Nora," she whimpered, cowering in the bottom of the boat.

"Now," I yelled to Mr. Massive.

"Stop." At a wave of his hand, the six thugs stopped. But one gave Jesse a final violent shove. Jesse staggered, then fell at the water's edge. I glanced at him, my gun still trained on Giselle. He was beaten and bleeding, but his eyes looked our way. He was alive.

And he knew we were here.

Mr. Massive glared at me from above. "Thanks," I yelled,

glancing at his crotch, "Mr. Teeny Weenie."

Mr. Massive turned purple as he went apoplectic. Eyes bulging, jaws flapping up and down uselessly, he looked like a volcano about to blow. His guys stood frozen, waiting for direction. Mr. Massive went for his gun, but since going apoplectic takes a little time, he lost precious seconds. I shot him before he shot me.

"Go, Giselle, go!" I yelled.

Giselle grabbed the throttle. We flew toward Jesse. He staggered up, floundering into the water for where we'd intersect. But he was moving too slowly. If we got much closer to shore, the propeller would hit bottom. I bent back, smashed my finger on the button that raises the motor. Had I been quick enough? I moved forward, held onto the boat with one hand, and stretched the other as far as I could reach out over the side to Jesse. He grabbed it as we went by. He was hurt, badly hurt, and I misjudged his remaining strength. For a split second, I thought I would lose him. Then Giselle reached out and grabbed him too. We yanked him partway into the boat. I felt the propeller hit bottom, but we churned through it. I hit the button to drop the motor. Jesse's legs still trailing over the side, Giselle rocketed away.

I focused my attention on Jesse in a frantic struggle to get him the rest of the way in the boat. But a tiny piece of me steeled myself, waiting for a bullet to rip through my body.

Chapter Thirty-Four

But there were no gunshots. As soon as I'd hauled Jesse in, I looked back. Now I knew why. Giselle was half-standing, using herself as a target, protecting Jesse and me.

But we weren't out of trouble. I'd hit Mr. Massive in the arm he used to hold his gun. His wound would need attention, but it'd be a serious underestimation to think he was down for the count. There was a reason they hadn't shot at Giselle.

They were going to come after her again.

I looked at Jesse. "Oh God." He was bleeding from his nose, cheeks, his forehead. His eyes lolled. He was barely conscious. Did he have a concussion? Something worse? I bent toward him. "Stay with me, Jesse," I whispered.

The storm intensified. We had to get to shore fast. And Jesse needed medical attention. "Giselle, round Castle Point and head for the dock on the other side."

I got in the bottom of the dinghy and held Jesse's hands. He squeezed my fingers for a second, then his grasp weakened. We needed help *now*. Moments later, I saw the dock come into view. Gently, I removed my hands from Jesse's. Grabbing the dock, I heaved myself on, pulled the dinghy in, and tied it up.

The waves bashed the boat, but somehow Giselle and I got Jesse onto the dock. Supporting him between us, we fought our way toward the castle, the wind pushing us with terrific force, each step a battle. The door seemed impossibly far. As Jesse lost his grip on consciousness, we were half-dragging him. Suddenly out of the mist two monks appeared, rushing to us, taking over for Giselle and me. A minute later, we were inside the castle.

A nun strode toward us. Thanks be to God, it was Sister Aggie.

"Sister, please," I implored.

She nodded instant understanding and beckoned us to follow. We boarded an elevator, stopping on the second floor. The monks held Jesse up, his chin on his chest now. They had to carry him as we proceeded a short way down the hall. Glancing into a room, I realized this was where the nuns and monks lived. Sister opened the door to a room on the right and gestured for us to enter. The monks gently lay Jesse on a bed before leaving. Sister Aggie disappeared, returning with a black bag. She opened it and began pulling out bandages and other supplies.

"Are you a doctor?" I asked.

"Nurse," she said.

I said a little prayer of gratitude Jesse had some medical attention—and hoped that it would be enough. Sister attended to Jesse, rousing him enough to ask him questions as she dressed the wounds on his head and face. My arm hurt like hell where I'd been shot, but the bullet had grazed me, nothing compared to Jesse's injuries. I didn't realize Giselle had seen me glance at my arm until she sat down beside me, a damp cloth in her hand. She hesitated. She was helping now, but she'd gotten us into this mess, and a part of me wanted to jerk away. But I lifted my arm a little in her direction, and she gently cleaned off the hardened blood.

A radio on a nearby table played softly. A weather report detailed storm damage. Downed tree limbs made many roads across the island impassable. It would have been impossible to get Jesse to a hospital immediately anyway. I listened to the rest of the forecast.

When Sister finished bandaging Jesse's wounds, I asked, "Will he make it?"

She looked up, very serious. "It's too soon to tell."

I wrestled with my emotions and exhaustion, swatting at the tears slipping down my cheeks. I wanted to rest. I wanted to lay down beside Jesse, cradle him in my arms until I was sure he was all right. But I couldn't stop now, and I couldn't break down.

I had too much more to do. Mr. Massive and the guys who had done this to Jesse topped the list. "Giselle, stay here with Jesse."

"Wait, where—"

I slipped into the hall. Mr. Massive and his boys had their own wing, so I had a general idea of where they were. They would have had to attend to Mr. Massive's gunshot wound and figure out their next step. They were probably gathered in some common room, maybe a dining room. Dining rooms were usually on the ground floor. I found a stairwell and bounded down. On the ground floor, I scooted across the foyer. Ignoring the "Private" sign on the door leading to their wing, I grabbed the door handle. Locked.

Hiding behind a plant on a pedestal, I waited. A few

minutes later, a monk with a serving tray came through the door. I stayed where I was until the last possible moment, then ran to the door, snagging it just before it clicked shut. Voices sounded from a room midway down the hall on the water side. Pulling my gun out, I hurried down the hall. Outside the room, I stood, ear to the door, intent on finding out what I could about how many people they had, how badly Mr. Massive was hurt, what the next step was in their—

Hands grabbed for my gun. I struggled to keep control but other hands gripped me around my middle, forcing my arms to my sides. I kicked back but the person holding me lifted me off the ground, my feet flailing in the air. I tried to jam my elbows back, but the grip around me tightened, and my effort had little impact. I stopped struggling. The person holding me turned me away from the room, toward another man.

"Nice to see you again, bitch," Tommy the Twitch whispered, inches from my face.

I kicked him in the balls. "Ohhh," he groaned, doubling over.

"Don't call me a bitch," I hissed. "And keep it down, will you?" I gestured toward the room.

Dom appeared beside Tommy. "Can I kill her now, boss?" he asked softly.

"Not yet," Tommy said, straightening. The implied "but soon" hung in the air.

"Can I?" Carlo asked, his voice right next to my ear. He was the one holding me. "I could try squeezing her to death, you know, like a python." He squeezed, demonstrating his python-like abilities.

With the air leaving my lungs, I gasped, "He didn't say 'yes.'"

"Not yet," said Tommy.

Carlo's hands loosened just enough for me to speak. "What the hell are you doing here? Couldn't this wait until another time? I'm in the middle of something now."

"I'm in the middle of something more important than anything you're in the middle of," Tommy said. "My life's in danger and you're the reason why. I don't think I'll be waiting."

He raised his hand to knock on the door.

"Hey," I said, "don't—"

The sound of feet running down the hall made us turn. Giselle barreled into Dom, knocked him to the floor. She jumped on him and socked him in the face. Blood spurted from his nose.

"Go, Giselle, go!" I cheered.

She pulled her hand back, ready to give him another, but he grabbed her wrist, muscled her off him. In seconds he had her under control. He stood, and yanked her to her feet.

"I'm sorry, Nora," she whispered.

Giselle was weak from all the ways she'd abused her body. And without a weapon, she'd taken on three guys to try to help me. "I think you broke his nose," I said to her, grinning.

"Yeah." She grinned back.

Tommy knocked on the door, opened it a foot, poked his head in. "Hi there. It's me."

"You know these guys?" I asked.

"Mr. Massive financed the shipment that, thanks to you, didn't go."

"Mr. Massive is your partner?" I said. "Oh hell."

"Which is why he wants to kill me. And why I want to kill you."

From the room came the sound of cocking guns. Tommy

looked grim. He swallowed, then gestured with his head that we should follow.

Carlo put me down, shoving me forward as we entered a large dining room. I stumbled across the room toward the floor-to-ceiling windows. As I got to my feet, I looked out over the raging seas. Closer in, I could make out the path we'd taken from the dock to the castle. Lucky they hadn't been in this room when we'd arrived. They'd have come after us and captured us all.

I turned toward Mr. Massive and his guys. They sat around a dining table. Massive's arm was in a makeshift sling. Another one of his guys had a large bandage on his head.

Mr. Massive glared at Tommy. "Where's my freakin' stuff?"

Tommy lifted his hands in a conciliatory gesture. "I can explain. I've got the stuff."

"The problem is, *I* don't got the stuff."

"It's on the boat."

Mr. Massive threw up his hands. "If you got the stuff and it's on the boat, then why didn't you send it?"

"I... I can't find the boat."

"It's forty feet long!" Mr. Massive said. "Kinda hard to misplace."

"My wife took the boat. Probably on a shopping spree or something. She doesn't know the stuff is on it."

"You better find it fast. Or you're gonna end up..." He reflected for a moment. "You're gonna make the unfortunate decision to go swimming during a dangerous tropical storm."

"I'll find it. I just need a little more time."

"You're gonna have to leave someone as collateral. To

make sure you come back."

"Keep her." Tommy nodded at me. "It's her fault for messing things up in the first place."

"What? That's such a bad idea," I said.

"It works for me," Mr. Massive said. "He wants to kill you, so he'll come back. We'll keep Giselle, too. I have plans for her." He licked his lips as he stared at Giselle. She turned white. Her knees shook. She looked like she was going to topple over any second.

Out of the corner of my eye, outside in the storm, I saw two drenched people stumbling along the path from the dock. One of them had a bedraggled *beehive*. Forcing myself not to let on, I registered that the two were Lenny and Mrs. T. It was a miracle they'd made it back. Castle Point was the northernmost part of the island; this must have been the first dock they came to as they tried to outrun the storm and get back to land. They must have had a devil of a time docking in this weather.

"Wait," I said. "For the right price, I can lead you to the boat."

"You can not," Tommy said.

"Can too," I declared.

"Can not."

"Can too."

"Can—"

"What's the right price?" Mr. Massive shouted.

"Umm. Two hundred thousand dollars."

Tommy looked at Mr. Massive. "Let's just torture it out of her."

Uh-oh. I hadn't thought about that. "Sorry to ruin your fun, but you don't have time."

"It wouldn't take that long," Tommy said with a

malicious smile.

Since I'd probably last about a minute and a half, they actually did have plenty of time. "Tropical storms can be dangerous and unpredictable," I said quickly. "Do you know how many boats go down in storms like this?"

"How many?" Tommy asked.

"Oh. I'm not sure. A lot I'd think."

"She's right. It's too risky," Mr. Massive said. "Okay, you got a deal."

"All two hundred thousand? I started high. I thought you'd try to negotiate down."

"Don't worry about it," Mr. Massive said. He turned to Tommy. "Give her the money."

"Me?" Tommy asked.

"Yes, you. You lost the goddamned boat."

Tommy gave me an icy stare, then nodded to Dom and Carlo. They opened their jackets and started pulling out packs of hundreds, one after the other, and stacking them on the table.

"Now you got what you asked for," Mr. Massive said with an evil look, cocking his gun and pointing it at my head, "you better deliver."

I pointed out the window. Through the driving rain we watched the *Greasy Palm* being bashed against the dock. With every second the wind escalated.

Everyone gathered at the window. "Geez," Mr. Massive said, "that's millions of dollars of stuff gettin' thrown around out there. If that boat goes down... Let's go!"

Mr. Massive, Tommy and their thugs raced for the door. For an awful moment, I thought they'd run into Lenny and Mrs. T in the lobby. But they took off in the opposite direction. There must be an exit directly from this wing to the outside.

"Are you just going to let them go?" Giselle asked. We were cramming the bundles of money in our pants.

"After everything we've been through? Not a chance."

Chapter Thirty-Five

We caught up with Lenny and Mrs. T at the front desk, told them what was going on, then returned to Sister's room. Jesse was still asleep. I bent down, caressed his cheek.

Giselle and I sat down with Sister. "Getting the drugs off the boat in this weather will take a little time," I said. "But once they're done... The cops can't get here. If we're going to stop them, we need weapons."

Sister Aggie walked to the bed, stooped down, and yanked out an oversized suitcase hidden underneath. She flipped it open. The case was filled with guns. She pulled open a closet door. Guns toppled from the overflowing closet.

I stared at her in amazement. "You collect guns?"

She shook her head vigorously.

She was conserving her words. Let's see. "You keep guns for protection?"

Again, the no, although she looked a little annoyed this time.

"You sell guns?"

"Of course I don't sell guns!" She yanked her word counter from her pocket and clicked hard six times.

I could see she was aggravated she had to use up words. "Well, I'm out of guesses and we're out of time," I countered.

"Grrr."

"Does that count?" I asked.

She pretended she didn't know what I meant, then reluctantly clicked the counter. "Shit," she said softly.

I raised my eyebrows and tapped my foot. She narrowed her eyes at me, then clicked again. "Now tell me about the guns," I said.

"With the exception of the Chief and a handful of others, the police are... lax, let's say. So criminals love this island. But if they arrive at the castle with guns, I take them," she said, clicking away.

"They just give them to you?"

"A surprising number attended parochial schools, so of course their spirits are broken. For the others, I mime the wrath of God."

"Oh," I said.

She mimed my "oh" with a decidedly sarcastic demeanor, for a nun.

"Do they work? Are they loaded?"

She tried to figure out how to mime that to me so I'd understand.

I threw my hands up in the air. "Just tell me, for crying out loud!"

"Yes! As soon as I confiscate them, I put them right in here, ammunition and all." She clicked.

"The time I saw you after you took Lenny's gun, you still had it on you."

"I left it in my habit pocket by mistake. I didn't wear that habit again until the day I saw you. But I was late for prayers because I got to doing my nails, so I had to dress in a hurry. I didn't have time to put the gun away." She clicked.

"You didn't have time?" I asked.

She hesitated. "All right, I had time, but it would have ruined my manicure." Click, click, click, click, click, click.

"Are nuns allowed to be vain?"

"Manicures are categorized as semi-vain, so they're allowed," she said, smug. "I hope you're satisfied. I've used my word allotment up until next Tuesday."

I waited while she clicked. "Tell me about the layout of the building."

She narrowed her eyes at me. "After today, I won't be able to talk again until Christmas!" She put her thumb on the clicker.

I grabbed it, threw it on the floor, and stomped on it. "Now talk your head off. There are lives at stake here."

She wavered, then made the sign of the cross. "All right." She pulled out a castle map and launched into a detailed description of the castle, complete with secret passageways exactly like the original. "In the olden days in Ireland, the monks were always getting attacked. Vikings, Goths, Normans, you name it. Pillaging was all the rage back then. So the castle includes hidey-holes for weapons to poke out. Knights who lived with the monks would fight back. They could shoot arrows but not be seen."

"Oh, that's good. That's really good," I said. "Do you think the monks and nuns would be willing to help?"

"I can check."

***

Giselle and I sat in Sister's room, waiting. Suddenly war cries, yelling and pounding footsteps of many people sounded from the hall. I opened the door in alarm and we peered out.

Sister Aggie in the lead, a horde of nuns and monks, bandanas around their heads, war paint streaked on their faces, rampaged down the hall. At Sister's signal, they skidded to a halt where Giselle and I stood. Lenny, dressed as a monk, and Mrs. T, dressed as a nun, were right behind Sister Aggie.

"What are you doing?" I asked.

"Rampaging," Sister Aggie said. "We felt it would be helpful to get into the right spirit."

I waved them on. But as soon as they started rampaging again, I put up my hand. They skidded to a halt again. "Aren't you pacifists?" I asked Sister Aggie.

"Semi-pacifists. We won't shoot to kill."

"Will you shoot to scare the crap out of people?" I asked.

She turned around, conferring with the others in hushed tones, then turned back to Giselle and me. "Oh sure," she said. "That would be fine." They rampaged away.

When they'd finished rampaging, Sister returned. She grabbed her suitcase of guns. Giselle and I grabbed armfuls of the other guns and positioned them where we needed them. Sister got the nuns and monks into place.

Now, the next crucial step. Giselle and I had to do this. Sister provided us with a very long length of rope, which we cut into two pieces. I tied bowline knots on one end of each piece, tugging on them to make sure the loops were secure. We pulled on slickers and hats that would allow us to blend in with Tommy's and Mr. Massive's guys if we needed to. With the rope hidden under our slickers, we stood just inside the castle door on the ground floor. We inched it open, watching for our opportunity.

I looked up to see gun barrels slide out of hidey-holes all over the turrets. For a second, Mrs. T's beehive popped up, followed by Sister Aggie's head, the heads of Lenny and hordes of monks and nuns. Then they disappeared. I knew they were still there when I heard the sound of hundreds of guns cock.

Mr. Massive, Tommy and their guys boarded the *Greasy Palm* carrying big sea bags, obviously empty. Tommy had shown me the small bags of drugs when he'd given me the tour of the boat. The guys must be loading the small bags into the larger sea bags to get them off the boat. This had to be their second load. They moved as a group. We watched, waiting until they descended below deck to begin filling the sea bags again.

Giselle and I sneaked down the dock and stepped onto the boat. They'd kill us if they saw us. I pushed the fear aside. Striding across the deck and stepping up to the wheel, I grabbed the keys from the ignition and pocketed them.

Next, the lines. The boat strained against the fore and aft lines stretched between metal cleats on the boat and those on the dock. Giselle and I took out the lines we'd concealed under our slickers. I looped the bowline knot on my line to the fore cleat on the boat. She did the same aft. We jumped back on the dock. We took the other ends and tied them onto the cleats on the dock. These new lines were a hundred feet long. The original, short lines still held the boat close to the dock.

Now, the pivotal last step. We had to simultaneously cut the shorter lines. We stood together on the dock. We'd get out our knives. Then I'd give the sign.

"Nora!" Giselle screamed.

Mr. Massive's head was rising from the cabin. All heck broke loose as Sister and the monks and nuns started shooting—above the boat. I glanced up at them whooping and yelling. That practicing they'd done was paying off. They were really getting into it.

I focused on the son of a bitch who had made Jesse suffer, drawing my gun as I headed for him. He started to draw his gun as I stepped onto the boat. His injury slowed him some, but the sling seemed to really be getting the better of him. The more he tried to get out of it, the more tangled he became. I reached him. "You hurt Jesse," I spat out.

Mr. Massive fought with the sling, jabbing his fists left and right, trying to get it off. He was totally tangled now. "Jesse schmesse," he said, fixing me with a murderous look, continuing to swing at the sling. "I'm gonna kill you so dead, you won't give a damn. I'm gonna kill you and your whole family. I'm gonna kill everyone you ever met. I'm gonna fill you so full of holes you're gonna look like mozzarella."

I was pretty sure he meant Swiss cheese, but now might not be the time to mention it.

"I'm gonna—"

I dinged him in the shoulder.

He was whirling in circles now, trying to get his gun in spite of the sling constricting his movement. But he kept ranting. "I'm gonna cut you in itty bitty pieces and use the two of you for bait. I'm gonna—"

I sighed and dinged him again.

Finally he got a hold of his gun, but he was so tangled, he couldn't get it pointed at me. For the first time, his look went from murderous to scared. He glanced back toward the stairs leading below deck. "Hey," he hollered. "Hey, you guys."

I dinged him for the third time.

He lurched to the side and hit the deck, groveling there. He was weakening. "I'm gonna... Oh, just kill me already."

"Kill you? I wanna see you suffer. Besides, I can't just kill you. You've got to at least get your gun pointed in my general direction first."

I heard footsteps on the stairs from the cabin below. I didn't dare turn. I didn't want to take my eyes off Mr. Massive. He'd use that opportunity. Out of the corner of my eye on the other side, I saw a beehive rising from a turret, a gun pointed in this direction. Mrs. Tommy wouldn't shoot at me, would she? No.

But she would shoot at Tommy.

"Nora!" Giselle's voice from the dock. "NORA!"

Her voice held so much warning, I knew I had to risk turning away from Massive. I saw Giselle drop to a knee, gun wobbling. I kept turning, in time to see that Tommy had his gun to my head. "Oh no," I screamed. A shot rang out. My heart jumped. But it had been Giselle who fired, hitting Tommy in the arm. But it only stopped him for a second. I grabbed for him, but he stepped back and started to raise his gun again. I heard an "oof" of effort and a piece of metal— Giselle's gun—hurtled into Tommy's head. Giselle heaved the gun so hard, she lost her balance and fell into the water. As Tommy started to go down, I heard a gunshot. Mrs. T's shot. The bullet whizzed by, exactly where Tommy's crotch would have been if he hadn't fallen.

I whirled back to Mr. Massive. He had control of his gun now, and it was pointed at me. He hadn't expected me to turn so quickly. He fired, but a second too late and I ducked. He was getting ready to fire again. I rose from my stooped position, turned his gun toward him, his finger stuck in the trigger, and tucked it into the sling. The gun was now pointed at his throat. If he moved the wrong way, he'd shoot himself.

I hopped onto the dock, fished Giselle out. "Thanks," I said. "You saved my life."

"Hey, what are big sisters for?" she said.

The rest of the bad guys emerged from below, Dom, Carlo and Joey in the lead. They started firing at the turrets. One of the bullets whizzed through Mrs. Tommy's beehive, really close to her head. Lenny fired three shots in quick succession. He nailed Dom, Carlo and Joey. They dropped to the deck.

"I think he killed them," Giselle said.

"Oh no. He aims to maim."

All the shooting and yelling stopped. Dom, Carlo and Joey didn't move. Long seconds went by. I swallowed. Was it possible Lenny wasn't as good as he said he was? Or that he actually did aim to kill?

Then Dom, Carlo and Joey got up, lurching toward cover. Lenny stood and took a small bow. The shooting, yelling and general mayhem started again.

Tommy started to rise. "We gotta get away." He looked toward the ignition. "Hey, they got the keys!"

Bad guys headed in my direction, guns drawn.

"Giselle, the lines!" As we snatched our knives, I lobbed the keys high and wide above the boat. "Now!" I yelled to Giselle and we sliced through the original lines. As the men jumped, grabbing for the keys, the boat rocketed away from the dock, knocking most of them off their feet. The keys splashed into the water as the boat continued moving to the full hundred-foot length of the new lines.

The shooting from the turrets stopped. I looked up. The nuns and monks looked bummed out. All their excitement was over.

But a wild string of gunshots erupted from the boat. Tommy twitched like he was electrified. It looked like he hit every guy on the boat once, some of the guys a couple of times. They ran below, slamming the door on Tommy and on Mr. Massive, still too frightened to move.

Giselle and I raced back to the castle, turned and watched the boat. I wondered if at some point some of the guys would try to pull on the lines and get the boat back to the dock. They'd be nuts to even try. The tons of force on the lines made it a total impossibility.

I pictured them, crazed, trying to figure out how to get out of the jam they were in. If they cut the lines to get away? They'd never live to tell the story.

The *Greasy Palm* was a nice little floating jail cell now. The real one they'd be living in for the foreseeable future wouldn't be anywhere near that comfy.

"That's odd," Giselle said. "The wind is starting to die down."

"I may have overstated the case on the storm when I was talking to Mr. Massive and Tommy. The storm actually should be ending in a little while."

"You lied?" Giselle asked.

"Well, I said tropical storms can be dangerous and unpredictable."

"That much is true."

"Right," I said. "But according to the forecast, not this one anymore."

"I thought you'd be a lousy liar, but I totally believed you," Giselle said.

"With the right motivation, I guess anything's possible," I said to her.

We found Sister Aggie. "Thanks for helping, Sister," I said. "We never could have done it without you and your posse."

"I didn't realize it would be so much fun." Her eyes gleamed with excitement, and she didn't even try to click a word counter.

I picked up her now empty suitcase and the three of us headed back to her room. "The only possible problem I can see right now is if the police who respond just want to let those guys go. That's what happened to Tommy last time."

Sister opened the door to her room. Jesse still lay on the bed, eyes closed. "I don't think that will be a problem. The police chief is a friend of mine."

"I hope you know him pretty well." As I laid the suitcase down and shoved it under the bed, I noticed a piece of silky red material. I grabbed it, stood, and held it up. A sheer, very sexy negligee. I arched my eyebrows at Sister Aggie.

"Oh," she said. "Didn't I mention? We're semi-celibate."

"So when you said the Chief was a friend..."

She nodded.

I laughed. A little later, we heard sirens in the distance. We went to the window. Cruisers streaked down the road toward the castle. As the cruisers got closer, the whoop of the sirens got louder.

Jesse's eyes blinked open.

Chapter Thirty-Six

The next day, I left the hotel to do an errand in the morning. When I got back, I walked around the pool and plunked myself into the chaise next to Jesse. Giselle waved from the bar. I started to get up. "Uh-oh, Jesse. Giselle is at the—"

"She's getting a Pepsi."

"Oh," I said, plopping back down. "Thank goodness."

"Yeah. She's fine."

I smiled over at him.

He smiled back. "I have a surprise. We're bringing your whole family down here."

"No!" I said. He had no idea what he'd be unleashing. "You don't have to do that."

"I'd like to see them again."

Wanna bet? He'd change his mind pretty quickly if he got the full dose. Thanksgiving they'd been on their best behavior, for them. "They probably can't make it anyway."

"I called them already. They can make it."

Maybe it wouldn't be so bad. Maybe it was only one or

two. And maybe it was the sane side of the family. Wait. There really wasn't a sane side so... "Who's coming?"

"Everyone."

"What fun." I sank into the pillow propped behind me. I wanted to put it over my face.

"Yeah, I explained everything." He grinned. It was a look so sweet, and just a little goofy, and how could I help but smile back?

Bruises covering much of his body had turned purplish green. He was cute all the time, even the purplish green parts, but on pain medication, he was adorable. Hmm. Maybe this *was* the perfect time to meet my family. Maybe *I'd* take some of the pain medication. "When are they coming?"

I heard a commotion in the direction of the foyer.

Jesse glanced at his watch. "Any time now."

"You are still on pain medication, right?"

Jesse nodded. "But the Percocet is starting to wear off. It's mostly ibuprofen now."

The doors burst open. "That's too bad."

People streamed toward us. My mother and father and Aunt Deirdre and Uncle Ned slowed to take a look around.

"Where's our little star?" Aunt Deirdre said.

Giselle stood off to the side. I saw them register her presence, waited for them to run toward her. But they kept looking. Then they saw me. When they trotted in my direction, I turned in confusion to Jesse.

"Like I said, I told them everything."

The family swooped in on me. Past them, I saw one person I'd never expected to see. Kenny. This could be awkward, very awkward. I sat up. But he wasn't looking at me. He was looking at Giselle. The way she looked back? That was the way I looked at Jesse. I knew then that Giselle really was going home to Portsmouth. She hadn't ever wanted to leave.

I'd almost married a man who only wanted to be near me because I was the closest thing to Giselle. No wonder I'd felt like I was settling. I would have been, and it would have been for life.

Glancing at Jesse, I felt happy. I knew what love felt like now. I felt sad, too. It wasn't going to work out for us. Our lives were too different. Agents never had normal lives, and that was the life he'd chosen. Maureen had backed down from her threat to fire him. But now that I knew what real love felt like, I'd never settle for anything less.

For now, I'd enjoy what time we had together.

Jesse and I sat with the others at a couple of tables the waiters pulled together. Everyone talked at once. They didn't notice Giselle and Kenny approach. The pair stood quietly, holding hands.

When there was silence, Giselle said, "Kenny and I want to get married."

All eyes slid in my direction. "It's fine with me." They kept looking. "Really. Look at them." The eyes slid back to Giselle and Kenny.

"One other thing," Giselle said. She held her breath for a moment. "I don't want to be a spy. I want to be a bookkeeper."

"No problem," Uncle Ned said. "Even a CPA if you want."

Giselle stood speechless with surprise. That wasn't the response she'd expected.

Uncle Ned tugged her arm. "It might take you a while, since you've been a spy all this time."

"I... I—"

"Tell them, for heaven's sake!" I said.

"Most of the time, I wasn't a spy at all. I was doing the

books, and administrative stuff." She hunched slightly, bracing for their reaction.

"That's perfect, dear," Aunt Deirdre said. "You can get life-and-work credit for those years, you know. You'll be a CPA in no time."

Giselle looked around for a second, wide-eyed in surprise. "It's... It's okay? You don't care that I'm not your little star?"

"Nora can be our little star for a while," Aunt Deirdre said.

***

Later that afternoon, I skipped down the stairs of the Barlanadana courthouse and hurried to the hotel where Jesse waited. We walked down the street toward the castle.

"How'd it go?" he asked.

"Great. The judge said that because of the bug I placed on the *Greasy Palm,* he had crystal clear conversations of Mr. Massive, Tommy and their guys offloading the drugs. Convicting them was a slam dunk."

"It helps they don't use the jury system."

"That sure speeds things up." We turned toward the castle, walking along the lush green grass of the manicured grounds.

"What about Ma?" Jesse asked.

"Now Ma says she wants to be the queen."

"Instead of a dictator?"

"No, she wants to be queen of England. Even her supporters knew that was a non-starter. They got her a princess costume and tiara and—"

Dressed in a sequined white dress with a ruffled skirt and long train, Ma paraded by, followed by a line of strutting chickens in tiny royal uniforms. The swear words she muttered seemed at odds with the dress, but the chickens didn't seem to care. We bowed as she passed.

"What about Dom and Carlo?" Jesse asked as we continued on.

"Fifty years apiece. Remember Purple Shirt, the guy they threw off the pier? He's the judge's golf partner. The judge didn't appreciate almost losing the only guy he can beat."

"So they'll be, what, around ninety when they get out?"

"Something like that," I said. "Oh, and I talked earlier today to Sister Aggie."

"Yeah?"

"She had such a great time rounding up the bad guys, she's considering joining the agency. Made her realize life as a nun might be a little too quiet for her. And she said she'd forgotten how much fun it was to use full sentences."

"Think she'll really do it?"

"I'd say she's semi-serious."

"Any other news?"

"I noticed at the court house that Mr. Massive and Tommy have already developed a very close friendship. They're going to be in jail together for the rest of their lives, so they're going to try to make it work. They were playing footsie in the courtroom, but it was hard with all the chains. The important thing is Tommy's already given Mrs. T a quickie divorce."

"Oh. I was wondering about today."

We arrived at the castle, walked into the small chapel, and sat down. A few minutes later, the bride proceeded down the aisle. I cried as her husband-to-be met her at the altar and they said their vows.

Jesse took a tissue. Dabbing his eyes, he whispered,

"That's so beautiful."

The bride and groom placed rings on each other's fingers. The minister intoned, "I now pronounce you Lenny and Mrs. Lenny."

***

Sister Aggie had given my family and Kenny a tour of the castle while Jesse and I attended the wedding ceremony. Lenny and Mrs. Lenny invited them all to the reception. We were having drinks outside while pictures were taken of the happy couple.

When the others ambled over to take a look at the labyrinth, Jesse and I had a few minutes to ourselves. "Where'd you say you're from?" I asked. "You've got kind of a twangie thing going there, don't you? The Midwest somewhere, right?"

"Gaping Wound, Kansas."

"You come from a town called 'Gaping Wound'?"

"Yeah, the Indians and the Europeans used to go at it quite a bit out that way. There's an old story that tells how the leader of the Indians ended up with a huge shotgun blast to his midsection, and the leader of the settlers had a great big old gash in his head from a tomahawk. They fell to the ground side by side with these gaping wounds and got talking. They decided then and there that the violence wasn't helping much and everyone would just end up dying. So they settled their differences. Both recovered, which was considered nothing short of a miracle. People took it as a sign from God it was meant to be. The peace held."

"Nice story."

"Yeah, the town name kind of stinks, but it serves as a

reminder of what happened, so whenever it comes up for discussion, the town votes to keep it."

"Funny what images a state brings to mind."

"What did you think about when I said Kansas?"

"Oh, big sky, simple living, nothing artificial. Good values. Family values, I guess." I blushed. I pictured Jesse running around with a bunch of kids in a grass-covered yard. The kids looked surprisingly like him and me. I pushed that impossible scenario out of my mind.

"That's what it's like, pretty much."

"So what made you choose your career?"

"I didn't really choose it. The agency recruited me. My degree was in teaching, but I'd taken a course in Russian history and that was enough for them. I tried to tell them I took it because the ancient history class was filled, but they didn't want to hear it. And I already knew how to shoot."

"Ahhh." I nodded. But what I was thinking was too bad. He would have made a great husband and father. But not with that kind of lifestyle.

"But I don't think of it as a career."

"You don't?" I asked. "But you've been at it... How long?"

"Let's see. I got in when I was twenty-two. Now I'm thirty-five. I never meant to stay in that long."

"The years get away from you." That had been true in my life, too. Sometimes it took a lot of time to figure out what you wanted in life and to finally make it happen. "Let's take a walk," I said. "I want to show you something." He picked up on my somber tone and took my hand as we made our way toward the waterfront.

The others had returned from the labyrinth. "Where are they going?" I heard someone say. I glanced behind me. They all followed along.

I looked out toward the dock. There she was. I smiled as we approached a large sailboat—a sixty-foot schooner, to be exact. "I bought this when I went out this morning."

Jesse scanned the boat. "She's badly in need of a paint job. She only has one sail, and that one has holes in it." But he was smiling with excitement when he said it. "What's the upside?"

"She floats. And she's all mine." I hopped aboard. Jesse followed. So did the others. "Can you see her majesty, Jesse? Just below the surface?"

"I can see it, Nora."

"I'll paint her, replace the rigging, get new sails and cushions. I'll do whatever it takes to make it happen." I caught the tone in my own voice. The doubt was gone. I'd never wanted to be a spy, but I'd learned a lot about believing in myself and doing whatever it takes to get the job done, no matter what the odds.

I'd learned about living my dreams.

I faced Jesse. "There are lots of places I want to visit, exotic spots to learn about, so when I start my school, I know the best places to take the kids. Here's where I want to go before the school year starts." I pulled out a dog-eared list.

He looked over my shoulder. "How many places on this list?" Jesse asked.

"Twenty. That's where I want to start." I pointed to a spot marked with a red "X."

"That country can be pretty—"

"—exciting, I know." From the alarmed look on his face, I was pretty sure he'd been about to say dangerous. But hey, every country in the world could be a little dangerous, right? No sense worrying the family. And who knew what amazing adventures might await me there?

Jesse's lips moved as he did math in his head. "If we leave tomorrow, there's time to spend two weeks in each country."

"We? What about your job?"

"I've already done something about that."

"You have? What?"

"I resigned this morning. But when I did, Maureen offered me a lot of money to stay."

I didn't want to ask, but had to know. "Are you going to?"

"Hell no, Nora. Sooner or later, you could get killed in a job like that. She tried to talk me into occasional special projects. Those can be even more dangerous, but I said I'd think it over."

This was all happening so fast. I must have had that deer-in-the-headlights look. As Jesse put his arm around me, I felt his phone vibrate. He took it out and put it on a seat. I saw the caller name: Maureen.

"I told you my degree's in teaching," Jesse said. "What I forgot to tell you is I minored in math."

"I hate math."

"Well, someone's going to have to teach the kids algebra."

I looked at him, hope dawning in my heart. Could this work?

Jesse pulled me into a snug hug. "And correct me if I'm wrong, Nora, but isn't this thing too big to sail alone?"

"Yes," I whispered.

"I love you, Nora." Then he kissed me, and every tingle made me sure it was true.

I had my dream boat, *and* my dreamboat.

That night, the rocking on the boat wasn't from the waves.

THE END

Thank you so much for reading *Suddenly Spying!*
I hope you had as much fun reading it as I did writing it.

If you enjoyed this book, would you please consider writing
a short review on Amazon? You would? YAAAAAAY!
Good reviews mean a heck of a lot to us writers!
Please know that I'm very grateful for your support.

To learn more about me and my writing, please visit:
www.ginmackey.com

All the best to you, dear reader!
from
Gin Mackey

Made in the USA
Middletown, DE
27 July 2019